Wolf Tales V

Also by Kate Douglas:

Wolf Tales

"Chanku Rising" in *Sexy Beast*

Wolf Tales II

"Camille's Dawn" in *Wild Nights*

Wolf Tales III

"Chanku Fallen" in *Sexy Beast II*

Wolf Tales IV

"Chanku Journey" in *Sexy Beast III*

Wolf Tales V

KATE DOUGLAS

APHRODISIA
KENSINGTON PUBLISHING CORP.
http://www.kensingtonbooks.com

APHRODISIA BOOKS are published by

Kensington Publishing Corp.
850 Third Avenue
New York, NY 10022

All Kensington Titles, Imprints, and Distributed Lines are available at special quantity discounts for bulk purchases for sales promotions, premiums, fund-raising, and educational or institutional use.

Special book excerpts or customized printings can also be created to fit specific needs. For details, write or phone the office of the Kensington special sales manager: Kensington Publishing Corp., 850 Third Avenue, New York, NY 10022, attn: Special Sales Department, Phone: 1-800-221-2647.

ISBN-13: 978-0-7582-1870-4
ISBN-10: 0-7582-1870-2

First Kensington Trade Paperback Printing: January 2008

10 9 8 7 6 5 4 3 2 1

Printed in the United States of America

The new Kensington imprint, Aphrodisia, and the very first *Wolf Tales* debuted exactly two years ago, and my life has not been the same since. This has been a most amazing time in my career, and I have to thank two of the people who made it possible: my agent, Jessica Faust of Book-Ends LLC, who refused to give up on me, and Kensington editor Audrey LaFehr, who saw something in my stories that made her willing to take a chance on a relatively unknown author. Ladies, you have given me an amazing opportunity, and I will be forever grateful to both of you.

I also want to thank my readers, those adventurous souls who took a chance on my Chanku. Your wonderful notes and encouraging comments make it so much more fun when I sit down at my computer every day, wondering where the story will take me next. This one is for all of you.

Acknowledgments

My thanks, as always, to my amazing critique partners who take time from their own very busy schedules to read my manuscripts. Their comments and suggestions always make my stories better, and I am more than grateful for their help. Cassie Walder, Devyn Quinn, Sheri Fogarty, and Ann Jacobs, talented wordsmiths all, are part of a most amazing village I call on for help, and they always come through for me. Thanks also to my husband, who, in the thirty-five years we've been married, may have thought of murder but has never followed through. Honey, I couldn't do this without you—nor would I want to!

Chapter 1

Manda stood motionless beside the window but she didn't dare part the shades. Not even for a peek. No, that was much too risky, but she listened. Listened and flinched at the double backfire that always reminded her of gunshots, listened to the slow, steady tread of heavy boots climbing the twelve steps to her front door.

Still, when the loud knock broke the silence, she jumped. Then she caught her breath and moved away from the window and shuffled closer to the door. Leaned the side of her head against the solid wood. "Is that you, Harry?"

Damn. She so wished her voice sounded normal. The scratchy, rasping growl wrapped around her words only added to the rumors.

"Yes, Ms. Smith. I have your order. Do you want me to bring it in?"

Bring it in. It would be so simple to show herself and be done with it. Manda sighed. "No, that's okay, Harry. The check for the groceries is under the mat. Your tip, too. Thank you."

She listened for the scrape of the rubber mat as it was pulled aside. Heard the crinkle of paper and knew he'd probably shoved the check into a pocket, and one of the last of her crisp five dollar bills into his wallet.

"Thank you, ma'am. I'll be going now."

"Thank you, Harry." Manda leaned her back against the door and listened for the solid clump of Harry's boots as he walked down the stairs. She sensed the long pause he made at the bottom and imagined him looking up toward her closed door.

Pictured him standing there, scratching his bald head and wondering what kind of freak she was. Manda waited until the unmistakable double retort of backfire told her Harry's truck was truly gone. Still, she waited a full ten minutes longer, her senses open to any disturbance, any suggestion Harry, or even someone else, might yet linger on the stoop.

Finally, stomach rumbling in hungry protest at the long but necessary delay, she cracked open the door and peered down the empty staircase. Then, hooking her long, black nails into the sides of the cardboard box, Manda slowly dragged the goods inside and closed the door.

The aroma of fresh, raw meat brought a rush of saliva to her mouth and made her throat convulse. She tried to stay in control, but the blood scent found a deeper level. She caved to her needs, the visceral reaction to fresh blood, to meat. Snarling deep in her throat, Manda ripped open the box with teeth and claws and used her sharp canines to tear into the first package on top. Raw sirloin steak. Almost two pounds of bloody meat.

She shoved the plastic covering aside with one curved nail, then fell on the steak, tearing at it as if it were prey, alive and struggling to escape. Growling, snapping at the bloody flesh, she devoured the slab of meat in seconds.

Hunger assuaged, Manda sat back on her haunches, breathing heavily. She glanced at the torn wrapping, the bloodstains on the floor, then at her hands. At least, what had once been hands. They were paws. Okay, so she had rudimentary opposing thumbs, but still, they were nothing but paws and she was cursed. Cursed for whatever sin she might have committed, cursed to live as a beast. She stared at the fur-covered paws, the extended black claws, the bits of meat caught on the sharp nails. Stared at them until the form wavered and her eyes watered, though no tears fell.

Damn Papa B and damn the people who followed him. Damn Mother and Father, the rebels and their guns, the hill people and God and His ugly curse. Damn them all.

Then she bowed her head, whimpering like a lost puppy, and curled into a shivering, shaking ball of fur and bone and flesh.

* * *

Baylor Quinn stepped out of the elevator and stood patiently in the doorway to San Francisco's elegant Top of the Mark restaurant. He tucked his motorcycle gloves inside his helmet and stuck the helmet under his arm, trying to look as inconspicuous as possible in his full-body black leather riding suit and heavy black motorcycle boots. While he waited for the maitre d' to seat him, Bay studied the large, laughing group sitting together on the far side of the restaurant and wondered once again why he should presume to feel a part of such an illustrious assembly of individuals.

Each one of them, perfect in every way possible.

All of them mated to someone . . . loved by someone. Even his sisters had found mates. Sisters from the same dysfunctional beginnings as his own, yet they laughed and loved as if they had every right to so much happiness.

The maitre d' grabbed a menu and gestured for Bay to follow. Baylor looked beyond the small, neatly attired man and glanced through the large windows. The skyline of San Francisco was almost lost in the low-lying fog below the top floor of the hotel, but the misty view out the windows created a perfect backdrop for such a gathering of the obviously rich and beautiful.

If only the other patrons seated nearby had a clue. Bay bit the inside of his cheek to keep himself from grinning like a fool. Shapeshifters all, from the handsome older man with white hair to the young African American mother gently cradling her newborn daughter.

Chanku. Creatures with the ability to leave their human bodies—if not their humanity—behind, and run as wolves. They might hunt and kill without remorse, yet they were just as comfortable sharing a linen-covered table set with the finest crystal and silver, conversing quietly over coffee in an elegant dining room.

It looked as if everyone had made it to brunch this morning. Considering the amount of alcohol consumed at the wedding reception the night before, Baylor'd had his doubts. He nodded to Anton Cheval, the obvious occupant for the space at the head of the table, shook Ulrich Mason's hand at the other end, and pulled out the vacant chair between his two sisters, across from Stefan Aragat, who sat beside his lovely mate, Alexandria.

She looked about ready to pop. Bay wasn't sure, but her baby had to be due any time . . . like maybe now? He gave each of his sisters a quick kiss. Then, for some obscure and probably foolish reason, he leaned across the table and kissed Xandi's cheek.

He sensed more than heard the low snarl coming from her mate. Bay sat, and at the same time flashed a quick grin when Xandi rolled her eyes at Stefan's purely wolven response.

"How're you feeling this morning, Xandi? You've got to be getting close." Spreading his napkin over his lap, Bay nodded to the waiter who poured his coffee.

Xandi laughed. "Definitely close. I feel like a beached whale about to burst." She glared at Stefan. "And it's all your fault!"

Stefan raised both hands in surrender. "Not completely," he said. "You did have the choice."

Xandi merely snorted and laughed, but Bay noticed the white lines around her mouth and the strain in her eyes. It was true—all Chanku females had a choice to breed or not. Pregnancy required the conscious release of an egg for fertilization. As miserable as she looked right now, Bay wondered if Xandi regretted choosing motherhood.

Stefan certainly seemed excited about the impending birth. What would it be like, knowing the woman who loved you carried your child? Bay sighed. It was doubtful he'd ever find out. There were so few of them, so very few Chanku of either sex.

Bay's odds of meeting the perfect mate seemed insurmountable. He sat back and listened as the others teased Stefan and Xandi about her impending delivery, but as he sipped his coffee, Bay felt once more that sense of being apart from the whole. Even with a newly rediscovered sister on either side of him, he remained the one lone wolf among the group.

Bay glanced up and caught Stefan watching him, smiling broadly. "Take a look at this," Stefan said. "I may have found you a woman." He handed a folded newspaper across the table, a cheap tabloid from the looks of it. The headline screamed across the front, WOLF GIRL TERRIFIES RURAL NY NEIGHBORHOOD!

Below was a grainy photo, obviously retouched, of a snarling wolf with just enough human features, including long, blond hair, to look truly hideous. Anger shot through Bay. Did everyone find it humorous that he among them was alone and hating it? It took him a minute to find his voice. He tossed the paper back on the table and snarled, "Not funny, Aragat."

Still smiling, Stefan shook his head. "You don't get it, do you? I'm not kidding and this is not a joke. Xandi, tell Bay how you found me."

Xandi reached across the table and covered Bay's clenched fist with her soft hand. "It wasn't that long ago, Bay, that Stefan looked almost exactly like the woman in that photo." She flashed her mate a wry grin. "Other than the hair. He was already going gray."

"Watch it, woman." Stefan smiled at Xandi, obviously urging her to continue.

"He'd been stuck like that, part wolf, part human, in mid-shift, for over five years. That picture's probably not real, but there's often a kernel of truth to tabloid stories. We found Keisha through an article in that same publication. It was just as lurid, but there was enough truth to send us searching for her. Point being, don't discount the possibility of this woman being real, and very much in need of help."

Bay felt as if someone had tilted his reality. He looked carefully at Stefan and tried to imagine the horror of being caught between shifts. "What happened?"

Stefan shook his head. "It's a long story and too intense for a 'breakfast after the wedding' conversation, but the point is, it can happen. There just might be a young woman in upstate New York, living the same horror I lived. And you, my friend, might be able to find her and save her."

Bay picked the paper up and looked at the article with a new sense of purpose. It named a small town in the Adirondack Mountains in New York. He read the entire piece and then glanced at his packmates, Jake and Shannon. Shannon smiled, Jake gave him a thumbs up.

Suddenly breakfast with the group didn't seem nearly as important. Nor did the day ahead loom so bleakly. Bay stood up, chugged the last of his tepid coffee and grabbed his helmet and gloves. Already his mind spun with plans and possibilities. "It's been wonderful to see all of you, to meet you," he said, nodding to the members of the Montana pack. "It's been especially wonderful to see you two rats." He leaned down and gave both Lisa and Tala another kiss on the cheek. "But it looks like I'm going to take a little trip east. I'll be in touch."

Xandi felt a catch in her breath, remembering Stefan, remembering the night she'd found and learned to love the man hidden within the body of a wolf. She watched as Bay tucked Stefan's tabloid into a side pocket on his leather suit, saluted all of them at the table and strolled out of the restaurant with the black helmet under one arm.

Damn, but the man was hot. She glanced at Stefan and smiled. Her mate was thinking exactly the same thing as he watched the tall, dark-haired Chanku leave the restaurant. He wasn't even trying to hide his thoughts.

Another twinge crossed Xandi's middle. She realized this had nothing whatsoever to do with Baylor Quinn or her mate.

Oblivious as only a man could be, Stefan leaned back in his chair, slipped an arm around Keisha on one side and Xandi on the other. "Well, folks. My work here is done," he said, grinning broadly.

"No, Stefan. It's not." Xandi gasped as another contraction stole her breath away. She rubbed her palm along one side of her taut belly. "I think it's just beginning."

* * *

Ulrich Mason waited outside the delivery room with Anton Cheval. Stefan and the women had gone into the birthing room with Xandi, while Jake, Tinker, Mik, and AJ, cowardly males all, went off in search of lunch. Anton's gaze hardly left the closed door, but he'd declined Stefan and Alexandria's invitation to join them for their child's birth.

He sat beside Ulrich instead, holding his own newborn daughter while Keisha and the other women used their Chanku skills to ease Xandi's pain.

Ulrich brushed his fingertip over the baby's satiny cheek. "It's frightening, isn't it, the responsibility you feel holding one that tiny? I remember when Camille delivered Tianna. The doctor handed that tiny bundle to me and all I could do was stare and worry about her future."

Anton sighed, but it was a contented sound. "I know. I can already feel the changes fatherhood has made in my perceptions, the sense I have of myself and those around me. It's good, though, my friend. All good. These little ones won't grow up wondering why they're different, wondering what drives them to be so unlike their friends. They'll know their heritage, their potential."

Ulrich nodded, lost in memories and old regrets. He'd not been so open with Tia. His daughter hadn't known a thing about the Chanku, beyond the fairy tales her mother had told her as a youngster. Thank goodness all had turned out so well.

"I have a favor to ask of you, but I'll not be unhappy should you refuse."

"A favor? Of me?" Ulrich sat back in his chair and looked closely at Anton, the acknowledged leader of the Chanku. He was a shapeshifter as well as a powerful wizard adept at many arcane skills, and it was difficult imagining Anton needing anything from anyone.

He smiled at Ulrich, obviously aware of his thoughts. "The High Mountain wolf sanctuary in Colorado has an interesting director. Her name's Millie West. She's lived in the area all her life." Anton glanced away from Ulrich's direct gaze and brushed his daughter's fuzzy head. "I met her briefly, a few weeks ago. She's Chanku. I'd almost swear it, though obviously I have no proof. I want you to meet her, see if my suspicions are correct. If she is, I want you to help her, to bring her over. She's got to be at least fifty . . . to my knowledge, she's never married."

Anton turned his attention back to Ulrich. "I know how you feel about Camille, but your wife's been gone for a long time. Chanku mate for life, but once a mate's life ends, I believe we can still find love."

It might have been merely his imagination, but Ulrich was almost sure his heart skipped a beat, skittered a little and then settled back into rhythm. He'd never imagined another woman and love in the same thought, never allowed himself to consider loving anyone but Camille.

He raised his head. When he stared into Anton's amber eyes Ulrich saw both compassion and encouragement. "Was this your goal," he asked, "when you brought Camille's spirit back for me? To free Keisha from her presence, or was it to free me?"

Anton's smile was bittersweet. "Couldn't it do both things? Camille needed to move on, Keisha needed peace, and you, my friend, needed to remember that, while your wife is no longer alive, you are. What are you? Fifty-nine? Sixty?"

"I'm sixty-four, and on days like this I feel every one of my years and then some." Ulrich chuckled, but there was little humor in his heart. Damn Camille. He'd hoped that one magical night he'd spent with his long-dead wife's spirit would help him move beyond the grief, but he still missed her. At least the anger was gone. For that, Ulrich would be forever grateful to Anton Cheval.

"Do you realize you're only a dozen years older than me, and I'm holding a newborn?" Anton leaned down and kissed the sleeping baby in his arms. "You have a life to live, Ulrich. A future ahead of you. Think about it. I need someone to bring Millie over, if she truly is Chanku. You're the one to do it."

Anton watched Ulrich where the older man stood by the window, staring out across the city. His thoughts were as clear to Anton as a written page. Anton debated whether or not to intrude. It was so easy, this slipping in and out of the minds of others, but he honored privacy whenever possible. From this distance, it would be almost as easy to tell by Ulrich's body language what the man thought.

The door to the birthing room opened and Stefan slipped outside. Anton bit back a grin. His packmate, usually so carefree and lighthearted, looked rumpled and exhausted. Stefan rubbed his injured shoulder, still healing after their plane crash just a few weeks earlier.

"How's she doing?"

"Better than me." Stefan flopped down on the chair beside Anton and ran his finger over baby Lily Milina's silky cheek. "But, if this is the reward, I imagine I'll be able to cope." He chuckled quietly. "The women are amazing. They sit beside Xandi while she labors, touch her body gently and take her pain. All of them are showing the strain of her efforts, yet she looks wonderful, still rested and strong."

"How's Keisha?" Anton caught a flicker of regret in Stefan's eyes and immediately frowned. "Is she okay?"

"She's tired. She wants me to bring Lily in so she can nurse. Said her breasts hurt."

"Ah. I'm surprised she didn't contact me directly." Anton had thought of going into the room, but Keisha had asked him to keep Lily away.

"She's afraid to link." Stefan reached for the baby. "She doesn't want Xandi's pain to spill over onto the baby. She's blocking now, but you know women. No way is she going to leave the room and maybe miss something. She said she'd be careful to block while she's got Lily with her. Xandi said you're more than welcome to . . ."

Anton shook his head and nodded in Ulrich's direction. "Later. Before your son arrives." He kissed his daughter's satiny cheek and handed her over to Stefan. Then he kissed his packmate, sensing Stefan's fear for his wife and his need to return to her side. Conflicted by his strong desire to be with Keisha and his equally powerful need to talk to Ulrich, Anton stayed behind. He watched his tall, handsome lover carry his only daughter to her mother and felt an ache in his heart when the door closed behind them.

Without the baby in his arms, Anton had only Ulrich to keep him busy. He studied the older man, reading his body language without trespassing on his thoughts. Ulrich had stepped outside. He sat alone in the small garden area easily visible through heavy glass doors, apparently lost in thought as he stared in the general direction of Golden Gate Park. Anton concentrated on Ulrich for a moment, and then settled back in the overstuffed chair in the waiting room and closed his eyes. To an observer, he would appear to sleep, but while Anton's body seemed to slumber, his searching mind silently, surreptitiously wound its way deep inside Ulrich's thoughts.

It was something he doubted he'd ever get used to, this sharing of minds without the other's notice. Bits and pieces of Ulrich's memories whirled in senseless disarray, slowly but surely falling into order as Anton's searching mind made sense of what he observed.

Within moments, he became Ulrich Mason, the Ulrich of memory. A younger Ulrich, walking hand in hand along a shaded path in Golden Gate Park with his beautiful African American wife. Her skin was as smooth and dark as bittersweet chocolate. When Camille turned and laughed, looking up at him with sparkling eyes and flashing teeth, his heart melted.

"I love you, Ric. I will always love you, but last night was truly spectacular."

They stopped and Ulrich pulled her into his arms. He breathed deeply of her scent, and Anton recognized the perfume of the ghostly specter that had so upset Keisha less than a year ago. It was hard to believe Camille, this beautiful, vibrant woman of memory, had been dead for over twenty years.

"I hate to admit it," Ulrich whispered, "but I enjoyed seeing you with another man. Watching his cock slip deep inside that sweet pussy of yours, then your ass . . . his hands on your breasts . . ."

Camille laughed. It was a sexy, throaty sound that caused an immediate reaction in Ulrich. Anton sensed Ulrich's cock swelling with the memory, felt the rush of blood to the other's loins. So intimate, to be this closely linked, to sense arousal through another.

"What about when his wife went down on you, and then sucked me off as well?" Camille raised her head, only this time her look was serious. "I've never been with a woman before, but that was so cool. I get hot just thinking about it. Especially when I think of all four of us together."

Ulrich chuckled and brushed his lips through her silky hair. His mind filled with images of the night before, images spilling softly, surreptitiously, into Anton's questing brain.

This had occurred before Tianna was born. They'd been traveling, on their way home from a trip north to their cabin near Mt. Lassen. They'd stopped for the night at a hotel along the highway. There was another couple, both young and attractive, traveling in the opposite direction. The man had broad shoulders and long hair tumbling almost to his waist. The woman was tiny and very fair, her blond hair short and curly.

Ulrich settled deeper into memory. Anton silently followed along. The two couples had started out with drinks in the hotel bar, but now the man lay back against the headboard of a large bed with Camille in his lap, her back to him. The man's legs were spread wide, his cock shoved deep inside Camille's ass.

The woman knelt between Camille's legs and feasted on her glistening pussy, moaning aloud with her pleasure, occasionally dipping her head lower to lick her mate's balls as he thrust slowly, rhythmically, in and out of Camille.

In his memories, Ulrich drew closer to the kneeling blonde. He knelt behind her, spread her thighs so he could fit his long legs between hers, and studied her hairless pussy. He'd never been with a woman who shaved herself before, and the smooth skin and visible contours of her swollen, flushed sex fascinated him. Her slit beckoned. Dark and inviting between thick lips, it glistened with pale cream. Her clit poked out of its protective hood, smooth and unusually distended. An invitation to taste.

Ulrich leaned down and ran his tongue along her sleek, wet opening. He felt her nether lips flutter when he circled the hard little bud of her clitoris. He sucked it for a moment, his nose buried in her damp folds, loving the way she squirmed against his face. Ulrich slowed and eased back. He didn't want her to come. Not yet.

He parted her swollen labia with his fingers and dipped two of them deep inside, buried all the way to his knuckles. She was slippery and wet and so very hot. Her muscles clamped around his fingers even as he pressed deeper. She arched her back as he slowly fucked her with his hand, dragging her juices out along her passage with each slow sweep of his fingers. When she was truly wet, her swollen lips dripping and glistening, Ulrich straightened up.

He wrapped his fist around the base of his erection and felt his abdominal muscles clench in response. Slowly he pressed his hard cock against her creamy sex, dragging the smooth crown back and forth over her slick opening. He was big, the head of his cock swollen with blood, round and dark as a ripe plum. He didn't want to hurt her. They'd never had sex before tonight—hell, he hadn't known her before tonight—and he wasn't sure how pliable she was, how much of him she could take.

Her mate was average, his erect cock not all that big—around six or seven inches in length. Camille had taken him with ease, merely sitting back on his erection until he'd slipped beyond her tight sphincter muscle and arrowed deep inside her dark passage.

Concerned for his unfamiliar partner's pleasure, Ulrich pressed forward, carefully forcing his cock's broad crown against hot, wet flesh. The woman continued feasting on Camille's snatch and he pushed harder, until she raised her hips and shoved back against him.

His cock slid part way in and he felt her sex enfold him like a warm glove. Her slick tissues parted, then tightened around his length in undulating waves of pressure. Ulrich wrapped his big hands around her slim hips, grabbed hold to anchor himself and thrust harder, pressing forward until his balls slapped against her smooth lips. She grunted, raised her head, and turned to look at Ulrich with an expression of surprised pleasure. "You're a big one, aren't you? I like that." She arched her back and practically growled. "Give it to me. Do it hard."

Then she turned back to Camille, licking and sucking with such total abandon that Ulrich heard the wet, slurping sounds she made, the low hum of pleasure that seemed to vibrate out of her throat. Her mate continued slowly fucking Camille's ass with a look of utter bliss on his face.

Ulrich caught the man's rhythm and fucked his partner, slamming his hips against her smooth buttocks, rotating his pelvis against her for even more penetration. The pace sped up until they'd become a virtual fucking machine, the four of them there on the bed in a cheap hotel where'd they'd met purely by accident.

A chance encounter in a bar, one they'd never had the opportunity to repeat. But Ulrich recalled the feel of the stranger's smooth, tight pussy clenching his cock. He still heard the sounds they'd all made—grunts and moans and breaths catching, the smells of clean bodies and hot sex. Most of all, he remembered watching Camille climax, sharing the rippling spasms of her clenching pussy, the woman's busy tongue licking and twirling through slick folds of flesh and, through their mindlink, feeling Camille's orgasm all the way to his toes.

The man had come next. Ulrich could still see the way his mouth twisted in a silent rictus, a soundless cry of release, remember how he'd worried the stranger's fingers might have gripped Camille's breasts too tight, that she'd be left with bruises.

The woman's climax had surprised him. She'd suddenly arched her back and screamed, then thrashed wildly against his cock as if trying to break free. Some sixth sense had made him hold her, made him ramp up his speed until he was slamming into her spasming pussy with everything he had. His long fingers dug into her slender hips, his balls hit her clit on every downward stroke, the head of his cock rammed solidly against her womb.

He'd raised his eyes just as his own climax began and looked directly into Camille's beaming smile. "*I love you,*" she'd said, the thoughts whirling in his mind while the hot coil of orgasm tightened his balls and blasted out the end of his cock.

Later, they'd bathed and, with hugs and kisses, parted ways, all of them sexually satisfied but realizing there was nothing more to hold them together. He didn't even remember their names. It was the seventies, after all, the height of the sexual revolution. Swinging probably wasn't the smartest activity for a young police lieutenant or his wife, but the memories were precious to him, even now.

He'd held that night in his fantasies for years, pulling it out when the time was right. But here and now, in these memories Anton secretly shared, Ulrich missed only Camille. Missed her scent, her taste, her touch and smile, her sass and her brass.

His memories slipped back to that walk in the park, the day after. "I wish they'd been Chanku." Ulrich's soft words carried a lifetime of pain. "I wish we knew of others like us, others we could share this amazing world with. As good as the sex was, it can never be anything more."

"If we find someone, I hope it's a woman with a tongue like hers. I'd be willing to share our bed with someone like that."

Laughing, Ulrich grabbed Camille's hand and they'd walked on through the park. A private, very personal memory between a man and his beloved wife.

Feeling much like the voyeur he was, Anton slipped free of Ulrich's memories, arched his spine and stretched as if coming awake from a brief nap.

When he opened his eyes, Ulrich was walking back inside the hospital. There was a smile on his face and a bounce to his step. Anton reached for his wallet and the card with Millie West's phone number. It looked as if he was going to need it.

Chapter 2

Bay climbed off of the big GS 1200 motorcycle in front of the small diner Anton had suggested he check out, slipped his helmet off and stretched. The pop of vertebrae crackling as he arched his back sounded overly loud, but it felt so good he did it again. Just three days to cover almost three thousand miles from San Francisco to New York and he was absolutely exhausted. Still, he felt energized. He practically vibrated with a sense of expectation.

Anton's call this morning had given Bay a destination much more specific than what he'd managed to glean out of the newspaper article and off the Internet at the hotel where he'd stayed his first night on the road.

Hell, he couldn't even recall what state that one had been in, much less the town. The trip itself was merely a blur of miles covered, a few hours' sleep at roadside hotels and meals best forgotten when he actually remembered to eat. He'd crossed mountains and desert, wide open plains and thick forest, changed two flat tires and gotten lost once when road construction sent him on an impatient detour, but he stood here on the sidewalk in Rome, New York with the firm belief he was only a couple hours at most from his destination.

All roads lead to Rome. Maybe, but with that thought

in mind, Bay felt positive this spot was really the beginning of the final leg of his journey. He locked his helmet to the bike and stuffed his thick leather gloves into the tank bag. Then, rubbing his bare palm over his stubbly chin, he headed inside the diner. A cold wind blew but the late spring sun heated his leather riding suit. Still, it felt good to close the door on the chilly morning. He nodded to a redheaded waitress behind the counter, noted the half dozen patrons seated about the small restaurant and then grabbed a loose newspaper lying on a chair by the front door. He took a seat near the window where he could keep an eye on the bike.

It was only eleven in the morning, but he'd been riding since around four and it felt good to sit on something that didn't vibrate. The redhead brought him strong, black coffee without being asked and handed him a menu printed on plain, white paper.

Bay smelled bacon cooking and his mouth watered, but he flashed a grin at the waitress and got an interested smile in return. He glanced over the menu and sipped at the surprisingly good coffee, then opened the newspaper. His breath literally caught in his throat when he saw the picture.

Not the same shot, but similar. A wolf with humanoid features and scraggly blond hair. There was a haunted expression on its face that wrapped a fist around Baylor's heart and squeezed. When he finally set the cup down a minute later, his heart pounded in his chest and he was almost certain he heard a ringing in his ears.

The waitress came back, pad and pencil in hand. She glanced at the open newspaper and snorted. "Ugly sucker, isn't she? Folks think it's all made up, but she's real, poor thing. Lives just an hour northeast of here, up in a little town in the mountains."

Bay schooled his features into a look of disbelief. "You're kidding, right? That looks like something someone did on their computer. You know, mixed a picture of a wolf and a really ugly woman . . . ?"

The waitress shook her head. "My cousin Harry owns a little grocery up in the Adirondacks. He delivers an order twice a week to a recluse. She never comes out, but her orders are for almost nothing but meat. Lots of red meat. He leaves the box of groceries by the door, takes his money from under the doormat and leaves. She never lets him come inside to deliver it proper. He said he caught a glimpse of her through the blinds one time and just about screamed like a schoolgirl, she scared him that bad."

Bay shook his head. "Poor thing. Can you imagine being that deformed? Trying to live in a society that reveres beauty?"

The waitress nodded and shook her long red hair back over her shoulder in an obviously flirtatious manner. "Nope. Can't imagine it." She smiled brightly with a lot more than mere interest in his order. "Anything I can get for you?"

That certainly sounded like a loaded question.

Bay pointed at the special typed at the top of the page. Three eggs, fried potatoes, sausage, bacon, and biscuits. Thank goodness cholesterol didn't appear to be a problem for Chanku.

"Another buck and you can get a slab of fried steak with that. A man your size must need to eat a lot to keep up his strength . . ." She smiled as her comment trailed off.

Bay smiled back at her and winked. "Sounds good. I appreciate the suggestion. Thank you. I like mine rare."

He watched her walk away and almost laughed at the pronounced sway to her ass. Jake was right, though. Flirt a little, learn a lot. When she brought his breakfast a few minutes later, Bay got the name of the town where Cousin Harry owned the local grocery.

* * *

Ulrich looked at the card Anton had given him, then at the map he'd spread out across the steering wheel. The past few days felt like a prolonged drug trip . . . the downed plane and Keisha's birth of a perfect little baby girl, Tia and Luc's wedding, Xandi's precipitous labor and delivery of a very tiny but healthy baby boy, Baylor heading off in search of the mysterious wolf woman, and now this.

How the hell he'd let Anton talk him into hunting down a woman who might be Chanku was beyond him. Actually, Ulrich wondered if Camille's spirit had a hand in the process. He hadn't thought of that sexual encounter with the other couple for years, but remembering how Camille had loved being with another woman had finally convinced him to look for this Millie West and see if she really was Chanku.

He was tired. Damn it all, at sixty-four he was ready to think about rocking chairs and puttering in the garden, not hunting down a sexy woman who might just be a shapeshifter.

So why did his cock suddenly swell and his heart begin to race when he thought of the slim blonde? The photo Anton had given him felt seared into his brain, the woman's image a polar opposite to his one, true love, Camille, but fascinating just the same.

Ulrich ignored his body and concentrated on the directions, found the High Mountain wolf sanctuary marked in pen and folded up the map. He had to stop obsessing over his concerns, quit projecting a future that existed purely in his imagination. He'd go and check out the woman, see if she was the real thing, and then he'd figure out what to do.

It took him another twenty minutes to find the right road, ten more minutes to make it to the sanctuary, and at least two seconds to fall in lust.

The minute Ulrich stepped through the door into the sanctuary office, the woman from the photograph lifted her head from whatever had held her attention and smiled at him. Her scent was pure wolf. Powerful, an aphrodisiac all on its own. It took Ulrich a moment to get his bearings, to catch his breath and rediscover the ability to form a complete sentence.

He cleared his throat, giving himself more time. "I'm looking for Millie West."

Her smile widened. White teeth, perfect cheekbones, long blond hair streaked with gray . . . and amber eyes. He felt her smile all the way to his balls.

"I'm Millie. Can I help you?"

Oh shit. Could she ever. He held out his hand and noticed it was shaking. Concentrated on holding it steady. "I'm Ulrich Mason. Anton Cheval asked me to stop in and see how things were going since the new board of directors took over. He wanted to make sure you had everything you need."

Millie stood up. She was taller than Camille, even taller than he'd imagined from her photo. Ulrich guessed Millie stood about five seven, with a slim, athletic build, but part of her height could have come from the well-worn roper style cowboy boots on her feet. Her faded blue jeans fit her like a second skin and she wore a pale yellow cotton blouse with long sleeves rolled back above her wrists.

She held out her hand and Ulrich wrapped his fingers around hers. The scent of her body reached out to him, subtle yet demanding. The moment they touched, he felt the connection race along his arm, a sense of destiny no doubt only he experienced.

"It's a pleasure to meet you," she said, releasing his hand and smiling naturally, as if her touch hadn't just rocked his world. "Mr. Cheval called yesterday and said to expect you. I've got the books ready. We can tour the compound either before or after you look at the records."

"I drove all the way out here from San Francisco. I think I've been sitting long enough." Ulrich laughed, a low chuckle meant to put her at ease. "If you have a moment, can we walk through the compound first? I'd love to see, firsthand, how you have everything set up."

"Of course." She walked to the door and opened it, looked out and called to a young man working nearby. "Seth, I have to be out of the office for a bit. Can you keep an eye on things, answer the phone if anyone calls?"

"Yes, Ms. West." The kid sort of slouched into the office, but he nodded politely to Ulrich and went straight to a pile of papers where he started sorting and filing. Millie watched him a moment, then led Ulrich outside.

"Seth has just gotten off probation after the problems here with Tinker McClintock and Lisa Quinn. You've heard about that?"

Ulrich nodded. So that was the young man who'd almost gotten Luc and Tia killed. He felt the hackles rise along the back of his neck and quickly suppressed the urge to attack. Okay, so the kid had thought he was saving wolves, not sending them to be slaughtered by wealthy hunters, but that didn't excuse him. Obviously, Millie had been able to forgive.

Ulrich wondered if he had that in him, that ability to forgive. As angry as he felt toward Seth, a young man he'd never met before today, Ulrich doubted forgiveness was one of his virtues. Probably another sign he was getting old and crotchety. Damn it all, where had the years gone?

Putting Seth out of his mind, Ulrich followed Millie, walking just far enough behind her to enjoy the gentle sway of her slim hips as she headed across the parking lot toward a shaded area of holding pens.

If anyone had asked him, later, what he'd gleaned from the tour of the compound, Ulrich would most likely have drawn a blank. Not because he wasn't paying attention . . . no, it was more than that. So much more.

His senses were fully engaged. He smelled the pines and the cedar and the sun-heated granite, the musky scent of wolves and the acrid odor of unwashed bodies as he passed the workmen cleaning pens and caring for the wolves.

There was the soft sweep of wind in the trees, the harsh call of a jay, the musical trill of a small stream bordering their trail, and about it all the scent of wild wolves, the echoes of their grunts and growls and heavy breathing.

Millie's scent mingled with the musky aroma of their wild brethren. Ulrich inhaled, felt his nostrils flare as his lungs expanded, and realized he was grinning like the village idiot.

Millie led him deeper into the woods, carrying on an in-depth discussion of the various types of wolves housed here, the strength of the pens, the quality of care. Ulrich heard her words as if she stood at the bottom of a deep well and he at the top, as though her voice surrounded him but the language, the meaning of what she said, remained a mystery.

He felt the sound of her voice, a vibration akin to fingers tapping out a tune on the low notes of a piano. Musical, with a slight drawl borne of the country and life among men. There was nothing overtly feminine about her, yet she screamed *female* with every step, every word. Screamed it loud enough that his cock now fought the confines of the denim jeans he wore, trapped as it was along his left inner thigh.

He wanted to shift. Wanted to run beside her and howl his need, take her hard and fast in the dark woods, his teeth nipping at her shoulder, his nails scraping her fur-covered shoulders.

Except he didn't know. Couldn't really tell if it was the scent of the wolf in Millie or his own frustration. The proximity of so many caged wolves confused him. Did the alluring perfume his sensitive nostrils caught really come from the woman? Maybe it was his own wishful thinking, the hope that he would some day, once again, find a mate to ease the aching loneliness he'd lived with since Camille's death.

There'd been women. Lots of women, and just as many men. No Chanku was capable of celibacy. Not with a libido as powerful as theirs, needs so strong. Needs . . . had his life always been one of needs?

The sound of their boots tramping along the edge of the service road was muffled in new grass and rain-dampened earth. Millie talked with her hands emphasizing each word as she explained the habits of the various wolves in each fenced compound they passed.

Ulrich smiled, watching her fingers, hearing her voice, feeling something unravel deep inside himself. He tried to ask questions apropos to Millie's comments, but knew he'd failed miserably when she turned around with her hands planted firmly on her hips, and burst into laughter.

"You're not listening to a word I'm saying, are you?"

"Excuse me?" He felt his cheeks grow hot and knew he was blushing. "Of course I am."

"Then what did I just tell you about the pack in that compound?" She pointed toward a heavy chain-link fence where three unusually small wolves waited in the shadows.

"You said . . . um . . ." He did the one thing he hoped would save his sorry ass. Ulrich grinned and held his hands out in surrender. "I don't know. I'm sorry. What did you say?"

Millie didn't appear to take offense. "That our breeding program appears successful. These are Ethiopian wolves, one of the rarest lupine species. The bitch is pregnant. They're part of our rescue program. There's been a rabies outbreak among Ethiopian wolves in the wild and we're hoping to keep the species alive through programs like ours."

"I thought they looked smaller than the timber wolves. They're more like coyotes."

Millie laughed. "Don't let them hear you say that! They'd be highly insulted." She glanced at her watch. "I had no idea how long I've been dragging you around." When she looked up at Ulrich and smiled, he felt her warmth. "It's almost one."

"No wonder I'm starving." As if on cue, Ulrich's stomach growled. "Is there a town nearby where I can find a sandwich?"

"The nearest town is at least a half hour's drive up the road." She stared at him for a long heartbeat, then appeared to come to a decision. "Why don't you just come with me and I'll fix something for both of us. I live just over the hill."

Her gaze lingered on him a moment longer. A dark stain spread over her high cheekbones, and then Millie turned away and started back down the road the way they'd come. Her back was ramrod straight and Ulrich wished he could see into her mind. Obviously something about her casual invitation upset her.

"If it's not too much trouble," Ulrich said, but inside, he was singing. Her scent rose to meet him, luring him forward, and there was no confusion now between her and the wolves.

Millie West was every bit as aroused as Ulrich.

Why now? She was an old woman, for crying out loud. Much too old to feel this amazing attraction to a man, though Ulrich Mason was, without any doubt, the sexiest male she'd ever seen. His interest in her was almost palpable, and when she'd turned around and actually looked at him, it had taken all her willpower not to stare at the sizeable bulge running down the inside seam of his left pants leg.

He must be hung like a bull and he was obviously hard as a post. Hard for her? She'd laugh if it wasn't so pathetic. Here she was, old enough to get a senior citizen discount in most places and, unless she counted the well-used collection of vibrators in the table beside her bed, she'd not had sex since 1970.

Tell that to your pussy.

Damn. She was so wet she prayed the dampness between her legs wouldn't leak through her jeans. How embarrassing would that be? The denim rubbed her swollen clit through her sopping panties with every step she took, and her breasts felt unusually restrained within her plain cotton bra. She wondered if the batteries in the new vibrator she'd ordered online were fresh, and almost laughed aloud.

What kind of woman took a gorgeous stranger home with her and worried about batteries?

A woman who'd learned her lesson the hard way.

That excuse didn't work anymore. She was fifty-six years old and pregnancy wasn't even an option, much less a worry. So what if she wanted sex with a man?

More important, what if he wanted sex with her?

She felt a low throb in the pit of her belly and took a deep breath. Her libido had caused trouble all her life—it was something her fanatically religious uncle had tried unsuccessfully to beat out of her.

She still remembered the spankings that had lasted well into her teen years, spankings requiring her bare bottom and the flat of her uncle's broad hand. By the time she was twelve or thirteen, she'd realized the punishment had taken on an overtly sexual tone, something that disgusted her even now.

For all his prayers and rules, her uncle had taken perverse pleasure in punishing her. She hadn't understood everything that was going on, but she'd known it was wrong. In their rural community, though, where his family name was among the first settlers, she'd had no one to turn to.

Thank goodness there'd always been the wolves. Why they fascinated her so, Millie would never know, but she'd sensed a link between herself and the animals long before the sanctuary had grown so large, long before the property that had been her only home had become the property of the High Mountain nonprofit organization. She'd been alone, except for the wolves.

There'd been one man. One sexy, long-legged, itinerant cowboy. He'd not lingered time enough for her to fall in love with him, but he'd certainly managed to change her life.

She wouldn't think about that now. Couldn't. Not with Ulrich Mason walking silently behind her, his big body still straight and strong in spite of his snow-white hair. He was a handsome man, ageless in the way of the very fit, with amazing eyes. Dark gold. No, she thought. Amber.

Similar to her own, but where her eyes were nothing special, his sparkled with an inner fire.

She wished she'd known him when he was young.

Wished she'd met him when she was younger, but it was too late for regrets. She slowed her pace at the top of a small rise. The sanctuary and offices lay to her right, but she took the trail to the left. It followed a narrow creek that gurgled and raced beside them.

"You live close enough to walk to work?" His voice was just over her shoulder. His nearness startled her so that she stopped and turned to reply.

"Every morning. It's a challenge in the winter, but I use snowshoes then." She took a deep breath. "I love the woods. I especially love the wolves. I've always felt a kinship with them, a sense that we practically communicate on some level."

Ulrich's hand suddenly rested on her shoulder. Millie stopped in midstride. "Maybe you do," he said. "Maybe you do."

She cleared her throat, felt her heart thudding in her chest, the hot coil of desire coursing from breasts to belly to sex. She thought of the dreams, the sense when she awakened of having run through the woods on four legs, the ache in her muscles, the tightness in her legs. The need, the overwhelming desire that had her reaching for her favorite vibrator. Such a cliché, the older woman alone with nothing more than her battery operated boyfriend, but it had kept her sane all these years.

"I wish," she said, and meant it. Then Millie turned and walked away from Ulrich's touch, well aware he followed closely behind her.

The cabin was small and neat, a square log structure nestled in the deep forest, surrounded by ponderosa pine, thick cedar, and old growth Douglas fir. Ulrich took a deep breath, inhaling the scent of centuries, the damp mix of rotting leaves and fresh grass, pine resin and wet earth that tickled his nostrils with ancient memories. The forest brought out the wild side of his nature and the wolf clamored silently for freedom. He would have to run at some point during this visit.

He wished he could run with Millie beside him, but the sense of her wasn't quite as strong now. Of course, she'd put more distance between them, opening the door and stepping inside the cabin while he stood outside and inhaled the fresh air.

Feeling somewhat sheepish, Ulrich followed her indoors. The interior was as neat as the outside. Bare logs aged to dark gold formed the walls, and the plank floor was covered with hand-woven rugs. The kitchen had obviously been added more recently, and a small room tucked behind the woodstove was most likely the bathroom.

Tiny, immaculate, serviceable . . . with comfortable, well-worn furniture and beautiful watercolors decorating the walls. "Are these yours?" Ulrich walked across the main room and studied a painting on the far side. A pride of wolves led by what was obviously the alpha bitch. She stood beside her mate, but her eyes were alive and seemed to be watching Ulrich, not the large wolf beside her.

Millie moved closer to Ulrich and nodded. "Yes. I paint them on my days off. They're such wonderful subjects."

"You have a lot of talent. This is beautiful."

She dipped her chin and blushed, then abruptly turned away. "I've got some leftover roast from last night. I'll make us each a sandwich. I hope you like your meat rare."

It was more than rare. It was still blood red, exactly the way Ulrich liked it when he couldn't just eat it raw. She'd cooked it the way every other Chanku preferred their meat when they dined in public. He watched while Millie sliced the beef thin and piled it high on sliced sourdough French bread with lots of horseradish and mustard. She moved with an economy and grace he admired.

They sat close at a small café-style table obviously designed for one person, not two. Conversation came easily. They talked a bit about the sanctuary, the changes Millie hoped to make over the coming year, her hopes for expanding into some of the unused property.

When their plates were clean, though, they found there was nothing else to say. Ulrich reached across the table and covered her hand with his. "Thank you. That was delicious. I know it's rude to eat and run off, but I'm going to need to head back to town, find a place to stay. I came straight to the sanctuary without finding a room first, once I realized how close I was. We can go over the books tomorrow, if that's okay with you."

Millie glanced down at their hands, his larger one covering hers entirely, then up at Ulrich. He saw questions in her amber eyes. Even more, he saw her need, felt her powerful desire for his touch. He inhaled and scented the sweet perfume of her arousal.

Silently placing his heart in Millie West's hands, Ulrich leaned across the small oak table and softly pressed his lips against hers. Her quick, indrawn breath told him she'd not expected this, but her lips softened, parted. He felt her sigh against his mouth.

He pulled away and cocked an eyebrow in her direction. She blushed and looked down at their hands. "You have no idea what you're asking," she said.

"Ah, I believe I do." He cupped her cheek in his palm and forced her to look at him. "You're a beautiful woman, Millie West. You're funny and smart and very sexy, and your heart is good."

She shook her head. "How can you say that? You hardly know me."

Ulrich raked his thumb along her cheekbone. "I know you've cared for the wolves as if they were your children. You've given Seth an extra chance at redemption when most people, including me, would turn him away. The sanctuary is well run, the animals healthy and content, your employees look at you as if you hold the sun and the moon in your hands and you've done all of this in just a matter of weeks since the problems with the last manager. What more do I need to know?"

She turned away. Her cheek still rested against the curve of his palm. Ulrich felt her sigh. She opened her mouth to speak, but no sound emerged. Finally she backed away, far enough to put herself out of his grasp, and looked him straight in the eye. "You need to know that I'm a freak, Ulrich Mason. I'm fifty-six years old and I've not been with a man for over thirty-six years." She stood up and pushed the chair back, then turned around and wrapped her arms around her slim waist. "I'm not normal, Ulrich. There's something about me that's so strange, I'll never have a normal relationship, never be able to . . ."

He circled the table and caught her up in his arms. She fought him at first, but he felt her embarrassment and knew her heart wasn't in the struggle. Her resistance ended on a sigh as she pressed her face against his chest, body trembling, breath catching in her throat. He felt her shoulders shake and knew she cried softly, silently, in his arms.

He held her close, rubbed her back slowly and smiled into her blond hair while she quietly brought her emotions back under control.

Standing there, with Millie pressed close against him, Ulrich felt the lust that had been burning in him all morning long suddenly shift and subside. His heart seemed to swell in his chest, his eyes blurred with tears. Somehow, over the course of the past few hours, pieces of his life that had long been sundered appeared to have found their way back to form a tenuous whole.

Unbelievable, he thought, rubbing his lips softly against Millie's thick crown of hair. After so many years as the pack's lone wolf, Ulrich Mason knew he'd suddenly, irrevocably, fallen in love.

Chapter 3

Baylor stood to one side in the small landing at the top of the stairs and watched as Harry Trenton carefully folded the crisp hundred dollar bill he'd just taken from Bay's hand. Harry had the good grace to look moderately guilty, but he lifted the door mat and drew a check and a five dollar bill from beneath it, then knocked on the door.

It didn't open, of course. Bay hadn't expected it to. He heard someone on the other side, a soft voice, low-pitched and slightly rough. "Thanks, Harry. I'll call next week when I need a new order."

"Sure I can't bring the stuff inside for you, Ma'am? The box is heavy."

"I'm sure. Thank you. Your check and tip are under the mat."

"Got 'em." Harry slanted a suspicious look at Bay and then turned and walked down the stairs to the ancient Ford pickup parked in the street.

He didn't look back, though he did pause for a moment on the bottom step, as if reconsidering his actions. Baylor held his breath. The last thing he wanted was a confrontation here, so close to his target.

Harry continued on across the cracked sidewalk and climbed into his truck. The engine growled, the truck rattled in place, backfired twice and then slowly headed down the narrow street.

Baylor stayed in the shadows and waited. She was in there. He'd heard her voice, rough and scratchy as if from lack of use. Her scent lingered, rich and inviting, an alluring temptation calling him close, but he knew better than to rush anything. He knew she stood just on the other side of the door. He heard a soft shuffle as she moved, the creak of floorboards, then finally, a good ten minutes or more after Harry had gone, the sharp click as a lock was turned, a handle moved.

The door lacked a traditional doorknob, but the accessible lever designed for those with physical handicaps slowly tilted downward. Bay pressed his back to the wall beside the door, saw the shadow of hands reaching for the box of groceries, then the fur-covered fingers themselves, tipped with dark claws that dug into the cardboard and dragged it slowly across the threshold.

Once the box was fully inside, Bay whirled around, stepped across the threshold through the open door and shut it behind him. The small, twisted figure crouched over the box, amber eyes wide, stringy blond hair hanging loose and lank, too frightened to scream—a creature out of his worst nightmares.

The photo in the paper had been kind.

She didn't even try to run. Instead, she collapsed and folded in upon herself, rolled into a small, cotton-shrouded, fur-covered ball, and whimpered like a lost pup.

He'd not thought beyond getting through the door. Had no idea what he would say or do once he finally found her, but the last thing Bay had expected was the heart-rending sound of such abject grief.

She was hardly bigger than a child and her tragic cries devastated him. He did the only thing he could. He leaned over and picked her up, cradled her unresponsive body in his arms and walked across the small living room to a big, overstuffed couch. Then he sat down with her in his lap, held her close against his chest and stroked her long, straggly blond hair.

She didn't try to pull away, though he felt her trembling and sensed her fear. "It's okay," he said. "I'm not going to hurt you. I'm here to help you. I promise."

She wore some kind of gray, shapeless smock that covered her body with long sleeves and a full skirt. He felt an awkward lump in his lap and knew it must be a tail, or at least part of one. She'd apparently started to shift and been unable to complete the process, leaving her body an awkward, obviously painful combination of human and wolf.

There wasn't anything remotely attractive about her. Thick wrists, rudimentary thumbs, long, sharp nails. Her face was buried against his chest, but she had more muzzle than mouth. Her ears were stuck midway between where a human's would be and the upright position of a wolf's, with tiny tufts of fur covering them.

He wondered how long she'd been caught like this, who had cared for her to allow her to survive, and most of all, if she was just too frightened to speak. He hated thinking he was causing her so much distress. He tried mindtalking but there was a wall as high and thick as any he'd encountered. She might not be fully Chanku, but the woman—or girl—managed to block.

For all he knew, she could be a child, but he hoped not. He'd been hard as a post from the first whiff of her scent, the purely feminine Chanku musk that had attracted him from the moment he'd entered the room. Richer even than Shannon's fragrance, this ugly little she-wolf had his blood thrumming in his veins.

She drew a long shuddering sigh against his chest. He waited for her to say something. Anything. Instead, she snuggled closer against him and sighed. Bay felt the rigid tension in her body relax as she finally surrendered to the safety of his embrace.

Manda figured that as long as she kept her mouth shut and didn't look the man in the eye, she wouldn't have to deal with whatever had just happened. Besides, it felt so good here, held snugly in his strong arms. She felt protected. Safer than she'd felt in many years, even though he was obviously up to no good. Why else would he have come for her?

Harry had betrayed her. He'd promised her keepers he'd deliver her weekly grocery orders and protect her privacy, but this beautiful man had obviously bought him off.

She wondered what newspaper or television station he represented. There was a price on her head, one she'd tried to ignore for much too long. The fact the man had found her told Manda she'd not been careful enough, but maybe this was merely one more example of God's punishment.

It would be nice to think otherwise. She'd never seen anyone as handsome as he was, even dressed in that strange, black leather suit. It made him look huge and powerful, but she liked the way the leather smelled. She even liked the way he smelled, but she didn't know a lot about men and their scents.

She'd never been around a man who didn't terrify her, except maybe Papa B, the man who rescued her so many years ago. Even so, she was almost sure she'd been punished enough for her sins, though she knew her father would never have agreed.

Whoever it was who held her, adjusted his position. She wondered if she was too heavy for him, if maybe his arm where she rested her upper body had grown weary. He stroked her hair with his right hand, an act so tender yet unbelievably erotic, she practically whimpered.

She'd never been held by a man. Not even her father

when she was small. He'd patted her head occasionally but left the affection and hugs to her overbearing mother. That was before the curse, when she'd still been just a normal little tow-headed girl living with her missionary parents in a small village on the Tibetan Plateau.

Of course, Mother had only been a pain with Manda and the help. Terrified of her overzealous missionary husband, Mother had taken her frustrations out on either Manda or the young village girls who came in to clean and cook for them.

Manda missed the girls from the village. She'd played in their homes, eaten at their tables. Life in Tibet had been a wonderful adventure. Wonderful until God cursed her for her sins.

"Will you talk to me now? Are you going to be okay?"

His voice rumbled from deep in his chest and she felt it against her cheek. Manda sighed. She'd truly hoped he would just go away, though she knew that wasn't about to happen.

"I'm okay. I can talk," she said, though her voice, twisting out through her malformed vocal cords, often slipped into squeaks and grunts. "I don't really want to, though." As much as she loved the warm comfort of his arms, Manda sat up and pushed herself away from the man. As quickly as she could, she scrambled off his lap and turned away. It was easier not to look at him. To know he couldn't see her face.

They'd let her wear a veil at the lab in California and when they'd flown her in private planes whenever she had to travel. Manda wanted to think it was more for her own comfort, but she knew the truth. It was so she wouldn't frighten the technicians or anyone else who might see her.

"Please. Don't turn away from me. I'm not here to hurt you. I don't intend to write stories about you or tell anyone you're here. I really am here to help."

Now that was a new approach. She almost laughed, but

choked the sound back at the last minute. She'd had all the help she needed over the years, thank you very much. Look what it had gotten her. Not a damned thing but pain and fear.

Manda heard him stand up and flinched. A warm hand touched her shoulder and fingers squeezed her lightly, as if caressing her. She trembled. Her entire body was shaking and there wasn't a damned thing she could do about it.

"Relax. I'm going to put your groceries away. I don't want anything to spoil."

She heard him walk away and her stomach growled. She'd run out of food early yesterday and was desperately hungry. Now the scent of the blood-red meat in the grocery order made her mouth water. She licked her muzzle to keep from salivating all over herself and slowly turned around.

He'd picked up the heavy box like it weighed nothing at all, and carried it into the kitchen. A package with two thick sirloin steaks sat on the top. He set that aside and began putting other perishables in the refrigerator—fresh hamburger and chicken, even some fish, though it wasn't her favorite. Manda focused on the steaks sitting on the table, slowly warming to room temperature.

She licked her muzzle again and inhaled the rich smell of fresh blood. A whimper caught in her throat and she realized she'd moved closer to the table. Had he noticed? She couldn't be sure. He put the last of the groceries away and she wondered if he'd forgotten the steaks, but when he moved the cardboard box to a corner, he went right back to the package of meat.

Manda glanced up at him and blinked. He looked at the raw meat the same way she did!

"You like it raw, too, don't you?"

Too? He liked his meat raw? She nodded her head.

"Good. Do you mind sharing with me? It's been a long journey, searching for you."

She shook her head, entirely confused now. No one else ever ate his meat raw. She was the only one. The freak.

He reached in the cupboard and grabbed two plates. Set them on the table without silverware. Grabbed a knife, tore open the plastic wrap covering the steaks and slid a thick slab of meat onto each plate.

"Do you want me to cut it up?"

She nodded. Carefully, he cut one of the steaks into bite-sized pieces. Then he held her chair for her and Manda slipped into it, resting on one hip to avoid that damned tail. He sat down across the table from her and waited.

Confused, she stared at him, then caught a strong whiff of the meat. Hunger took over and she practically attacked the steak, using one paw to hold the plate. Biting and licking up the pieces, tearing at them with her sharp canines. Swallowing the meat in huge gulping bites.

It tasted warm and rich and she thought of what it must be like, to hunt and kill and eat meat still warm from life. She'd rather think imaginary dreams than actually consider the implications of the man sitting across from her.

She knew he must be watching her, but the hunger was too powerful, her need too great. She licked the last remnants of blood from the plate, still holding it down with one paw. Finally, Manda forced herself to stop and raise her head. He'd left his piece of the steak intact. Now he sat across from her, holding the bloody slab of meat in his two hands, chewing thoughtfully as he watched her eat.

She licked around her muzzle with her long tongue. So what if he saw! He already knew what she looked like. Then she used both hands to pick up a napkin and carefully wiped the rest of the blood away from her face. Hunger assuaged, Manda watched the man finish the last of his steak with obvious relish. He wiped his mouth with his napkin and smiled at her, then rested his chin on his folded hands. "Do you want to tell me your story, or should I tell you mine?"

"Tell me who you are." Her voice sounded scratchy, as she so rarely used it anymore. Still, he looked pleased that she'd at least said something to him. Even more important, he didn't look frightened by her. He didn't look away.

"My name is Baylor Quinn. Bay, for short. I'm with a group called Pack Dynamics, and I'm here to help you."

"You said that already. There's no way to help me. Look at me." Belly full, finally more angry than frightened, Manda pushed her chair away from the table and stood up. She had to catch the edge of the table for balance. She held her arms out, displaying her smock-clad body as best she could. "I'm a freak. An example of what happens when you sin. I'm cursed. You can't help a curse."

"You're not cursed. You're caught halfway between shifts."

Manda shook her head. "That doesn't make any sense."

"I know it doesn't, but it can. It will. You have to trust me, though. I want to show you what I mean, but you need to trust me. Don't be afraid, don't scream. Most of all, don't run away."

She frowned. "I can barely walk. Running's out of the question. Where would I go? Besides, why would I want to run away?"

He laughed, but he stayed well back from her. "Because you're going to think I'm absolutely nuts. I'm not. Nor am I a pervert, but I have to take my clothes off if I'm going to do this right."

Manda laughed. She couldn't help herself. In fact, she realized that in some perverse way she was actually enjoying herself. What she'd feared for so long—discovery—had finally come to pass. The worst that could happen to her had happened and she was still alive. For now. "You're kidding, right? You think you're going to just barge in here, eat one of my steaks, and tell me not to weird out when you take your clothes off? I may be a freak, but you're certifiable."

"Maybe." He unzipped the heavy black leather suit and peeled it off. There were regular clothes underneath. Manda realized he was much slimmer than she'd first thought. Once the suit was off, he started unbuttoning his shirt.

"What I have to show you has nothing to do with being naked, and everything to do with who and what you are. What we are. For the record, I have a very good friend who looked almost exactly as you do. He's now a very handsome man with a wife and new baby . . . and sometimes he's a wolf."

She was still trying to process what he'd said when he slipped his muscular arms free of his long-sleeved cotton shirt and draped the shirt over the kitchen chair. Manda hadn't seen a man's chest for years, and she'd never seen one like his, so perfect it made her sex tighten in anticipation and terrified her at the same time. What was it he said? He had a friend just like her? Impossible.

He reached for his belt and she turned around.

"No," he said. "I want you to watch."

She snorted. "You really are a pervert, aren't you?" She didn't turn away. Couldn't. Just knowing how she'd reacted to the brief sight of his lean, muscled chest with the dark swirl of hair between his nipples warned Manda anything else might be too much. Still, shouldn't she be afraid? A stranger had forced his way into her home, eaten her food and now was undressing and asking her to watch?

She must be just as perverted as he was. Or maybe she was merely desperate.

"Please. You need to turn around and watch this. I'm not going to hurt you."

She heard the sound of his boots hitting the floor, then the rustle of his jeans. Tried to imagine the lean strength of his hips and whether or not the hair on his groin matched the dark pelt on his chest.

"You really do need to watch me if you're going to understand."

Manda sighed. What was the point? She pivoted slowly, awkwardly, and caught the briefest glimpse of him naked. Tall, lean, and muscular with the kind of body that could provide plenty of fuel for any woman's fantasy . . . even a freak's.

Then he was gone. So quickly Manda barely had time to gasp.

In his place was a wolf. Black overall, with amber eyes that glistened against the ebony fur, the beast sat patiently in exactly the same spot where Baylor had been standing.

Manda's twisted legs gave out. She fell to her knees, caught herself with one hand braced on the floor. She reached out and touched the animal's face, scooted closer and ran her fingers the length of an ear. "Baylor? Is that you?"

The wolf nodded. Such a human response was almost too much. Almost. She touched him with both hands now, hands that weren't nearly as much like paws as his. He held up one foot, almost as if he knew what she was thinking. Manda took his big paw in her own, compared the ebony nails, the thick pads on his, the longer fingers on hers.

It couldn't be. It was impossible, but then wasn't she impossible as well? "How?" She sat back on her fanny, hard, and it hurt because the stub of a tail that had never quite become anything other than a stub got in the way. Scrambling to her feet, Manda held out her hands. "Tell me. How?"

Then, as if she'd blinked and missed something miraculous, Baylor Quinn stood in front of her again. He was closer though, his lean body so sleek and perfect she wanted to weep at the wretched ugliness of her own.

She clasped her hands in front of her waist to keep from

touching him, stared unabashed at his male perfection, the lean cut of his belly, the thick length of his dark penis. It wasn't quite flaccid, nor as hard as she knew it could be, resting there against the heavy weight of his testicles.

Manda knew all about those parts of a man. Knew they were supposed to bring pleasure but in reality gave only pain. Knowing what she did, why did she still want to touch him? Another part of that damned curse? It must be.

He bent over and grabbed his underwear off the floor and quickly stepped into the cotton boxers. He pulled on his jeans and his shirt, but didn't say a word. He buttoned the fly on his jeans, left his shirt undone, his feet bare. Manda practically quivered with the need to know, but she didn't ask again. He'd come here to help her. She had to believe.

She had no choice.

Bay sat down on the couch and patted the seat beside him. Manda limped tentatively across the room and sat on the soft cushions, but as far away from Bay as she could. He knew she'd tried to make it look as if she merely wanted to be comfortable, but her barriers had fallen when Bay shifted and she'd broadcasted her thoughts like an open book.

He still terrified her, but for different reasons. He wondered what had happened to make her so afraid of men. Whatever, it went beyond the mere fact of her appearance or the fact he was a stranger. He tried probing her mind, but her chin snapped up and she glared at him, obviously aware he intruded.

Bay took a deep breath and wondered where to begin. It hadn't been all that long ago that Jacob Trent had done to Bay exactly what he'd just done to this young woman. Shifted from man to wolf, and in the process, turned Baylor's world upside down.

Then, just as quickly, Jake had righted it. Answered the

questions that had plagued Baylor all his life. Questions that couldn't possibly be as confusing as the ones this young woman confronted. He couldn't imagine going through life looking the way she did. Well, he had to start somewhere. "Will you tell me your name?"

She looked oddly vulnerable and at the same time, almost pleased with his question. "I thought you knew. My name is Manda. I figured that was how you found me."

Bay shook his head. "No, Manda. The folks here are working damned hard to protect you. Even Harry, the guy who brought your groceries, only agreed to tell me where you lived when I convinced him I could help you. He wasn't real happy about it, but I think he finally believed me."

"Did you do that for him? Change into a wolf?"

Bay shook his head. "No. That's a secret we're not allowed to share."

"You shared it with me."

He laughed, reached out and ruffled her tangled hair and realized he'd frightened her with the friendly gesture. Immediately he withdrew his hand. "I'm sorry. I didn't mean to startle you."

"It's just . . . I'm not used to people not being afraid of me. Or disgusted. I'm not used to other people, period." She looked down at her paws crossed in her lap, then raised her head again. "I haven't always been like this. I was cursed when I was twelve years old. Up until then, I was just a normal girl."

"Why do you think you were cursed?"

"I sinned." She looked away. "My father caught me . . ." She sighed, then looked directly at Bay and the words spilled out. "He caught me touching myself. He said it was an abomination. A sin against God. If I didn't pray for forgiveness and promise never to do it again, God would curse me. I didn't ask for forgiveness because it felt too good and I knew I'd do it again, so I lied to my father. That night the rebels came into the village. They killed

Mother and Father. It was all my fault, for lying, and I was cursed. I became this creature."

"How long ago was this? How long have you been . . ." He couldn't call it a curse, though to Manda it must be worse than death.

"Like this? It happened almost twenty-five years ago. I'm almost thirty-six years old and I've looked this way my entire adult life. I've been studied, poked, experimented on, and raped, all in the name of science. You try telling me it's not a curse. If not, then what? Tell me, Mr. Quinn. You seem to have all the answers."

He wanted to smile at her anger. She still had spirit. No matter what had happened, that hadn't been broken. "Actually," he said, leaning back against the padded arm of the sofa so he could see her better, "I probably have as many questions as you. What scientists? What happened?"

She clenched her hands and glared at him. "No more. You said you have answers. Damn it, tell me what happened. I have to know. Why? What made me this way? If not God's curse, then what?"

He liked her already. "Genetics. Your breeding. I believe you, just like me, are Chanku. An ancient race of shapeshifters that first appeared on the steppes of the Himalayas, probably not that far from the village where your parents were missionaries. We don't know if the first ones evolved naturally or might even have been left here by some alien race millennia ago. What we do know, however, is that the species loses the ability to shift from human to wolf and back again without certain nutrients found in that one isolated area of the world. I can only imagine you ate some of the local vegetation that allowed your Chanku genes to awaken. We can't shift until reaching puberty. You were twelve years old. About the time when a lot of girls begin puberty, right? What happened the night your parents died?"

Manda stared at him a moment, amber eyes wide, yet

Bay knew she tried to process what he'd just told her while she focused on her memories. Somehow she would have to reconcile an entirely different history for herself, but now she relived her own reality. Horrible memories of blood and death and abject fear. He felt them, saw as she remembered, experienced her agony through the thoughts spilling out of her now unblocked mind. Bay felt her horror of the men on horseback and on foot slipping into the small, walled village late at night, moving from hut to hut, burning and murdering.

He saw her father standing at their doorway, his Bible held high as he defied the raiders. Saw the blood spatter from the back of his head when a bullet entered between his eyes and split his skull. Her mother was next, though her death wasn't nearly as clean as her husband's. She, like the other women, was raped by many before one of them finally killed her.

Manda saw and heard it all, hidden in a secret closet designed for just such an attack, watching through the woven, wicker door. When the battle ended, when soldiers came in the morning to find what was left of the village, they'd found her by the sound of her whimpering. One of the men opened the door and he'd screamed. Screamed and run from her in fear.

There'd been a young congressman on a fact-finding mission. He'd obviously been repulsed by her appearance, but when he heard her speak English, he'd been kind to her. He'd managed to smuggle her out of the country and back to the United States, where he'd kept her over the years. Moved from lab to lab around the country, she'd spent the last two dozen years being studied as a freak of nature.

She'd called him Papa B, but he'd been dead now for what seemed like forever and the visual Bay got of the man was fuzzy and indistinct. Manda opened her mouth to speak. Bay moved closer to her and touched his finger to the side of her muzzle. "I've been in your thoughts. I don't want to make you talk about what happened. It was truly awful, but what I saw in your memories explains a lot."

She blinked, almost as if she were coming out of a trance. "How do you know what I remembered?"

"I am Chanku. So are you. We share our thoughts with one another. It's a form of telepathy we call *mindtalking*. It's even easier with a mate, but just getting to know each other will make it easier for us. Living there in Tibet, you probably ate enough of the local foods to enable a small gland in your brain to begin to develop. Probably not fully, which would account for your partial shift. The trauma of the attack and your parents' deaths would have forced the shift on you. You're not a freak, Manda. Not at all. You are Chanku. A shapeshifter. Part of an ancient species that exists secretly among humans, but they have the most amazing abilities. I can help you find your true self, but you'll have to trust me. Can you do that, Manda? Can you trust someone you've barely begun to know?"

She reached up and touched his cheek with her paw. Bay felt the sharp nails against his face, the rough pads at the end of each finger, and looked into eyes the image of his own. "The two men who've cared for me since Papa B died didn't come back from their last mission. They've been gone more than two weeks now. I'm almost out of cash and running out of money in the bank to live on. I don't have enough to pay my next month's rent, and I don't know where the money has been coming from in the first place. The men who watched me took care of all that. You're proof that Harry can't be trusted to keep my secrets, even though he hasn't got any idea what they are."

Manda dropped her hand to her lap and took a deep, soulful breath. Bay held his. When she looked at him again, there were tears in her eyes, though he noticed that none fell. Wolves didn't cry . . . though the girl in her obviously wanted to.

"You're the first man I've known who hasn't recoiled from me in absolute horror. I don't know you, but for some reason I want to believe you and your unbelievable story. It's a much nicer one than my own explanation, that God has cursed me. I'd prefer being part of a secret, yet ancient race. It's much more romantic. Maybe it's merely for my own self-preservation. God knows, I've wanted to die often enough over the past twenty-five years."

"I don't want you to die, Manda. I want to show you what life really can be like. You have no idea how wonderful it is to embrace that part of yourself you've probably hated all your life. You are wolf, Manda. You have the wild heart of a predator beating in your chest. I want you to learn to love the wolf as much as the woman."

She stared at him for a long, heart-stopping moment. Then she nodded. "Fair enough. What do I have to do?"

Bay laughed and reached for his jacket. He pulled the pill bottle out of his pocket and opened the lid. The big brown capsules smelled like dried grass, and he put one in Amanda's oddly shaped palm. "Just a minute. I'll get you some water."

He went into her kitchen, looked in a cupboard and saw a couple of glasses. He thought better of it, filled a bowl with water from the tap, and took it back to Manda. She sat on the couch, sniffing at the pill in her open hand. "It smells like grass, or maybe dry hay."

"It's a combination of dried grasses from the Himalayan steppes. We take one every day, though no one knows if we would revert without them, once the change occurs. I'm not sure how long it will take you to make the shift fully to either wolf or woman. If you take one of these a day, I imagine just a couple days should do it, especially since you've obviously already started."

She popped the pill into her mouth without hesitation and then leaned forward and lapped water from the bowl Bay held in his hands. He'd guessed right, that drinking from a glass would be difficult for her. She raised her head and there were droplets of water glistening at her muzzle. He tried to imagine her as a woman with lips and cheekbones and smooth skin.

"Do we just wait, now?"

"No. Now I need to figure out how to smuggle you out of here without anyone seeing you. I want to take you to our cabin up in Maine. I want to have you far from town when you finally make the complete shift. You're going to want to race through the forest and I don't want anyone or anything to get in your way."

"Can't I just tuck down in the backseat of your car?"

Bay laughed. "Well, that would work. Unfortunately, all I've got is my motorcycle. There's really no place at all for you to hide."

He pulled her back into his lap. He was surprised but greatly pleased when she let him hold her close. As horrendous as she looked, Bay realized he was fascinated by her appearance as much as her resilience. Drawn to her addictive Chanku aroma, her feisty personality, her core of strength that nothing appeared to have shaken.

For better or worse, he held her against his chest and accepted the fact he was falling, fast and sure, under Manda's spell.

Chapter 4

Ulrich gently brushed Millie's hair back from her eyes and she raised her head to look at him. He was so handsome standing there, the shock of white hair hanging down over his forehead looking incongruous with his otherwise youthful appearance. His skin was tan yet unlined, his eyes dark with worry. When he leaned close and kissed her, it seemed perfectly natural to kiss him back.

She had, after all, known him for at least three hours now.

Their mouths connected and heat spiraled from lips to womb. There was no thrust of his tongue, no groping of hands. He held her steady, one palm resting in the middle of her back, the other gently cradling her head. He moved his lips over hers softly, gently, sucking at her mouth with little sips and nips.

She angled her hips forward, found the hard edge of his belt buckle, the long swell of his cock. His heat radiated through the heavy denim of his jeans and her sex creamed in response.

She had so little experience with men. The few times in recent history when men had tried to entice her, their rough groping and hard thrusts had turned her away.

Ulrich was pure gentleness, his touch merely a guide for

Millie to follow. She angled her mouth against his, tested the seam of his lips with her tongue and smiled against his mouth when he opened for her.

They kissed. Tongues twining, lips pressing and nipping. When Ulrich pulled away, he was breathing hard but obviously still very much in control. He rested his forehead against hers and his voice carried a promise. "It's up to you, Millie. I'll not take you anywhere you're not ready to go."

She felt the tears start in her eyes. It was hard to talk around the lump in her throat. "I have no idea what I want, Ulrich. No idea at all. My body is reacting to you as if we've known each other forever, but my mind is throwing up all kinds of roadblocks."

He laughed, took her hand and led her to the sofa. "How about I give you another roadblock? I didn't expect anything like this between us, and I'm not prepared. I didn't bring any protection, so there's only so far we can go."

Now it was Millie's turn to laugh. "I think I'm a bit beyond worrying about pregnancy, Mr. Mason. Those parts retired a few years ago."

"There are other things to worry about in this day and age. I'm just trying to protect you." He twirled a curl of her hair around his finger, slipped it free and watched it spring back against her throat. "I would never want to put you at risk."

"Oh." She hadn't even thought of disease or any of the other reasons folks used condoms. It hadn't entered her mind. Not in 1970 and not today. She raised her chin and smiled at Ulrich. "That just goes to show you how long it's been for me. I never even thought of needing protection."

"We probably don't, but it's a good way to make sure we don't rush things. Let me touch you, Millie. I'd love to spend an afternoon lying in bed with you, just touching."

His voice vibrated with what could only be desire. His jeans swelled with his erection and his visible need spread heat everywhere throughout Millie's suddenly pliant body.

She really should go back to the office. Really hadn't planned to be away . . .

Ulrich's broad palm covered her breast. She moaned and arched her back, forcing herself into his grasp. "I need to call the office, tell Seth I won't be back." Her words exploded in a breathless whisper.

"Good." With a satisfied smile, Ulrich removed his hand from her breast, laced his fingers behind his head and leaned back against the sofa. He reminded her of a self-satisfied cat.

She should have felt insulted. She didn't. She'd never felt more gloriously feminine, more powerful, in her life.

Millie called Seth and asked him to cover for her. When she said her business with Mr. Mason was taking longer than she'd planned, she heard Ulrich's soft chuckle. She tried frowning at him when she turned around, but all she could manage was a silly grin. She'd never done anything like this. Ever.

It was about damned time.

Ulrich stood up and held out his hand. She looked at his long fingers for a moment, imagined them slipping inside her hungry sex, knew how much he would fill her, and had to bite back a needy moan. Without another moment's hesitation, she reached out and allowed Ulrich to fold her smaller hand within his. Then she followed him down the short hallway to her bedroom.

Narrow shades kept the room in semi-darkness, something for which Millie was thankful. She might still be slim and trim, her muscles firm and her breasts small enough not to sag, but she was a fifty-six-year-old woman. As kind as the years had been, she had no illusions about her looks.

Ulrich didn't even hesitate. He began unbuttoning his shirt before he was even into the bedroom. He untied his hiking boots and kicked them off, stripped his shirt off his broad shoulders, peeled off his undershirt and slipped his jeans down over his lean hips.

Millie's mouth went dry. Her fingers stilled against the first button on her shirt and she stared at the monstrous bulge between Ulrich's legs. He wore soft, knit boxer shorts, the kind that clung to every bump and crease, and the pale blue shorts outlined a penis much larger than anything Millie had even imagined.

Ulrich seemed unaware of her hesitation. He slipped his shorts down his legs. His heavy erection jutted out from the thick nest of dark hair covering his groin. Millie swallowed, and moved on to the next button, but she couldn't take her eyes off Ulrich's perfect body.

The hair on his chest grew in a frosted mat from nipples to groin. Darker than the hair on his head, it made a perfect V over the finely honed muscles of his chest. He didn't have the body of a sixty-four-year-old man. Not at all. From his well defined pectorals to the ripple of a neatly formed six-pack, Ulrich could have been a man in his thirties. Only the shock of white hair on his head, the smattering of gray mixed with the darker hair on his chest, hinted at his true age.

With trembling fingers, Millie slipped her shirt off and reached behind herself to unfasten her bra. She tugged it over her arms and let it drop to the floor. Ulrich watched her with such profound hunger in his eyes that she forgot the size of his cock, forgot the age of her body.

He'd said he only wanted to touch her. Imagining the intimacy of his body close to hers made her shiver. Ulrich stepped close and reached for the snap on her jeans. "May I?"

Millie broke into a huge grin. "Please." She held her hands out to her sides. "I'm all yours."

He laughed then, a big, booming sound of utter joy. "I was hoping you'd say that. My God, Millie. You're absolutely lovely."

There was no hesitation in his voice. None in his actions. She felt the snap give way at her waist and bent to tug the jeans down her hips, but Ulrich stopped her. "Allow me. Please?"

She nodded. He knelt in front of her and untied her boots first. She stepped out of them. When he tugged her thick socks off, his fingers wrapped around the arch of first one foot, then the other. He rubbed each one for just a moment, but it was long enough for Millie to break out in chills. His touch was perfect—gentle, but firm.

He looped his fingers into the waistband of her jeans and tugged. Her plain white cotton panties came off with the denims. She should have felt some sense of shame, some knowledge of sin as this man, who was essentially a stranger, slowly but surely stripped her naked, but Millie gloried in his touch, in the avid attention he paid her. She grabbed the hard ridge of his shoulder for balance when he tugged her pants off first one leg, then the other. When she was naked, he smiled like a small boy who'd just unwrapped a priceless package.

Her skin tingled with her growing arousal. She looked into his amber eyes—eyes shimmering with an inner fire that must surely match her own. Caught in their glow she sucked in a huge breath, then another, and suddenly it was too much, too soon.

Too intimate.

She tensed. Her fingers dug into Ulrich's shoulders while her heart tumbled in her chest, but before Millie could move away, Ulrich grabbed her hips in his big hands. He steadied her with his powerful grasp and then leaned forward and kissed her just below the navel.

Millie gasped as all the air escaped her lungs. Ulrich nuzzled the soft skin of her lower belly. He brushed the edge of her pubic curls with the very tip of his tongue, then slipped lower, just to the beginning of her cleft. He exhaled and his warm breath flowed over her swollen clit.

Millie's heart stuttered. The muscles in her belly clenched and a convulsive spasm rippled between her legs. Ulrich lowered his head, licking softly until his tongue suddenly became the entire center of her universe.

No man had ever done that before. She'd fantasized about the soft touch of lips and tongue, but not once had she ever experienced what she'd so thoroughly and explicitly imagined.

Imagination had nothing on Ulrich. He leaned close and ran his tongue between her labia. Millie whimpered and almost collapsed in his grasp. He pulled back and grinned at her. "Like that, eh?" Then he lifted her as if she weighed nothing at all and propped her butt against the edge of the bed. "This is better. Can't have you falling down, can we?"

She shook her head. Words failed her.

Ulrich slipped between her legs and somehow she ended up stretched back on the mattress with her knees bent over his shoulders and his hands cupping her butt. She felt totally exposed, completely vulnerable and more aroused than she'd ever been in her life.

This time he lifted her hips and held her to his mouth. His tongue stroked once more between her swollen lips and then delved deep inside. She felt the tip of his tongue curl against the inner walls of her pussy and closed her eyes to the intense pleasure, drifted with the fantasy of his tongue and lips, the small, gentle nibbles of his teeth.

She heard moaning and realized the sound came from her own throat. She heard similar noises from Ulrich. In fact, he wasn't at all quiet. Wet, squishy sounds of his mouth on her sex, the low groan of arousal when she tilted her hips just a fraction to give him more room to savor what he so obviously enjoyed.

She raised her head and watched him for just a moment, his white hair between her thighs, the strong curve of his muscular arms, but when he found her clit with his mouth she lay back and cried out. He sucked her clitoris between his lips and licked the compressed bundle of nerves with the tip of his tongue.

There was no warning, no sign her world was about to collapse in upon itself. Her climax hit hard, an explosion of sensation, streaks of fire along her spine, a spasm of muscles in vagina and rectum, and still he suckled and licked until she screamed and rolled forward, grabbing at his shoulders, clutching the sides of his head, her legs clenching and holding him against her.

Then, to her absolute humiliation, Millie burst into tears.

He brought her down slowly, licking, kissing, nuzzling her sex and lapping up the rush of fluids that spilled along her inner thighs. She should have been embarrassed at such intimacy from a man who was essentially a stranger, but he'd rocked her world and left her in a state of shock.

When her body no longer trembled, when the tears still flowed from her eyes but her sobs had quieted, he moved slowly up her prostrate form and kissed her full on the mouth. She tasted herself on his lips, smelled the earthy sent of her release and broke into fresh tears.

Ulrich slid higher on the bed, leaned against the headboard and drew her into his arms. Millie curled up and cried against his chest, too embarrassed to look him in the eye, too overwhelmed to even think of taking control of her emotions. It had never been like this, not even in the bloom of youth with her dashing young cowboy. Nothing she'd ever felt, ever experienced, compared to what Ulrich Mason had just given her.

With his mouth, his hands, his intimate touch, he'd led Millie into an entirely new world.

A world she'd wondered about but not truly imagined, pleasure she couldn't, even now, describe. Her muscles still pulsed with a deep, steady rhythm, her heart pounded in her chest, her lungs, only now, began to slow their frantic pace.

Ulrich rubbed his chin against her crown. "You've just given me a most special gift. One I will never, ever forget. One never to be duplicated."

His slow, deep words seemed to rumble up out of his chest. Millie turned in his arms so that she could see him, confused by the depth of emotion in his voice. She was shocked to see silver streams of tears on his cheeks.

"Ulrich?" She touched a damp streak and, without even wondering why, brought her fingertip to her mouth and tasted the salt. "What's wrong? What do you mean?"

He scooted higher on the bed, taking Millie with him, and stuck a pillow between his back and the headboard. Millie sprawled bonelessly across his body, intimately aware of the solid length of his erection trapped between their bodies. For all the pleasure he'd given her, he'd not taken any of his own. She'd never met a man like him, one who put her first. It was frightening in some indefinable way.

"You've never climaxed during sex before, have you?"

She felt her skin grow hot with shame and shut her eyes, totally humiliated by his astute—and accurate—observation. "I . . ."

"Millie! It's not meant as criticism." His arms tightened around her body and she felt his lips against her hair. "What you just gave to me was more important than any gift I've ever received. More precious. You gave me trust, Millie. You let me love you in a most intimate way without any hesitation, and I know that's something you don't take lightly."

"Never lightly. Not that." She tangled her fingers in the silky hair on his chest. "There's something else I want from you though."

"What's that?"

She felt his chin nuzzling behind her ear and broke out in chills and giggles. Damn, he made her feel like a young girl, not a woman old enough to be a grandmother!

"I want you to make love to me." She rolled to one side and freed his trapped penis. She wanted to touch it, to wrap her fingers around the thick length and touch the silky crown, but she was afraid. What would he say?

"I'm too old to get pregnant, I've not been intimate with anyone for years, so I can't give you any diseases. I want to feel you inside me. I want the freedom to touch you . . . but I'm afraid. I've never . . ."

"I want you to touch me. Oh Lord, do I ever!" He laughed, but she sensed the powerful arousal behind his words. "You'll not catch anything from me, I can promise, so long as you're not able to become pregnant. Millie, you are such a treasure, but I want to make you as comfortable as possible."

"I don't know what to do. Where to start." She glanced away, suddenly feeling unaccountably shy and awkward. "Maybe this wasn't such a good idea. Maybe . . ."

Ulrich paused for a moment. He twisted a long strand of her hair around his finger, then smiled as if he'd discovered answers to a deep, dark secret. "I have an idea that might make you more comfortable."

Millie tilted her head back to see him better. He was such a beautiful man, his features so perfectly shaped, his eyes absolutely mesmerizing.

"I think you need to feel some control," he said, slowly twisting the lock of her hair. He tugged gently, released the curl, then started all over again. "It can be disconcerting, that loss of self that occurs during orgasm, the feeling someone else has taken over your body, taken away your freedom of choice." He tugged again, as if to emphasize the control he held over her with that one lock of hair.

"I understand, but I tell you what. Pretend I'm tied and can't move and you can do whatever you like, touch wherever you want. If it makes you more comfortable, put a blindfold over my eyes." He pulled his finger free of the curl and brushed her hair down flat.

"You'd let me do that?"

"Millie, I'll let you do whatever you want. If you feel more comfortable tying me up for real, do that. Do whatever you want. You are in charge."

The thought of tying this big, powerful man brought a fresh rush of moisture between her legs. She'd never thought of tying a man up before, never imagined the sense of power it would give her. The spike of arousal was exhilarating. "I think I'd like that." She shoved herself away from his warm length and knelt beside him on the bed with one palm planted in the middle of his chest. "I really think I'd like that. If you're sure you don't mind. Don't go away."

He laughed again. She loved the sound of it. "You're kidding, right?" He gestured toward his erection, at the powerful length of it thrusting upward from his groin, the head swollen and dark. "I'm not going anywhere."

Surprised at her own lack of self-consciousness—she was, after all, naked—Millie crawled off the bed and opened the top drawer on her dresser. She pulled out a handful of colored scarves and held them in her hands for a moment while she admired the man in her bed. Damn, he was absolutely perfect.

And he had the most amazing erection. Long and thick, too heavy to stand completely upright, it curved toward her, practically begging for her attention. Grinning at the image, Millie approached the bed and carefully tied each of Ulrich's feet to a corner post on the bed. A red scarf for the right leg, purple for the left. She spread his legs wide and made sure the knots were tight, all the while fighting the urge to giggle at her own audacity. She noticed that his erection not only seemed to get bigger, it went from a long curve over his thigh to a completely upright position. Millie stared at the thick, blood-filled shaft and swallowed. He was huge.

She clutched the remainder of the scarves against her breasts and glanced up at Ulrich's face. He lay with his arms folded beneath his head, a big grin on his face. He cocked one eyebrow at her, looked at his erection and shrugged his shoulders. "What can I say? You have a powerful effect on me, Millie West."

She snorted. Not the most ladylike thing, but she was at a loss for words. She tied his right arm to the headboard with a swirly orange scarf, then straddled his body and tied his left arm to the opposing side. She picked a dark blue one this time. Then she held the last scarf in her hands and stared directly into Ulrich's dark amber eyes. "I want to blindfold you, too. Are you sure you won't mind?"

He chuckled and she felt his belly move beneath her sex. His erection touched her back. "You're kidding? Do I appear to mind?"

All she could do was shake her head. Then she folded the one black scarf she owned until there was no way anyone could see through it, and wrapped it carefully over Ulrich's eyes. He lifted his head so she could tie it at the back. Feeling unaccountably kinky and moving as if she were part of one of her own intricate sexual fantasies, Millie crawled off of him and off the bed. She stood back to admire her handiwork.

Ulrich was truly confined in multihued bands of silk. She watched as he tugged lightly at the scarves holding him down. Watched his swollen staff swell more with each tug, as if the thought of being restrained excited him as much as it did her.

"Are you comfortable?" She had to ask, but she certainly didn't expect the wide grin that spread across his face.

"Very, thank you. I do need to tell you something, though. It might be important. Maybe not." He paused and took a deep breath and Millie could have sworn his penis grew another inch. "This has been a fantasy of mine for years, being tied up with a beautiful woman in charge. I've never done it. Not even with my wife."

"You're married?" Millie grabbed the dresser to keep from collapsing. She'd never thought to ask.

He laughed again. She expected him to say he was divorced. "No," he said. "My wife died over twenty years ago. I've been alone since then."

Alone? Had he had sex? She couldn't imagine a man remaining celibate. "You mean you haven't . . . ?"

"I have. Very circumspect, very carefully. Never with anyone important to me. Never with a woman who attracted me the way you do. I'm single, I carry no diseases, and I'm growing quite anxious, lying here on your bed with my arms and legs tied and my eyes covered. Anxious because I have no idea what your intentions are."

He was single. He thought she was attractive. She had him tied to her bed. This time it was Millie's turn to laugh. "I'm still working on my intentions. Give me time. I'm out of practice. I've never had a man tied anywhere before, much less in my bed, and I don't intend to waste the opportunity."

"I was hoping for that. Any idea what you're going to do first?"

"I'm going to touch you. I've never really touched a man's . . ." She couldn't say it. Even the word *penis* stuck in her throat. No way could she use any one of the more popular euphemisms.

"It's my cock, Millie. Say the word. I imagine it's sort of empowering, to use those words that you were told nice girls don't say. I call it my dick, or prick or, when I'm really feeling nasty, it's meat. Hard, big, and really hot meat. And it's waiting for you."

He practically growled the words. Millie felt her skin growing hot and cold and wondered if she'd suddenly bitten off more than she could chew.

"Okay. It's a cock." She almost strangled over the word. "It's very . . . well, it's not pretty, not with all those big veins running along the sides. It's big. It looks hard and I can't imagine that much of anything fitting inside me, so it looks like regular sex is out."

"You might be surprised."

She crawled up on the bed to get a better look. It was nice having him tied. Even better having him blindfolded.

"You can touch me, you know. I really am tied pretty tightly."

She glanced at him once again, decided he was stuck where she'd tied him and reached out to touch the solid length of . . . well, his cock. She said it, silently, a few times and decided she liked the word after all. Her fingers wrapped around the length of him just beneath the bulbous head. He jerked when she touched him. Moaned when she tightened her fingers around his bulk. When Millie glanced at Ulrich's face, he was smiling, but there were beads of sweat above the blindfold.

She ran her thumb over the silky head and he actually moaned again. A little burst of courage had her scooting closer. She took a deep breath, straddled his chest and turned her back on Ulrich's sinfully attractive lips, but the position was even more intimate. She actually felt his heart beating beneath her left thigh, a steady metronome pounding out a counterpoint to her own throbbing pulse.

As she rubbed her thumb across the crown of his cock, a tiny drop of white seeped from the slit at the top. She smoothed it over the silky curve and another took its place. This one she took with her tongue, leaning over and licking slowly across the broad crown.

Not only did Ulrich moan, his cock twitched. Feeling a new sense of power, she ran her fingers down the long length to his full sac lying between his wide-spread thighs. She cupped him in her palm, feeling the two, separate balls within the wrinkly sac, separating them with her fingers, rolling them gently in fascinated curiosity.

"I'll give you about two more hours to quit that."

She laughed at his dry comment and continued her tender, exploratory caress. "I'm just familiarizing myself with your parts. They're a bit different than mine."

"Damn, I sure hope so."

His voice sounded strained. Because of her touch? Millie took a deep breath and let it out. This entire experience had a surrealistic sense to it, the feeling it couldn't possibly be happening to her.

But it was.

Ulrich had nailed it. Touching him like this, thinking those words she'd always thought of as dirty, Millie truly felt empowered. Brave in a way she'd never felt before. Without thinking it through, she leaned over and licked the next pale drop of fluid from the top of Ulrich's penis . . . *cock*. She had to think of it as a cock. That sounded more intimate . . . less formal.

Definitely less formal. Nothing formal about kneeling naked over a stranger's chest, licking the end of his cock. She almost choked on the thought. Instead, she ran her tongue over the silky crown, lapped up the white pearl of fluid at its tip and closed her eyes to better examine the taste. Salty, a little bitter, but somehow fascinating, and she was almost certain it could easily become addictive. She wrapped both her hands around him, squeezing gently and sliding slowly up and down.

Ulrich groaned and lifted his hips into her touch. Another pearly drop squeezed out. She licked that one as well, then, before she could talk herself out of it, opened her mouth wide and wrapped her lips around the silky crown.

He groaned aloud and thrust his hips up, catching her by surprise. His cock slipped past her lips and all the way to the back of her throat.

She gagged, pulled him out a bit and suckled with all her might, holding him in place in her mouth, pressing against the topside of his cock with the flat of her tongue.

There was a pulse beating in the big vein along the bottom and she trailed her fingers along it, down the full length to the wrinkled sac beneath. She felt the tension in Ulrich's thighs, as if he fought his restraints. The more he struggled, the more in control Millie felt. She cupped his testicles in her hands again, rolling the hard balls inside between her fingers.

His sac felt tighter and harder, as if the balls inside had drawn closer to his body. There was a subtle rhythm to Ulrich's movements now, a thrust and retreat that mimicked sex and triggered an immediate, visceral response in Millie. She felt the welling up of fluids between her legs and an overwhelming desire to impale herself on Ulrich, condom be damned.

Desire won out. She slipped her mouth free of his cock and let go of his balls. Carefully, refusing to think of what she was really doing, Millie turned around to face him and straddled his thighs. She used her hands to guide his straining cock toward her needy, greedy sex.

She was so wet she'd be embarrassed if Ulrich could see her, but he was lost there, hidden behind her black scarf and she was preparing to fuck an anonymous lover, no one she knew, no one who could question anything she did.

She rubbed his cock against her swollen labia. There was so much moisture, between his pre-cum and her thick fluids that he slipped back and forth with each stroke as if she'd slathered herself in some kind of lubricant.

As large as he was, Millie prayed he'd fit. She couldn't wait a moment longer, knew if she did she'd be climaxing all by herself.

Not this time.

She pressed the broad crown against her ripe sex and slowly lowered herself over his long, rock-solid length. He was so big but oh, so much better than her best sex toy. Her inner muscles clenched and spasmed around him and it hurt, at first, to force so much inside her vagina, but it was wonderfully thrilling, so amazingly exciting to be in control, to know that how deep and how far was totally her call.

She pressed down, lifted, then pressed again. Ulrich's hands strained at the scarves holding him. The muscles in his forearms, the veins covering his wrists and the backs of his hands were all extended with his efforts. Her bed creaked but the knots held.

Her scarves, however, would never be the same again.

Neither would she.

Millie realized Ulrich had grown silent. After all the chatter earlier, now he didn't say a word. A trickle of sweat ran down his right temple. She heard the rush of his harsh breath, felt the rise of his chest beneath her palms and it all came together in a brilliant flash of understanding.

She did this to him. Her touch, her body. She turned this man on until he struggled for control.

Suddenly it became a matter of pride more than desire, that she make him fit. She wanted him all the way inside, no matter if it hurt or not, wanted to feel the thick mat of his pubic hair against her labia, wanted to give him the same pleasure he'd shared with her.

Slowly, carefully, raising up and then lowering herself just a fraction more, Millie managed to take more of him. To her surprise, her body responded, her nipples peaked once more, her sex seemed to soften and expand, as if in invitation to this huge, male intruder. She opened her eyes and looked at Ulrich, but his eyes were still covered by the scarf, his lips set in a determined line. He'd wrapped his fingers around the scarves holding him captive and the strain showed in white knuckles and bulging forearms.

He was utterly silent, but his body language spoke volumes. With a final wriggle of her hips, Millie seated Ulrich's cock fully inside. She felt his balls beneath her butt, the pressure of his cock pressing against her womb. He was in. Completely inside, and she did what her body directed.

Curling her fingers into the hair on his chest, Millie began to move.

Ulrich thought of all the woman he'd fucked, all the men he'd taken or who had taken him, and none compared with the innocent, untutored exploration Millie West made on his exquisitely aroused body. It wasn't that her mouth was so soft, her hands naturally talented, her body warm and willing. It wasn't even the tight, clasp of her sex as she slowly, surely took him deep inside.

It was the awe, the amazing mental experience she shared with him, her thoughts as free and unfettered as a bird on the wing. He might be tied to the bed, his eyes covered, his body immobilized and his cock spearing a perfect, warm pussy, but his mind was one with Millie's, and her thoughts were soaring free.

She was totally, completely, without any reservation at all, in tune with her experience. She was enthralled with the fact she was fucking a man. In control. Her body taking him all the way inside, but at her own bidding.

He wanted to know her. Wanted to know the secrets that drove her. He had to know. Needed to know everything there was to the story of Millie West. Why, at fifty-six, was she practically a virgin? How had she managed without sex for so long?

She settled herself fully on his cock. He felt her inner muscles clasping him, releasing, clasping again. She leaned over and her lips found the nipple on his left breast, just over his heart. She suckled hard and licked at the same time, and Ulrich moaned. He'd tried to keep quiet. More a matter of pride than anything else, but she unmanned him. Owned him, for what it was worth.

Hell, he was sixty-four years old, yet he felt like a kid. Millie's tongue swept over his nipple again and then she nipped him with sharp teeth. The nip was unexpected, the pleasure of her tongue and lips soothing the bite unbelievable. With a final groan of surrender, Ulrich gave freedom to the swift coil of heat that erupted along his spine, burned through his balls, and burst from his cock.

He thrust his hips upward, catching Millie by surprise. Pumping hard and fast he filled her, felt her sex clench his throbbing cock and felt her thoughts slip completely into his.

He'd not expected this, either. Not expected the amazing sharing of climax with this woman, this amazing person, this Chanku bitch who cried out with the thrill of orgasm and carried him with her into the abyss.

Chapter 5

Manda blinked, surprised awake by the brilliant flash of sunlight spilling across the bedroom. She'd slept, as she often did, curled up on top of the bedspread, but generally her blinds were tightly drawn and the room stayed in semi-darkness throughout the day.

She stretched, aware of a sense of well-being, a rush of energy about the coming day . . . and the sudden awareness she wasn't alone in her room.

She raised her head and saw Baylor lounging against the door frame with a cup of Starbuck's coffee in his hand. He was fully dressed. She wasn't. No, she was lying here atop the spread, covered in nothing but her patchy gray coat of fur and tangled mop of blond hair, her freakish body fully visible to the perfect man in the doorway.

Manda yelped, rolled quickly to cover herself with the spread, and glared at Baylor. "Where are my clothes? How did I get into bed?"

"Good morning to you, too. Do you drink coffee? I brought extra." He grinned and pushed himself away from the door, then held the tantalizing brew just under her sensitive nostrils.

"I have to let it cool, then lap it up." She held a paw to her muzzle. "I don't do cups well."

"I thought so. There's some cooling in a bowl for you in the kitchen. And as far as how you got into bed, I brought you in after you fell asleep on the couch. Your smock is hanging in the closet but I was afraid it would be too warm for you, especially since you had to share your bed."

"You slept with me?"

He shrugged. "The couch is too short. In case you hadn't noticed, I'm a big boy."

Oh, she'd noticed all right. She just couldn't believe a man had slept beside her all night and she hadn't known. Why did that make her feel like crying? It wasn't as if he could possibly be attracted to her. She should be grateful he didn't look at her as if she were a hideous freak, even though Manda knew that description was putting it kindly.

As difficult as it was to believe, Baylor treated her as if she were his friend. She didn't think she'd had a friend since the curse, couldn't recall anyone, even Papa B, looking at her with anything beyond curiosity. Most people reacted with horror.

"I need to wash up. I'll be out in a minute." Still holding the bedspread around herself, Manda limped to the closet and grabbed her smock, then went into the bathroom. She'd long ago thrown a towel over the mirror, unwilling to face herself each morning. Today, though, she pulled the towel aside and studied her reflection.

Definitely more wolf than woman, though just enough humanity showed through to make her look truly abnormal. Her body was twisted, caught between a creature that walked on four legs and one that stood upright. What would it be like, to finally be a complete woman . . . or a complete wolf? She'd never really thought of becoming wholly wolf. Never thought it possible, but Baylor had been utterly beautiful when he shifted.

When she finally left the bathroom, covered once again in her shapeless gray smock, Baylor had left the room.

Manda found him in the kitchen, drinking coffee and reading a newspaper. He looked up and smiled when she sat down across from him. "I think I've figured out how we're going to get you to Maine. Take a look."

He shoved the newspaper across the table to her and pointed at an ad in the classifieds section. She read the ad, then looked up at him. The man must be nuts! "A sidecar? You want me to ride all the way to Maine in a sidecar?"

Bay pressed his hand over his heart as if she'd insulted him. "It's not just any sidecar. It's fully lined, completely enclosed, and comes with all the hardware to adapt it to my bike." He wiggled his eyebrows and pretended to hold a cigar to his lips. "It's got the classic BMW double pin-stripe," he said, as if that alone should convince Manda. Then he paused and looked at her like she was nuts. "You should be swooning by now. How come you don't look thrilled?"

Manda burst out laughing and slapped her paw over her mouth. The sound startled her and she realized it was the second time she'd laughed with Bay. She never laughed. Never.

"Okay, now I am insulted." He grabbed the newspaper back and glared at her, but it only made her giggle.

At least Manda knew she was giggling. The strangled noise that escaped from her twisted vocal chords sounded as if she were choking. Manda clamped her mouth shut. "I'm sorry." She swallowed and got herself under control. "Now, will you please tell me more about his amazing sidecar?"

She said it in all seriousness, then realized she was flirting with Bay. Flirting! He'd think her even more pathetic than she already was.

"I'm not sure you're worthy, but if you're real nice to me, I just might tell you that this is the perfect way to get you up to Maine in complete creature comfort . . ."

"Well, I am a creature and I do like my comforts."

Bay reached out and covered her paw with his big hand. She was getting more and more used to his touch, but this time she felt more from him, emotion beyond mere compassion. "You're an amazing creature, Manda, and you deserve every comfort."

He studied her a moment, watching her with those piercing, dark amber eyes, then he seemed to catch himself. She wondered what he'd been thinking.

"I need to call and see if the guy's still got this for sale. Is this a local number?" He shoved the paper across to her once more, and Manda studied the phone number.

"One town over, I think. About fifteen miles away. The phone's there." She pointed to a small desk in the living room.

Bay pushed his chair away from the table and went in to make the call, but he handed her one of the big brown capsules before he left the room. Manda lapped at her cooling coffee, drinking slowly while she thought of the changes in her life.

All of them revolved around—and were happening because of—Baylor Quinn . . . but was it her interest in the man or what he said he could do for her?

When she swallowed the pill, Manda realized that, for the first time ever, she was taking control of her own future.

She actually missed him. Bay left shortly after breakfast and took all the sunshine with him. Considering the fact she'd lived most of the last twenty-five years alone, it made no sense that she should miss the company of a man she'd known less than twenty-four hours, but she did. Terribly.

She actually chanced a look out the window, parting the blinds just enough to see when she thought she heard his motorcycle pull up out in front, but it was only her neighbor's car. The motorcycle didn't arrive until well after dark. By then she'd convinced herself he was never coming back, that he'd either changed his mind or been killed in an accident somewhere along the fifteen mile stretch of country road he'd had to travel.

When he knocked quietly on the door and called his name out to Manda, she almost fell over herself in her haste to let him in. She flipped the lock and turned the latch and he was standing there in her doorway, grinning at her. He held his helmet under his left arm and the big heavy gloves were tucked into the front of his one-piece leather suit with the zippered pockets all over it. She would have hugged him, but he leaned over to pick up bags of stuff he'd set on the floor, and she was glad for that. Hugging would have embarrassed both of them.

"Did you miss me?" He brushed by her and, as if it were the most natural thing in the world, leaned over and planted a kiss on top of her head.

Manda stood stock still, staring at the door he'd closed behind himself. It took her a moment to find her voice. "I was worried when you didn't come back."

She felt him move up behind her, felt his hands on her shoulders. She held her breath and prayed for him not to move. She wanted to savor the heat and weight of his hands for as long as she could.

"I'm sorry. I would have called, but I was halfway to the guy's house before I realized I hadn't gotten your phone number and you didn't have my cell phone number. I wish you could come out and see, though. Here. Maybe the streetlight's bright enough."

He took his hands off her shoulders, much to Manda's regret, but then he turned off the lights in the front room, and opened the shades. No one would be able to see her, not standing here in the dark, but Manda peered out the open window from behind Bay and saw his big motorcycle parked in front of her apartment. There was a bullet-shaped contraption stuck on the right side. It looked like a small rocket ship.

"That's what I'm going to ride in?"

"Yep. And if it's okay with you, we're going to leave really early tomorrow morning, before dawn. That way no one will see you getting into the sidecar, and we should be able to beat the worst of the traffic."

"I'll need to pack some things." She hadn't realized he intended to go so quickly. Suddenly the enormity of what she was doing hit Manda—the fact she was going off with a stranger, away from everything familiar.

Putting all her trust in Baylor Quinn, a man she hardly knew.

"I brought you something to wear besides that gray smock. It looks really awful on you." He laughed when he said it, but it didn't take the sting out of his words.

"It's comfortable." Manda felt her spine straighten and knew her voice sounded waspish. She hated the thing herself, but there wasn't much in her closet to choose from.

"I'm sure it is, but this should be, too." He dumped one of the bags on the living room sofa and shook out a long, black jersey dress. It had a high neck and no waist, but the fabric was so soft that Manda's first reaction was to hold it against her cheek. "Go try it on. I hope it's not too long."

She slipped it on in the bedroom. The fit couldn't have been better. Full enough for her stumpy tail, sleeves long enough to cover her wrists, a high neck and a hem that rode a bare two inches from the floor. She'd never owned anything as nice.

"Let me see."

Manda limped back into the front room. She would have modeled it for him, but turning in place wasn't an easy move on her twisted legs. She should have felt more self-conscious. In fact, she should have felt absolutely ridiculous, trying to act like a normal woman. She didn't. Not with Bay. He was, after all, a wolf in man's clothing, right? She giggled. He made her feel almost normal.

"I like it. It looks good on you. Here." He reached into

another bag. "You can wear this over it. It's going to be chilly when we leave."

Feeling close to tears at his generosity, Manda choked back a snort of laughter when Bay drew a long, red cape with a hood out of the bag. Fashioned out of suede, it slipped over Manda's hands like silk. She cocked her head and looked at Bay. "I'm supposed to be Little Red Riding Hood?"

He laughed. "Why not? I'm feeling sort of like the big, bad wolf, dragging you out into the forest."

"Yeah, but I'm the wolf."

Bay shook his head, and the tender expression in his eyes had Manda blinking back the unfamiliar sting of tears she couldn't shed. "Not for long, sweetheart. If you're anything like the other women who've taken the capsules, you could change as quickly as tomorrow night. That's why I want to get us out of here. When you shift, I intend to take you to wolf form first, since that's what you're closest to. You really are more wolf than woman."

He looked at her with so much emotion in his eyes she wanted to weep. "I can't wait to see you run," he said. He sounded almost wistful, as if he wanted it as badly as Manda. "You're going to fly on four legs. Manda, you are going to be so beautiful." He blinked, as if catching himself admitting too much. His chest expanded with the deep breath he took, then he cupped the side of her face. His palm felt warm, so comforting against the long line of her jaw.

She'd longed for human touch her entire adult life. Now she rubbed her face against his hand as she soaked up the promises he made. "I'll want you in the forest so you can figure out how all your wolven parts are supposed to work. We'll run together, just you and me. Then we'll go back to the cabin and you can shift to human once we're back inside. I imagine you'll want to be near a mirror so you can see what you look like."

Manda's heart thudded in her chest. Once again there was the sense of too much, too soon. But was it really too soon? She'd lost a lifetime, and now, after so many years living as a beast, she might actually see herself as soon as tomorrow night.

She shook her head in denial. "You make it all sound so simple."

"It is, sweetheart. It's the simplest thing there is. It's who and what you are, your nature. You are a shapeshifter. Trust me."

Then he did something so amazing, Manda thought she might faint. He put his arms around her and hugged her close against his body, just as if she were a real woman. She felt his lips in her hair and even more unbelievable, felt her body responding, softening, readying for him.

Manda shivered, as much from arousal as from fear. It was too much, too soon, and trusting was so hard to do.

He should feel pity for her but he couldn't. She was too brave, too willing to risk all to follow him. He couldn't imagine how her life had been, but the mere fact he might be the one to show Manda for the first time how she looked as a woman, what her true soul was like as a wolf, absolutely terrified him.

He wanted to think this need to hold her was out of sympathy, but already Bay knew she had changed his life. How could he fall in love with someone who looked like Manda?

How could he not?

She fit so perfectly in his arms, felt so warm and alive and full of hope. The responsibility he'd taken for her life practically unmanned him, yet deep in his heart, Bay knew she made him stronger, better, more complete.

The women he'd lusted after had always been beautiful. The men as well, their bodies strong and healthy, faces, hair . . . Shannon and Jake were perfect examples.

He loved them both. Loved them with all his heart, but already the feelings he had for this brave creature made his love for Shannon and Jake seem shallow, almost meaningless.

He'd never really looked beneath a person's appearance before. Never wanted to, never tried. Manda was so filled with hope, needy yet powerful, Bay felt driven to know more about her. Drawn to her both emotionally and sexually, though he knew sex wasn't even a possibility with her fragile, misshapen body.

He didn't want to frighten her, but there was no denying the fact he was hard and pulsing inside his leather riding suit. No denying it was desire for Manda that had him nursing the king of all erections. He wondered if she'd ever had sex and then he remembered her saying she'd been raped.

If that was the case, he'd definitely have to take special care with her. Maybe he could talk to Keisha . . . Anton's mate had gone through some horrible stuff before she met Anton, but she seemed okay, now. Somehow he needed to find out what the past twenty-five years had been like for Manda. Had to know what happened to her. No matter how awful, it hadn't broken her spirit, but he felt her past still trapped her far more than her misshapen body. He squeezed her tightly and felt Manda sigh against his chest. "You okay?"

She nodded. "It feels so good, to have your arms around me. No one has ever hugged me before. Not since I was little."

Bay closed his eyes and fought the sting of tears. Damn, she was killing him. "I like holding you. Manda, I like everything about you. I can't wait until you're able to pick one body or the other. It must be so painful to be caught the way you are. Do you hurt? Will it be hard for you to ride in the sidecar? I hadn't even thought about you sitting in that thing for any length of time."

She pulled out of Bay's embrace and shrugged her shoulders. "I'm used to hurting. My legs are the worst. My knees don't function properly and my ankles are all screwed up. The bones in my feet aren't placed for walking upright comfortably, but my arms and shoulders aren't designed for walking on all four . . . and I can't wear shoes. I have moccasins shaped to fit my feet, but even those hurt. Hopefully those disgusting pills of yours will take care of all that, right?"

Bay nodded. "Right." At least he hoped they would. How would either of them stand the disappointment if they didn't? "Let's get your things together and get some sleep. I've got the alarm on my cell set to wake us around three."

She stared at him, wide-eyed and incredulous. "Three? I am so not a morning person."

Bay swatted her lightly on the butt and followed her, still grumbling, into the bedroom.

Manda lay awake beside Baylor on the double bed that wasn't nearly long enough for a man his size. She'd been awake most of the night, so aware of him sleeping next to her. Aware of his strength and length, his scent and the sound of his heart beating. She kept waiting for him to snore, but he slept quietly.

Unlike Manda who didn't sleep at all. Her arms and legs kept twitching and itching and she felt as if her skin were crawling and trying to jump off her bones. She remembered the same sensation when she was still a normal girl and wondered now if it was caused by the changes in her body from the nutrients in her diet in Tibet.

The same nutrients, according to Bay, that were in those pills she took. Whatever was in them appeared to have kick-started her libido, as well. She'd spent much of her life in a state of frustrated arousal, but this was something even more powerful, more intense. Proximity to a man as gorgeous as Baylor Quinn wasn't helping matters a bit.

Baylor rolled over beside her and one heavy arm came down across her belly. Utterly amazing. The man didn't even seem to notice how she looked. He'd kissed her hair, hugged her, and even kissed her furry cheek when they'd crawled into bed. She wanted more. Her body wanted more, wanted something to ease the powerful desire that consumed her as she lay next to the most perfect man she'd ever seen.

He was nothing like the men she'd known at the various labs where Papa B sent her for testing. Definitely nothing like the men who had held her down and raped her, twisting her arms and pulling her misshapen legs wide. One of them, an ugly little man who talked with a lisp, had been the one who forced his penis inside her. It hurt so bad she'd tried to bite him, but someone had muzzled her. She'd been about sixteen and never once told Papa B what they had done.

At another lab, they'd tied her up and had a big wolf mount her, one of the captive animals in Papa B's collection of wolves and big cats. Nightmare images still haunted her—the lab technicians making jokes when she'd tried to fight them off, the huge animal growling, forcing his penis inside her. Thank goodness she'd passed out, but she'd never forget how the men hadn't cared when she screamed and begged them to help her. None of them had tried to stop something that went beyond depraved.

She couldn't remember everything that happened, but she'd awakened in her cubicle with blood on her inner thighs and huge scratches on her shoulders from the animal's nails. She wondered if she still had the scars beneath her fur.

The scars inside were even worse. She lay there in the bed beside Bay with his arm across her belly and wondered what would happen when she finally looked like a real woman. He'd want sex then. She was sure of it, but she wasn't sure she could handle it. Wasn't sure if she'd ever be able to accept a man inside her. Any man. Even one as wonderful as Bay.

Bay rolled over and dragged her close. He pulled her into the curve of his powerful body. She should have been afraid. Instead she felt his warmth and the quiet rise and fall of his chest. She wriggled around a little, burrowing even deeper into his embrace. Wondering why she wasn't frightened, Manda finally drifted off to sleep.

* * *

Ulrich wasn't sure what awakened him, but suddenly he was alert, staring into the silvery darkness. Moonlight filtered through the shades and cast long shadows across Millie's small room. He hadn't shifted tonight and he missed the chance to run in the woods, but Millie had kept him too busy to think about it until now.

She slept beside him, her hair a tousled mess, her face surprisingly young for a woman her age. He wondered if it had something to do with being Chanku. None of them appeared to age as quickly as normal humans. He'd have to ask Anton about it.

So many things to ask Anton. Like how to tell for sure the woman who was twining herself around his shriveled old heart was truly Chanku? He was ninety-nine percent sure and needed to get her started on the pills, but how could he get her to take them without telling her why?

He was just going to have to tell her, the way Camille had told him. She'd recognized his true self and shifted for him—and just about scared the shit out of him. Now it was one of his favorite memories, but at the time he'd been sure he was losing his mind. They hadn't had the pills then, but she'd known about the grasses and she'd given him enough to eventually shift.

He'd never brought a woman over, only the men. They were easy, pragmatic, accepting. The other guys hadn't had the same luck with their mates. Some of the women had been really upset about the fact they were given the nutrients without being told what they were, or how the pills were going to forever change their lives. Like Shannon had said, it wasn't that she didn't love being a shapeshifter, but it should have been her choice.

Ulrich smiled, remembering how Jake had paid for that move. He'd definitely tell Millie. Maybe after they made love in the morning.

"Ulrich? Are you awake?" Millie rolled close and kissed the side of his neck, nipping at the sensitive skin over his collarbone. Her hand slipped along his ribs and found his quickly wakening cock.

"I am now." He smiled in the darkness, comparing her familiarity with his body now to the tentative touches the day before.

They made slow, sweet love, touching and kissing in the dark, learning even more about one another's bodies with tongues and lips, fingers and teeth. When Ulrich finally turned Millie over and pulled her to her hands and knees so he could enter her from behind, the pale glow of dawn had replaced the silvery sheen of moonlight.

Millie was slick, gloriously aroused and practically dripping when Ulrich slid inside her heat. He knelt behind her, his hands on her hips at first, but as his need grew he moved to palm her breasts. Her nipples beaded and he pinched them between his fingers. Millie stiffened and arched her back, her sex rippling around his cock in yet another climax.

She was insatiable, uninhibited, and giving. Fighting his own growing arousal, Ulrich paced himself, thrusting in the age-old rhythm of lovers everywhere. Thoughts of shifting filled his mind, of the two of them as wolves in the deep forest, his cock swelling inside her slippery folds, holding them together, tying them.

He'd not known such arousal since Camille, had almost

forgotten the desperate Chanku desires after so many years without a mate. He'd never lacked partners, but they'd been nothing more than a means to an end. Sex with Millie was far more than anything he'd experienced since Camille's death.

His flat belly slapped the round globes of her buttocks on each downward thrust, her spasming muscles clenched his cock, holding him, pulling him deeper inside. She spread her thighs wider, directing the angle of his penetration, then turned and looked at him with a devilish wink.

He felt her fingers snake between their bodies, warm and searching. He shuddered when she found the taut sac between his legs, cupped him as he drove harder inside.

Her fingers were fire. She gripped his balls just to the point of pain, held him perfectly in her small hand. Her touch shot a coil of need through his gut, a blinding shock of current that threw him over the edge.

Whatever control he'd struggled to hang on to fled with the touch of Millie's fingers. He gripped her slim waist and drove forward, caught in time, trapped in a maelstrom of pure, mind-bending ecstasy, held there with the head of his cock pressed against Millie's womb, his balls caught in the gentle grasp of her fingers, the mechanics of sperm from balls to release as much pain as pleasure.

Heart pounding, breath trapped in his chest, Ulrich threw back his head and groaned. He felt her then, knew Millie went with him, free-falling into yet another orgasm. This time, though, her thoughts were his. He felt the thick length of his cock, the way he filled her and stretched tissues long untouched by any man. The brush of hair at his groin abraded the soft curves of her buttocks, her nipples tingled where he'd squeezed and pinched them during climax.

She was there, in his mind, sharing all these sensations as she experienced them. A part of his thoughts so natural, so welcome, that the two of them functioned as one. Not a bonding, but a sharing. Only another shapeshifter could climb inside his brain like this.

She was Chanku. She must be Chanku.

Practically weeping his relief, Ulrich leaned forward and nipped the back of her neck, marking Millie with his teeth. She didn't cry out. Didn't object. Instead, she turned and kissed him. Looked back over her shoulder at the man still buried deep inside and gave him a quizzical smile.

"Do you want to explain," she asked, "what just occurred? I have the strangest feeling I just got fucked by a wolf in the woods. Even more interesting, for the briefest of moments, I was the alpha wolf. You. I was you."

Laughing, Ulrich wrapped his arms around her and rolled them both to their sides. Still embedded in Millie, he threw one leg over hers, trapping her close to him. "In a way, Millie m'dear, that's exactly what happened." He kissed the tender spot between her neck and shoulder where he'd nipped her, then licked the reddened skin with the tip of his tongue.

Millie shuddered and rubbed her breasts against his forearms. He was already growing hard again. He kissed her mouth and snuggled her against him, nuzzling her neck and fighting the urge to make love to her all over again. "I want to tell you a story about an ancient race of people who once lived on the Himalayan steppes. People called Chanku, who were able to do something wonderful, something no other race before or after them could master."

Millie shifted her hips, tilting her body so that Ulrich could press deeper. "And what wonderful thing was that?"

Ulrich heard the smile in her voice. She thought he was telling her a fairy tale. If only she knew! "They had the ability to shift from human to wolf," he said. "The ability to become one with the forest. For some unknown reason, they wandered from their home and their magical ability to run as wolves faded into distant memory." He paused and let that thought sink in. Millie's mind was open to his, her curiosity growing more profound with each second that passed.

"The ability faded, Millie. But it didn't disappear. It was rediscovered, a combination, I imagine, of accident and research, only in the last thirty years or so, as far as we know." He waited, his thoughts open, his heart pounding in his chest.

Slowly, Millie slipped free of Ulrich's embrace, turned to face him, and pressed her hips against his. He slipped his reawakened cock between her swollen nether lips, connecting them once again. She snuggled closer and kissed the swell of muscle over his heart.

Her whisper tickled his chest and her lips moved against him. "There have been dreams. A lifetime of dreams. Running on four legs through the forest, the sense of communicating with wolves, a sense I carry with me during the day. Are you telling me . . . ?"

"Yes. I believe you are Chanku, as I know I am. There are pills we take. Nasty looking things." He laughed, tilted Millie's chin up and kissed her. He couldn't not kiss her. "They contain the nutrients our bodies need to shift from human to wolf and back again. There's a small gland at the base of our brains, different from that of humans. It lies dormant without the proper nutrients, but once it's brought back to life, it gives us the ability to shift."

"Different from humans? You're saying you're not human?"

Ulrich sighed. "More or less . . . without the nutrients, we are wholly human. We lead our lives in silent desperation, always aware of something incomplete, something missing. Once the Chanku part of us is enabled, life suddenly makes sense. Millie, I want you to start taking the pills. In just a few days, you should be able to fulfill all those dreams you've had. You should be able to run beside me as a wolf."

Shaking her head in disbelief, Millie tilted her chin to

look him in the eye. "That's a lot to swallow, don't you think? Why . . . how do I know you're not teasing? Show me. Will you shift for me?"

He nodded. He'd known she would want to see. Had hoped she would accept his story. Slipping the solid length of his cock out of her warm nest wasn't easy . . . he would much prefer to have finished what he'd once again started.

Standing beside the bed, Ulrich stared into Millie's amber eyes. There was no fear in them, no derision. She believed because she knew, deep in her heart, that what he'd told her was true. It was always that way. Those who carried the genes for shifting accepted what they'd always suspected yet not been able to put words to.

Damn, she would be so easy to love. With that thought in mind, Ulrich became the wolf.

Meeting Ulrich, taking him to her bed, making love with him most of the night . . . all of that had taken Millie far beyond her wildest, most sexual fantasies. But this . . . this was amazing.

She lay on the bed, arm bent at the elbow, chin resting in her palm and stared at the man who'd shown her the stars. She wanted to think all his talk of shapeshifting, of turning into a wolf, was just so much hooey, but he believed and so did she.

With that thought in mind, she still gasped when his form suddenly wavered, shifted, and changed. Before she was actually aware of what he'd done, a large black wolf stared at her over the edge of the bed.

A wolf with ivory canines and Ulrich's beautiful amber eyes. Millie pressed her fist against her mouth and stared at him, speechless. Then she started to laugh. Lying there on the bed, staring at the beautiful, amber-eyed wolf, Millie laughed until she cried. Then she slipped to the floor beside the wolf, wrapped her arms around his neck and cried until her tears had all been spent.

Chapter 6

"You okay?" Bay helped Manda crawl slowly from the sidecar. Even with all the pillows he'd stuffed around her, she had to be sore after so many hours in such cramped quarters. A trip that would have taken no more than eight hours had lasted almost twelve on back roads and blue highways.

"Stiff, yes, but I can't believe we're actually here!" She looked around, wide-eyed, obviously enthralled by the thick forest surrounding the cabin.

Bay slipped an arm around her waist while she arranged the folds of the red cape, then he swung her easily against his chest and carried her up the front steps. She wrapped her arm around his neck, a familiarity she'd been uncomfortable with when he'd first carried her this morning, in spite of the fact they'd shared her bed the past two nights.

He smiled, unable to remember the last time he'd slept in a bed with a woman without having sex. Then he thought back over the long miles they'd traveled, the intimacy of their conversation through the headsets each of them wore, the feeling he'd finally gotten to know a little bit more about Manda. He was attracted to her on so many levels, but the feelings were unfamiliar, so much deeper and more profound than he'd expected. No matter, he'd put his needs on hold while they gave the pills time to make their magic.

Now, at least, he knew more about the private side of Manda, how she'd gotten her view of the world through daytime TV and CNN. She never missed an episode of *Oprah* or *Judge Judy*, she loved to read the paper and was really good at crossword puzzles. Her political beliefs were liberal and she regretted not being able to vote. Her favorite pastime was chatting with her anonymous online friends on the Internet, where she lived an entirely fictitious life as a young woman with a job and a normal life in upstate New York.

It explained a lot, but not everything. Manda was obviously intelligent and well read, but still so terribly innocent, totally unaware of her potential as a woman. Once she shifted . . .

Everything was going to change for her. She would finally discover the real Manda, not only as a woman but as a wolf. Bay practically shivered with anticipation. He wished there were more signs of her impending shift, but he could only wait until Manda sensed she was ready.

The cabin was cold, with the chill of a building empty for far too long. No one had been here since Jake, Shannon, and Bay had taken off on their cross-country motorcycle trip to Tia and Luc's wedding in San Francisco so many weeks ago.

So much had happened since then.

It was dark and gloomy inside. Bay flipped a switch that fired up the battery powered lights, illuminating the large front room in a soft glow. Then he smiled down at the woman in his arms and shook his head. More things had happened than he'd ever dreamed. Manda gave him a quizzical glance as he set her down on the braided rug. "I need to get a fire going," he said. "If you're cold, there are some afghans and quilts around the room . . . go ahead and bundle up."

"I'm okay. I'm so stiff, I think I need to move around a little. Is it okay if I explore?"

Bay laughed. "Go ahead. Shouldn't take you too long, but *mi casa es su casa*. Here, take the flashlight. The lights here in the front room are the only ones that work until I get things started, and with all the shades drawn it's pretty dark." He grabbed a small flashlight off the hearth and handed it to her. "I'll get the generator fired up in a minute and we'll have real lights until I can check the batteries on the solar, make sure it's okay. Go ahead and look around. You might want to open up some shades and windows so we can air the place out."

He stripped out of his leather riding suit and started the fire in the big stone fireplace to ward off the chill, while Manda wandered through the kitchen and then down the long hallway where the extra bedrooms were. He heard the sound of shades drawing up, of windows sliding open, and felt the draft of fresh air warring with the heat from the fire.

After a few minutes, Manda came back to the living room and finally went into the master bedroom where Jake and Shannon slept. Bay hadn't talked all that much about his packmates. As innocent as Manda appeared, he'd been hesitant to discuss the sexuality of the Chanku, or his intimate relationship with both Jake and Shannon.

He'd been so afraid of frightening Manda away, but now, with her ability to shift growing closer with each pill she took, Bay knew he couldn't put it off much longer.

"Where do you sleep?" Manda stood in the doorway to the master bedroom. "There are women's clothes in this room. Do they belong to your friend?"

"That's Shannon and Jake's room. Jake's the one who actually owns the cabin. I expect he and Shannon will be back in another week or so."

Actually, he'd asked for two weeks and they'd agreed.

Two weeks to help Manda undo a lifetime of hurt and mistrust.

She looked at him now, her head tilted to one side, the expression on her wolven face as difficult as always for Bay to decipher. "But where do you sleep? I can't find a room that looks like it should be yours."

He sighed. Then he stood up and brushed the dust from the logs off his hands. "In there. I sleep in there. With them." The fire crackled and roared behind him. It couldn't drown out the sudden pounding of his heart. Manda's expression didn't change. "We're Chanku," he said, well aware of the defensive tone in his voice. "Pack animals. We mate for life, but we also have open sexual relationships within our own pack. Ménages of three or more are fairly common among us."

She blinked but said nothing. He wished her thoughts were open to him, wished he weren't making such a mess of this. "Our sexuality is a powerful, driving force. It's a big part of who and what we are." He walked across the room, careful not to get too close. He didn't want to frighten her, but he felt like kicking himself. There must be a better way to explain all of this.

"Remember when your father caught you touching yourself?"

Manda nodded.

"You said it felt so good you knew you wouldn't stop doing it, so you lied. Sweetie, don't lie to me. Do you still touch yourself?"

She looked down. He imagined she'd be blushing if she still had the ability. Finally, Bay noticed an almost imperceptible nod.

"Thank goodness. I was afraid you'd managed to bury that part of yourself." He held his arms out and she slipped into his embrace and buried her face against his chest. "Manda, baby . . . it's not a bad thing. For you, especially, caught halfway between your two selves, it's probably a necessity. You've had all the drives and no opportunity. After any of us shift, our sex drive is so powerful, so all consuming, that we have to find release."

He rubbed her back as he held her. Her slight body trembled, but she didn't pull away. Bay felt helpless and awkward, talking to someone who was so sexually inexperienced about the realities of the Chanku libido. Somehow he had to make Manda understand their sexuality was merely a part of their nature, not something prurient or evil, but he didn't want to shock or frighten her.

"That's why I stay with Jake and Shannon," he said, choosing his words carefully. "I share their bed and we have sex. They're not here and you are, but I know you're not ready for sex, your body's not ready. We've managed okay the last two nights, haven't we? I want you to sleep with me in the guest room in the back. No sex. Not until you're sure. Is that okay?"

Manda raised her head and stared at him for a long, uncomfortable moment. "You talk as if sex between us is inevitable. As if you're going to want to sleep with me. What if I'm ugly when I'm human, too? What if you're repulsed by me?"

Bay cupped her face in his palms and looked into her twisted countenance with a dawning sense of understanding tinged with awe. "You're not ugly now, Manda, and I've never been repulsed by you. You're different, but you have your own beauty shining through. As far as sex between us, when you're willing, it is inevitable. Even now, knowing your body hurts and your fears are stronger than your needs, I want you."

Manda shook her head and looked away. "I find that hard to believe. I've looked in enough mirrors in my lifetime."

Anger surged. It had been one hell of a long day, traveling so far along back roads and skirting cities whenever possible. He'd been terrified of a cop stopping him or someone seeing Manda when they'd pulled over in isolated areas to stretch tired muscles and relieve themselves. It pissed him off, knowing she still had such a crappy view of her worth, but part of Bay's anger was self-directed.

He had no right feeling the way he did about her, but her Chanku scent was making him crazy and the mess of emotions he felt for Manda that went so far beyond sex didn't help one bit. The least he could do was be totally honest. He grabbed Manda's hand and pressed it against his leg where his cock surged hot and hard, trapped beneath denim along his inner thigh. As if by instinct, she curled her fingers around the solid ridge beneath the denim and raised her chin to stare at him. "Because of me? You're hard because you want me?"

"You're the only one in the room, Manda. You figure it out."

She snatched her hand away as if it burned. "I can't." She slipped free of his embrace. "I'm afraid. You'll hurt me, I . . ."

"No. I will never hurt you and we're not going to do anything until you're ready. It's up to you, Manda. I've been frustrated before and it hasn't killed me." He laughed and shrugged his shoulders. "I might have thought I was near death, but I always seem to survive."

He turned away abruptly and it probably hurt her feelings, but his blood surged hot and his cock was hard and he felt so damned confused. He needed to get away from her. "I'm gonna get the generator fired up." Bay shut the door behind him, though it killed him a little, knowing he left Manda standing alone in the middle of the living room, staring after him.

The afternoon sun felt warm, but the air had a definite bite to it and a cold wind blew. At least it helped clear his head. Bay welcomed the chill. He needed to run. Needed the freedom of the woods as much as he needed to breathe. Instead he walked around to the back of the house and started the generator. He looked up at the brilliant blue sky, the air so clear it practically sparkled, and took a deep breath. Then he went back inside. Manda sat all curled up on one of the couches.

"I need to run," he said. She raised her head and stared at him, her eyes filled with longing but no sense of reproach. That was even harder. If she'd been angry with him, if she'd called him a selfish bastard, it would have been easier. Instead she merely blinked slowly and accepted.

Bay closed off the need to gather her once more in his arms. His voice sounded gruff, angry even to his own ears. He hated to think what he sounded like to Manda. "The generator's running and you can use any of the small appliances in the kitchen. The refrigerator is propane powered and we left it running, so the meat in the freezer should be fine if you're hungry. Thaw it out in the microwave. I'll be back in about an hour."

He shut the door before Manda could answer, and stripped out of his clothes on the front deck. He paused a moment, sensing her anguish, her vulnerability. The forest called to him. The clean air, the freedom. The chill wind washed over his bare skin and he shivered.

His balls ached and his cock was hard as a bat. Need throbbed through his veins like a physical thing, clawing at his gut. She didn't have a clue what she did to him, even in this form. Her human side called to him. So did the wolf. Neither one nor the other, but still very much a part of both.

Maybe if he ran, if he shifted and disappeared into the forest for even a short time, it would all make sense. This need he felt for Manda, the powerful sense that he had to make her his own.

Inside the cabin, Manda was silent, but her silence pulled almost as strongly as the sounds of the forest. Bay stared into the distance, felt the pull of freedom, of the wolf howling to run free, and made his choice. He took a deep breath, let it out, and turned his back on the dark woods. He had no idea what he was going to do, but there was no way in hell he could leave Manda alone. With a last, longing glance toward the forest, Bay opened the door and stepped back inside.

Manda jerked her head up at the sound of the door. Bay stood in the open doorway, naked, aroused. He looked every bit as confused as she felt.

"I thought you were going to run."

He shrugged his shoulders. "So did I. I couldn't leave you here like this."

She felt like snarling. She knew the fur stood up along her spine and that made her feel even uglier, more beast than woman. "I don't want your pity. I don't want anyone's pity. I'm tired of being the pathetic freak. Hell, I'm tired of everything, including being me. Go. Just go and let me have some time to myself."

She almost growled at him. Maybe she should have. She was, after all, merely an ugly animal, and animals growled.

He came closer. As much as his nudity frightened her, it fascinated Manda even more. She couldn't look him in the eye, no matter how hard she tried. All she saw was the length of that huge penis thrusting out of the nest of dark hair covering his groin. The same hair that shimmered across his broad chest.

She should have been terrified, especially with the waves of heat and emotion spilling from Bay's body, but she wasn't. Curiosity overwhelmed whatever fear Manda might have felt.

She'd never really seen a naked man this closely. Oh, there'd been brief glimpses when she'd been raped and even the first time Bay shifted and she saw him unclothed for that instant, but not like this. Not standing six feet away, almost close enough to touch. Definitely close enough to see.

She felt no fear. This was Baylor, the man who had promised to save her, the man who had slept beside her and held her in his arms. She finally forced her gaze upward and met his dark, amber eyes. "What do you want from me, Bay? I know you don't want sex with me. Not the way I am now. Maybe, if those pills of yours work and I ever look like a real woman . . . but not now."

"Have you ever been touched by a man?"

His question came out of nowhere. For some reason, it made her angry. "I was raped. Isn't that touching?"

He shook his head. "You know what I mean. Has a man's touch ever given you pleasure? Has any man held you, made love to you?"

She laughed. There was no other response. She realized her gaze was flipping back and forth from his eyes to his sex. She couldn't help herself. He was absolutely fascinating, almost close enough to touch and she wanted to. Damn, but she wanted to see if he felt as hard as he looked.

Manda got her nervous giggles under control. She wished she could do the same with her suddenly raging libido. "Right. Like some guy is going to want to make love to me. The one who raped me lost a bet. They had to get him drunk first, and then he did it from behind, so he wouldn't have to look at me. Bay, you're the only man who has ever touched me in any way, the only man who gives me hope that there might some day be a time when . . ."

"Today. Tonight. Nothing that will hurt you, nothing . . ." He paused, as if searching for the right words. "Nothing invasive. I know you're curious about me." He shrugged his broad shoulders again, and if she'd had the capacity to blush, Manda knew she would have been beet red.

"Well, of course I'm curious. I don't even know what a real woman should look like, much less a man. Even there, I . . ." She gestured between her own legs. God, this was so damned hard, talking about things like this, things she'd wondered about all her life. If not for the Internet, she might not know how different her sex was from every other woman, but images were just that. Images.

The real thing had just moved a couple steps closer. "Touch it," he said. "I won't hurt you."

Touch it? Just like that? Touch it? He stood directly in front of her now and his penis curved up until the tip practically brushed his belly. It was long and thick and Manda knew there was no way she'd ever want that inside her, but she did want to touch him.

Just this once. From her seat on the couch, she looked up into Bay's face and wondered what his expression meant. He almost looked as if he were in pain. Did it hurt a man, to be this hard? Manda reached out with one finger, careful of the long, dark claw at the end of it. She touched the very tip and he jerked back.

"Careful." Bay's voice sounded strangled. "I'm not circumcised, the way a lot of men are, so I'm really sensitive there. When I get hard, that skin pulls back." He pointed to a fold of skin behind the broad, plum-shaped crown. "That smooth skin on the end? It's usually protected, so it's really sensitive to touch. Sort of like your clit. Here." He gently took her hand and wrapped her fingers around the middle of the shaft.

The skin was hot and smooth. Manda was surprised at the way it slipped, just a bit, over the hard muscle beneath, like a satin sheath covering a steel rod. As short and stubby as her fingers were, she had to use both hands to completely encircle his girth. When she stroked him a few times, a tiny bead of moisture appeared at the tip. She heard Bay moan.

"You do that much more and I'm going to lose it."

Manda barely heard him. She was absolutely fascinated by the small, white pearl of fluid at the tip. It spilled from the part Bay said was so sensitive she couldn't touch it.

Without thinking, Manda leaned forward and swept

her tongue gently over the tiny slit. Bay gasped, but she swirled her tongue lightly across the slick flesh, licked up the drop and concentrated on the taste.

"You're trying to kill me, aren't you?"

"Not really." Manda tilted her head and looked up at him. "That would serve no purpose whatsoever." Bay's skin was a ruddy shade, much darker than usual. She wondered if the dark color meant he was aroused. Had the touch of her tongue felt that good to him?

She let go of his shaft and cupped the wrinkled sac beneath it in her palm. Her long nails gently scraped the spot behind his balls and she felt his muscles tighten in response, but she carefully rolled the hard orbs inside the sac between her fingers. *Fascinating!* The entire sac tightened within her grasp, as if it wanted to crawl up closer to his body.

"Does that hurt?"

Bay shook his head, but he grabbed the arm of the couch as if for balance. His legs trembled, and Manda noticed a lot more of the white fluid escaping from the end of his penis. Without thinking, she leaned close and licked it off again. This time, Bay's hips thrust forward and the tip knocked against her sharp canines.

Manda pulled away. She certainly didn't want to bite him. Bay groaned. "She really is trying to kill me," he muttered.

"No," Manda said, laughing. She'd never expected the sense of power it gave her, to hold his sex in her hands, to affect his body this way. He was actually shaking and she knew it was all from arousal. That much she recognized.

"If I were trying to kill you," she said, "I might do this." Without warning, without really understanding the needs that drove her, Manda used her long, wolven tongue to sweep the length of his shaft. Then she closed her elongated mouth around him and sucked, hard.

* * *

Bay's legs buckled. He tightened his grasp on the arm of the couch for balance and barely managed to stay upright. The rasp of her unusually shaped tongue, the scrape of sharp teeth and almost unbearable suction with her tongue pressing his cock to the roof of her mouth, took him right to the edge.

This wasn't what he'd wanted, not what he expected, but Manda seemed fascinated by the feel and taste of him and he sure as hell wasn't going to ask her to stop. He heard her moan and realized he was groaning right along with her. His vision glazed over. He felt the coil of heat start in his lower spine, the familiar clenching of his buttocks. Nothing was going to stop him, not now. He looked down at the wispy blond hair moving slowly against his groin, the narrow shoulders beneath the soft, black jersey dress he'd bought for her, and she looked young and fragile and, in her own way, uniquely beautiful. Suddenly it was too late to do anything but give in to the rush of orgasm, the heat of his ejaculation.

Manda grabbed his hips as he thrust forward into her mouth. She pulled him closer, sucked him harder. His legs gave out entirely. Bracing his arms on the back of the couch, leaning completely over Manda while she continued to suck and lick his cock, Bay waited for the tremors of his orgasm to ebb. The clenching, pulsing contractions seem to go on forever, soothed by the soft caress of Manda's tongue.

Finally he backed away and his cock slipped free. She looked up at him and ran her tongue along the sides of her mouth, licking her chops. "That was different," she said. Then she reached out and touched his cock.

He jumped, laughing. "I didn't expect you to take me in your mouth," Bay said. "Have you ever . . . ?"

Manda shook her head. "Never. I've read about it and I always wondered what semen tasted like." She snuggled back in her corner of the couch and gazed at him out of her wolven eyes. "It's good. I'd like to do that again."

Bay threw his head back and laughed. "Well, don't let me stop you. That was amazing." He plopped down next to her on the couch and put an arm around Manda's shoulders. "You're amazing, Manda. Totally, unbelievably amazing." He ran his finger along the side of her face and followed the long jawline that was almost entirely wolf. What was she going to look like when she finally shifted?

She watched him steadily, not saying anything. Her mental shields were solid as stone and Bay didn't have a clue what she might be thinking. He wished she'd open to him, but that would come in time. He hoped.

He didn't kiss her. Her mouth was all wrong for kissing, though he imagined she might like it if he touched her. How to do it without frightening her was the tough part. He wondered if the fact she was in control when she'd gone down on him made it easier for her? Not as scary, for her, anyway, knowing she held his balls in her hand and his cock nestled between very sharp teeth.

He felt a coil of heat in his balls and knew he was getting hard again. Manda's nipples poked against the soft black jersey, and without even thinking, Bay palmed one, gently rubbing his hand around her small breast and finally rubbing gently with his thumb.

He felt Manda's body stiffen and she jerked her head around to glare at him. He didn't stop. Instead, he smiled at her. "If you want me to stop, I will."

"I won't have sex with you."

"I didn't ask you to. All I want to do is touch you. Maybe give you some of the pleasure you gave me."

"I don't want your mouth on me, not down there. Not while I look like this."

Bay shook his head and his thumb kept up the slow, steady stroking. "That's fine. I won't do anything that makes you uncomfortable. I promise."

"How come your penis looks different?"

Her non sequitur threw him for a loop. "What?" He

glanced down at his semi-flaccid cock. The foreskin completely covered the glans. "Well, I'm not erect right now, so it's smaller."

She snorted. "Not that small. I meant, what's that over the end of it?" She reached out and touched him.

Immediately, his cock began to harden and the foreskin slipped back over the crown.

"Oh. My." Manda glanced up at him. "That's what you meant when you said it was covered. I wasn't sure." She reached down and wrapped her fingers around his quickly growing erection.

Bay covered her hand with his. "Nope. It's my turn to touch."

"No. I don't want you to see me." Manda wrapped her arms around herself in a totally defensive posture.

"I promise not to look." He flashed a big grin at Manda and rubbed his thumb over her nipple a little harder.

"No." The word came out on a moan, but she shook her head and tried to scoot away from him. Bay continued holding her against his side. Kept rubbing her erect nipple.

"I'll cover my eyes. Will that work?" He was biting back the laughter now. Manda glared at him.

"You blindfold me. I won't mind." He pinched her nipple gently between his fingers and tugged. She gasped and arched into his touch. "I can make you feel really good."

"Do I get to put the blindfold on you? Can I tie it really tight?"

He laughed out loud. "Tie it as tight as you want. I promise not to look."

"I've got a scarf in my suitcase. It's one Papa B gave me years ago. Wait here." Manda scrambled off the couch and headed for the bedroom where Bay had stashed her bags. He leaned back on the couch with his arms folded behind his head, long legs spread out in front of him. His once flaccid cock was back at half-mast, already anticipating Manda's response.

She was back in less than a minute with a long, black silk scarf in her hands. First she dimmed the lights in the room, and then she stood behind the couch and wrapped the scarf over Bay's eyes, tying it carefully behind his head. "Can you see anything?"

He shook his head. "Not a thing." He patted the couch next to him. "Okay, a deal's a deal. Your turn."

He didn't hear her move. "Manda?"

"I'm coming."

He felt the couch dip beside him as she sat down. "Maybe you think you're coming. I want to show you what *coming* is all about."

"Oh."

"Now, lie back and relax."

"You're kidding, right? What are you going to do?"

"Practice my Braille, I imagine. If you won't let me see you, I guess I just need to learn your body by touch." He reached for the spot where he thought her head might be and found the side of her face. Slowly running his hand along her long hair, Bay realized he was smiling. "I won't hurt you. I'll stop if you want. Please, Manda. Won't you let me give you the same wonderful feelings you gave to me?"

Manda lay back on the big leather couch and tried her best to relax, but it was impossible. Bay loomed over her. Big and masculine and so powerful looking, even more beautiful and mysterious with his eyes covered in black silk. The shimmering fabric emphasized the thick mat of hair on his chest, the same dark hair that trailed down his flat belly to his groin. He was all muscle and man and she felt her body responding in spite of her fear.

He slipped off the couch and knelt on the rug beside her. The first thing he did was press his ear to her chest. "I hear your heart beating. It's racing so fast. I don't know if it's because you're afraid of me, or because you want what I'm going to do."

His left hand touched her leg through the folds of the soft dress. There was something so intimate about his cheek pressed to her breast, his hand rubbing her leg. Intimate and yet comforting at the same time.

Manda felt herself relax just a tiny bit.

"I wish you could open your thoughts to me. Let me know what you're thinking. You've got such strong shields against me."

"I don't know how." She tried to hear Bay's mind, but something seemed to stop her.

"Imagine a window. Think of looking through the glass, of seeing me on the other side, then opening the window. Sometimes that helps."

His lips moved against her breast when he talked. His breath felt warm through the fabric of her dress. Manda thought of the window, pictured Bay looking through the glass at her. In her mind, Manda raised the window. She felt the warmth of the breeze, saw Bay even clearer.

Heard his thoughts.

I want to touch you, Manda. I don't want you to fear me. I promise not to hurt you. Let me know if I frighten you at all.

Okay.

That's a girl.

He slipped his hand beneath the hem of her dress. She felt his fingers tracing the misshapen contours of her right leg. How could he touch her and not be repulsed?

Bay's thoughts were as open to Manda as hers were to him. She sensed his need to please her, his desire not to frighten her. His fascination with her body, twisted though it might be. It was so hard to believe yet impossible to deny that he saw her as unique and beautiful in her own way.

He'd found her inner thigh. The fur grew lighter here and her skin was much more sensitive to his touch. He stroked her, slowly growing closer and closer to her sex.

She felt the tension building, the coil of need burning deep in her womb as his fingers burned a trail closer to her clit.

She grabbed the couch when one broad fingertip traced her soaking wet slit. She moaned and fought the strong desire to close her thighs against his intrusive touch, but he was so gentle and it felt so good.

His finger pressed deeper inside, moving slowly in and out, sliding on the thick fluids suddenly seeping out of her. Manda realized she'd closed her eyes when his touch became so intimate. Now she forced herself to open them, to watch Bay's face as he touched her. Pleasured her.

He still knelt beside the couch with his cheek pressed against her breast. One arm supported her back, the other was doing such amazing things to her body, she practically whimpered with the sensations.

He'd found her clit, sweeping gently over that small bud of flesh, and he smiled when he realized what he'd discovered. "I knew it had to be there somewhere. I'm not hurting you, am I?" His breath brushed a warm path across her breast. His fingers worked magic.

Manda's denial escaped on a gasp. She arched her hips into his touch and realized she'd found a rhythm, a slow, in and out thrust of her hips, careful to avoid that damned tail, opening herself to Bay's wonderful fingers. He thrust two inside her now, and his thumb brushed her clit on each down stroke.

Manda's breath caught in her throat, her fingertips had gone numb from grabbing on to the leather couch so hard, but her mind was singing with the sounds of Bay's encouragement.

She heard his voice as if he spoke into her ear, but the sound was in her head, a part of her experience. *Let it go, sweetie. Let it go. Feel the heat, imagine my cock inside you, imagine the heat and thrust, the pressure of our bodies pressing, one against the other. Feel me, Manda. Feel me touching you, making your body sing.*

Bay turned his head and took her nipple between his teeth, right through the fabric. She felt the sharp edge of his bite, the soft pressure of his lips as he sucked her into his mouth. Dampness spread across the jersey and it was cool against her skin, hot where he suckled.

His fingers went deeper, his thumb pressed harder, and he nipped her! Bit down on her painfully sensitive nipple and sent a blast of heat from breast to womb to clit.

Manda wanted to scream. Wanted to howl at the burst of sensation that coursed through her body, sent her sex into convulsions, arched her back and puckered her nipples, but all that came out was a long, low moan. Her hips lifted completely off the sofa and Bay held her close against his chest, sucking harder on her breast, his fingers buried deep inside her body.

He kept touching, gently rubbing and soothing her, murmuring low words that meant nothing whatsoever, but made her feel loved, made her feel safe. Finally, she relaxed against the warm leather, breath rushing from her lungs.

If she'd been able to cry, Manda knew she would have been awash in tears. Bay rested his face against her chest, the blindfold still in place. He nuzzled the soft swell of her breast and licked the damp fabric covering her nipple.

His fingers remained buried in her sex, an intimate connection even Manda was loath to break.

"Sweetie, are you okay?"

His voice startled her. She'd already grown accustomed to hearing his words in her head.

"I'm more than okay. That was amazing, like nothing else I've . . ." Her voice broke on a sob.

"Shhh. It's okay. It's wonderful. Manda, I've known you such a short time, but I want to tell you something I've never felt, never said, before in my life." He rubbed his cheek against her breast. "I love you. Even if you make me wear a blindfold for the rest of our days, I will always love you."

She tried to laugh, but it was too much. Too intense. Too unexpected. "I'm a freak, Bay. A physical mess. You can't love me."

He slipped the blindfold off his eyes and looked at Manda. She felt as if he saw inside her, beyond the patchy fur and the twisted limbs. He saw someone even she didn't know. "Yes, Manda. I can."

He sounded angry. His erection once again brushed against his belly and he obviously expected something of her Manda didn't know how to give.

Would she ever?

"Will you be okay?" Bay stepped back, away from her. It was as if a shutter had fallen over his eyes, as if the connection they'd just shared had never happened. He added a couple of pieces of wood to the fire. Adjusted the screen stretching across the hearth.

Even angry, he looked after her. He saw to her comfort.

Manda nodded, and he headed for the door. Still naked. Still very aroused. She pulled an afghan off the back of the couch and covered herself. Huddled in the corner of the big, leather couch, Manda watched Bay walk out the door.

Chapter 7

As soon as he closed the door behind himself, Bay shifted. He took a deep breath and felt the tension flow away from him. He needed this. Needed the wolf more than he realized. Belatedly, he searched his surroundings. Confident there was no one around, he leapt down the stairs and raced into the woods.

Manda's amazing reaction to his lovemaking had left him thoroughly shaken. He needed to think about that, about the way it felt to touch her so intimately, to know she still, on some level, feared him.

Running would clear his mind. It always had in the past. The forest was his, if only for a brief time, but he was alone. He'd never minded solitude before, but now something was missing. Bay wanted Manda running beside him. Wanted her voice in his mind, her scent in his nostrils, her humor and strength filling his heart. He realized he missed Shannon, too, and Jake—he missed the solidarity of his pack.

And damned if he didn't want to make love to Manda. Really make love to her. Wanted to bury himself in her warm and welcoming flesh and never come out again. It wasn't the body, the look or even the intoxicating scent of a Chanku bitch that drew him. No, it was the woman. It was Manda. Just Manda.

He stretched his legs out in front and raced the wind. Ran as fast as he could away from the woman, searching for answers without really knowing all the questions.

"What would Oprah do?" Manda pulled her red cape on over her dress for warmth and stared at the closed door. Bay was gone, already racing through the woods. She still wanted his touch, still needed the contact of his hands on her, his mouth on her breast. She felt her body react, though at this point she expected the spike of need, the dampness between her thighs, even though he'd just given her an orgasm unlike anything she'd ever experienced in her life. She'd been in an almost constant state of arousal over the past day and, as amazing as the climax had been, she still wanted, no, needed, more. It confused her at the same time she welcomed the sensations.

It had to mean the pills were working. She'd always had her *needs,* as she thought of that powerful force lurking inside, but never to this extent. When Bay looked at her, she teetered on the edge of control. Never, not in her wildest dreams, had she imagined she'd have to fight the urge to attack him and rip the clothes off that magnificent body of his. Hearing it from him, seeing him aroused and knowing he was actually attracted to her, twisted body and all, made Manda's heart sing. His touch was magic. Just thinking of his fingers inside her body made all those intimate muscles clench and ripple.

He said he loved her. Looking the way she did, being who she was, the most handsome man she'd ever seen in her life loved her. At least he thought he did. What if he merely felt sorry for her? She was definitely a pathetic creature. Hardly worthy of Bay's love.

Or was she?

Manda let out a huge sigh. Damn, she had it so bad. So, she asked herself again, what would Oprah do?

Everything she knew of life, of the world outside her

four walls, Manda'd learned from the media, but of all the programs on TV, she loved to watch Oprah, loved the way the star always encouraged women to find themselves, to be true to their desires. Well, Manda certainly had desires. Fighting back almost hysterical laughter, she got up off the couch and walked over to the fireplace. She stared at the flames and lost herself in the ebb and flow of color. As much as she agreed with Oprah's views, she had to admit that daytime TV certainly didn't cover situations like hers.

Manda rubbed her arms. The tingling had grown stronger in the short time since Bay left. She had a powerful desire to follow him, to go into the woods and search for his trail, but there was no way in hell she was going out in the dark by herself. Not as crippled, twisted, and helpless as she was.

The strange sensations in her arms and legs grew more intense. The desire to follow drew Manda to the front door. She had her hand on the latch before she even realized what was happening.

Was this it? She'd had three of the pills . . . it had been barely three days. She stopped and searched herself for any new bit of knowledge, something that would tell her it was time to shift, time to become the wolf.

All she felt was a strong need to shed her clothing, but the sun was slipping low on the horizon and the night would be cold. Manda hesitated, one hand still holding the door latch. She'd been afraid most of her life. Damn it, she was tired of always being a victim.

Bay had gone off into the forest without her. He'd brought her to this lonely cabin, far from everything Manda knew. He'd made her body sing, told her he loved her, and then he'd abandoned her to go off in the woods. It wasn't fair.

Not fair at all. Spurred by her growing anger, Manda pulled the cape off over her head and threw it on the floor. Then she slipped out of the long, jersey dress and kicked off the shapeless moccasins.

Feeling as if she were moving outside of her own body,

Manda pressed on the lever and threw open the door. The wind blew stiff and cold across the broad front deck. A porch swing creaked and clanked against the supports and she heard a raven cry nearby.

Scents assailed her nostrils and stirred something primitive deep inside. She shivered and her patchy coat of fur rose along her spine. Slowly, Manda closed the door behind her and stood naked and trembling, one hand still on the latch.

She picked up a feral scent and knew it was the way Baylor smelled when he was the wolf. His Chanku scent did something deep inside of her. She felt a hot coil of need in her womb, felt the nipples on her misshapen, mismatched breasts tighten until they ached.

Breathing deeply, Manda opened herself to the sensations of her strange, beautiful new surroundings. She felt the air currents rippling over her fur, fought the aching pain in her twisted arms and legs. Then, as if it had been there all along, Manda's mind filled with knowledge. It burst into life, flowering, filling every aspect of her being with the sense of who and what she was, what she was meant to be.

She raised her muzzle to the sky and howled, calling for all the world to hear. Calling for Baylor Quinn.

Then, as if she'd done this every day for all her life, Manda dropped to all four paws, finally, completely, from the plume of her perfect tail to the tip of her shiny black nose, a most glorious gray wolf.

Breath rasping in and out of wolven lungs, she held up her left paw and marveled at the perfection. Broad and bony over the top, with thick, black pads and long, sharply curving nails, it made a travesty of what she'd called her hands for so many years. Turning her head, she stared at the long, bushy tail, waving slowly behind her like a silken flag.

The stumpy, incomplete thing that had been her nemesis for so long was utterly transformed. Her back was long and straight, the fur thick and sparkling in the light from the setting sun. She was Chanku. Baylor was right.

Nothing would ever be the same again.

There was no pain, no sense of disbelief, merely the final acceptance of who and what she was. She felt power in her legs, power she'd only dreamed of, and it was a simple thing to launch herself over the railing and land lightly in the thick mat of spring grasses on the other side.

She raised her nose to the air currents and scented Baylor. He'd run far but his trail was clear to her Chanku senses and she knew he was no match for her speed and strength. Stretching her long legs out in front of her, running as she ran in her dreams, Manda sped across the open meadow in front of the cabin and slipped between the bushes at the edge of the thick woods.

There was no fear, no sense of anything beyond wonder. It was darker here in the woods, all shadows and thick branches and twisted brambles. The night not only waited, it called to her. Welcomed her with myriad scents and sounds she'd dreamed of her entire adult life. She practically burst with joy, with the newfound sense of strength in limbs that had long been twisted and misshapen. There was no weakness, no pain, no lack of power as she leapt over fallen logs, crossed rushing creeks and followed Bay's scent, drawing unerringly closer to the male wolf who had gone ahead.

Manda ran with her nose to the ground and her tail waving behind her. Ears pricked forward, long legs stretching out in front, she ran. After about a mile, she scented fresh blood and stopped, nose in the air, ears laid back. The smell was unfamiliar to her, but somewhere, deep in her long-buried instincts, Manda knew she scented the blood of a deer, freshly killed.

She growled, the sound reverberating from deep in her chest. Ears laid back, tail straight out behind her, Manda slipped beneath the thick brush and worked her way silently through the woods.

She heard the crunch of bone, the sounds of a solitary wolf feeding and picked up a familiar scent. Immediately, she knew Bay had hunted and killed. Saliva dripped from her jaws. They'd not eaten since around noon when Bay had picked up some sort of tasteless fast food at a small drive-in along the road. Now Manda wrapped her long tongue around her muzzle to catch the rush of saliva pouring from her jaws. She moved closer to the scent and sound. Crouching down at the edge of a small clearing, she finally spotted Bay. The large, black wolf tore into the belly of a dead buck. A gaping wound at the animal's throat gave evidence of the creature's violent death.

The scent of hot blood overruled every human thought Manda possessed. Snarling, she felt her muscles bunch into tight springs and launched herself out of the heavy tangle of shrubs, straight at Baylor.

Caught by surprise, he rolled away from the buck, snarled and snapped, and then backed off, tail tucked and ears flat. Manda stood over the carcass and claimed the feast as her own. Snarling with ears flattened and eyes narrowed, she stood stiff-legged with her tail straight behind her.

A sense of confusion emanated from Baylor as he paced back and forth a dozen feet away. Manda dipped her muzzle into the warm body and tore a huge chunk of flesh free. Gulping it down, she grabbed another, and then a third. As she choked down the bloody hunks of meat, she raised her head, licked her muzzle and stared at Baylor.

Are you still angry with me?

The black wolf halted in midstep. *Manda?* He stood with one big paw raised and stared at her in disbelief. *Is that you? Oh shit! It is you. Good Lord! You scared the crap out of me! I thought you were a wild wolf. You shifted! My God! You're beautiful, you're . . . oh crap . . . baby, I'm sorry. I wanted to be there when it happened. I had no idea you were ready to shift.*

He moved closer, his unspoken words tumbling frantically into her thoughts, yet sounding like a prayer in her mind. The dead deer appeared to have been forgotten.

Manda felt the intensity of Baylor's scrutiny, sensed the many levels of his interest.

Strongest was arousal, an intense desire to mount her now, to claim her as his mate.

Not gonna happen, big guy. Not now. Back off. Manda snarled.

Bay didn't even hesitate. He backed off and sat a few feet away. His cock bulged, red and pulsing, the knot already swollen at its base. Manda shuddered as memories of that long ago horror swamped her thoughts. She shook her head. *Eat. We're not mating tonight. Not as wolves. Not as humans.*

Bay cocked his head and looked at her, his amber eyes filled with questions Manda couldn't answer.

I don't know if that's something I'll ever be able to do.

Baylor nodded slowly, stood up and approached the deer. He drew closer to Manda and brushed her muzzle with his long tongue. *Nothing will happen until you're ready. How are you? Do you still have any pain? Are your legs strong?*

This, at least, was safe territory. *It's truly amazing. I ran, Bay. I ran through the forest and no one, not even you, could have caught me. I've never been so fast, so strong. The sights and sounds are unbelievable.* She sat back and looked at Bay with her long tongue lolling from her muzzle, then turned and twisted to look at herself. *I'm unbelievable.*

That you are. You're also absolutely gorgeous. Did you make the shift to human yet?

His question shocked Manda all the way to her core. *Would you believe I didn't even think of that? All I wanted to do was jump off the deck and run. I wanted to find you.* She turned away, then glanced back over her shoulder. Challenged Baylor. *Want to try and catch me?*

You think I can't?

Just try. Manda spun away and raced into the forest with Baylor close behind her. If she'd been human, she would have laughed, but she ran with her tail high and her jaws open, ears twisting and turning to catch the sounds beside the trail as well as the pounding cadence of Baylor racing behind her.

Was he trying to catch her, or just following her lead?

Did it really matter? This body was amazing. Strong and powerful and perfectly designed to cover vast distances without tiring. Sleek muscles bunched beneath rippling gray fur, powerful legs stretched to clear whatever lay in her path. Manda felt as if she could run forever, leaping over fallen trees, slipping through narrow paths in the tall grass, dipping her nose to the ground to catch scents of the varied denizens of the forest. Bay stayed about ten paces behind her, following easily but not attempting to pass, or even to crowd her. She sensed his exhilaration, his unbridled pride in her speed and agility.

Just as she sensed his arousal. Desire coursed through her own body as well, but fear tempered the sensual pleasure that should have flowed with it. If he'd wanted her before, when her body was twisted and ugly, he must be even more interested now that she'd become such a perfect creature.

Perfect in appearance, maybe, but the woman inside was every bit as twisted and damaged as before. Would she ever get past the fear? Ever be able to bury the memories?

Even now, in the midst of a sensual high over this most amazing experience, Manda was consumed by terror. Memories of that horrible night when Papa B had been away, when some of the workers had been drinking in the lab. They'd started out teasing her with their rude comments, but they'd gotten brave. They'd grabbed her, restrained her, muzzled her jaws. Forcing her down, they'd bent her over a low table and taped her arms up over her head. Two men had held her feet and spread them so far apart she'd thought she might split open. Then they'd smeared her between her legs with the scent of a she-wolf in heat.

She couldn't cry, could barely breathe when they brought the huge male wolf into the room. Muzzled so it wouldn't bite her, the animal had been crazed by the rich scent of the female.

She remembered laughter and crude comments by the men, the probing, stabbing pain as the wolf mounted her, the scrape and tear of sharp claws over her small shoulders. She'd felt excruciating pain when the animal penetrated and tied to her, then nothing.

The next day, it was as if it had never happened. The lab workers went about their duties, continued their studies and, other than avoiding making eye contact with Manda, pretended all was well. Terrified of their doing it again, Manda had kept her mouth shut. She'd never told a soul about that horrible night.

Now, though, the memories dulled the joy she felt in this new body. Would Bay want to mount her? Would he take her in wolf form, against her will?

Bay had promised he would never hurt her. Could she really trust him?

They'd come to a high ridge and Manda found a rocky outcropping, bare of trees. A pale moon cast its silvery light over the granite boulders and gave life to the oddly shaped shadows. Scrabbling over the rough granite, Manda found the tallest point and claimed if for her own. Squatting, she peed in the dirt near the top, then kicked leaves and dirt over the spot.

Bay marked a tree, but it was at a level below the rise from Manda. Did that mean he accepted her as the alpha bitch? This was all so new to her! He kicked dirt as well, throwing the torn pieces of turf out behind him, then he sat just below her, looking up with jaws gaping, tongue lolling. *You really can run. You're fast. It was all I could do to keep up.*

Really? His words of praise were the nicest thing he could have given her. Manda, the one who'd shuffled on malformed legs for two thirds of her life was fast? She wanted to laugh, to raise her voice to the heavens and give thanks.

Instead, she howled. Pointing her nose toward the moon, Manda voiced her joy in a long, drawn out cry. Bay joined her, pointing his nose skyward and singing along.

Two wolves howling in the darkness, a simple thing in a state once home to a huge wolven population, yet not so simple at all. It was beyond Manda's wildest dreams, a miracle of chance, that Baylor had not only found her, he'd saved her. She'd work through her fears in time. She was a survivor, wasn't she? Eyes sparkling, Manda gave up the hideously malformed woman with the misshapen body and consigned her to memories. Now, she was powerful. She was perfect, a child of nature.

She was Chanku.

* * *

Millie lay beside Ulrich and cataloged the way her body felt this morning. She ached, most deliciously, between her legs and her nipples felt so tender from his suckling mouth and pinching, twisting fingers, she wondered if she'd have to skip wearing a bra.

He slept soundly, his back to her, one arm thrown over his face, the covers tangled just below his hips. From the muscular line of his back to the firm curve of his buttocks, Ulrich Mason had an absolutely gorgeous body. She'd never have guessed him to be in his early sixties.

He certainly had the sexual stamina of a man half his years. Millie rolled to her back and fought a surge of giggles. She'd teased him after one particularly amazing climax, wondering if he was trying to make up for all her years of celibacy.

His answer had been to turn her over and gently take her last virginity from her. She blushed, still amazed by her powerful response to a sex act she'd always thought of as both prurient and disgusting.

Who would have guessed how sensitive her bottom might be to such slow, delicious penetration? Thinking about the sensation of Ulrich's huge cock breaching that tight ring of muscle made her sex clench and a shiver run over her breasts. She couldn't possibly want more sex. Not after a night like that.

What she really needed was a shower, a cup of coffee or three, and something to eat. Then she had to go back to work, as much as she would have preferred staying in bed all day with such a gorgeous man.

A gorgeous man who can turn himself into a wolf.

She'd really tried not to think of that. Tried not to remember the amazing sight of Ulrich beside the bed, amber eyes glowing out of the face of the most beautiful wolf she'd ever seen.

Tried not to think of the fact he'd promised Millie she would soon be able to do the same thing. Shift. Become a four-legged creature with the speed and endurance of any of the beautiful wolves now living here at the sanctuary. Had she really taken that pill?

Millie felt her heart rate speed up as the impact of what she'd experienced last night hit her like a gale-force wind.

"Sweetheart, what's wrong?"

Millie turned and saw that Ulrich had rolled over and propped himself up on his elbows. His white hair was tousled and stuck up on one side. He needed a shave. His lips looked as swollen from kissing as hers must be.

He was absolutely perfect.

And worried.

"I'm okay. I think the enormity of what I've learned about you—and me—is sinking in."

Ulrich leaned close and kissed her and Millie's pulse raced for an entirely different reason. She kissed him back and felt his warm palm cupping the swell of her breast.

"This has got to be the most perfect part of a woman's body." His voice sounded gruff from sleep as he looked at the spot where his fingers supported her right breast. "The curve fits perfectly into my hand. Your skin feels like silk and your nipple stands up to show its appreciation." Ulrich leaned over and kissed the nipple he'd been admiring.

Millie moaned and arched into his touch. "I have to get up and get ready for work."

Ulrich suckled her nipple between his lips while his hand stole lower. She felt his fingertip exploring her navel.

"I'm already up. Maybe I can help."

She laughed, but it sounded more like a whimper. "I've discovered you're always up."

"You say that as if it's a bad thing. We know better." His fingertip slipped lower and Millie tensed just before he brushed across her sensitive clit.

She clamped her legs together, trapping his fingers in her soft folds. "No more, or I'll never get back to my office." Laughing at his crestfallen look, Millie slipped out of bed. She felt absolutely no modesty around him. None, as if she'd wandered naked in front of a man before. She'd never really had the opportunity with her cowboy. She turned around and pointed at Ulrich. "Stay there. I'll be out in a minute."

Sunlight streamed through the open shades, shining over her body, spotlighting her. She felt like an actress on stage, aware of Ulrich's appreciative gaze. Suddenly his eyes narrowed and he looked up, frowning. "Do you have children, sweetheart? I hadn't noticed your stretch marks until the sunlight caught them."

Stricken, unable to answer, Millie spun around and raced into the shower.

Almost as stunned by Millie's reaction as he was at his own stupidity for such an inappropriate comment, Ulrich rolled to his back and clenched his fists. "Idiot. What a complete idiot."

He'd probably screwed up everything, but damn it all,

he'd been so surprised by the silvery tracings across her smooth belly that he'd spoken without thinking.

Obviously.

He heard the shower running and wondered what Millie was thinking right now. Probably devising the best method to get him out of her life. If she'd wanted to talk about her pregnancy, she would have brought it up. They'd talked about everything else.

Hell, he'd even told her about Anton Cheval, leader of the Montana Pack, and how Anton had made it possible for Ulrich to make peace with Camille, the woman he'd loved and hated with equal measure since her untimely death when their daughter was small.

That one night with Camille had been amazing, but not anything could compete with the night he'd just spent with Millie West.

Lying here grumbling about what an ass he'd been wasn't going to fix things. An abject apology for his insensitive comment would probably go a lot further. Ulrich crawled out of bed and headed for the bathroom. The door wasn't locked, so he considered that an invitation.

Of course, if it had been locked, he'd probably have opened it anyway. He stepped into the steam-filled room and saw Millie through the clear plastic curtain. She had her back to him. Her forehead was pressed against the tile wall and Ulrich suspected she was crying. He tried to find her thoughts, thoughts they'd shared openly all night long, but she blocked him.

Sighing, feeling lower than low, Ulrich tugged the shower curtain aside and stepped in behind Millie. She spun around at the sound and Ulrich slipped an arm around her waist so she wouldn't fall.

He expected a struggle, but she merely collapsed against him, sobbing as if her heart would break. He held her, stroking her back, whispering apologies for being such an ass, but she kept shaking her head against his chest.

"I should have said something, should have told you. I didn't know how, especially when you talked about Tianna and how hard it had been for you to raise her without her mother. I felt like such a horrible person, but I didn't want to give them up. Really, Ulrich. I wanted to keep them both and raise them, but I was young and my uncle took them away."

"Them? You had more than one?"

Millie nodded. "Twins. A boy and a girl. I was twenty and their father was a cowboy just passing through. He was my only lover, until last night. He was good to me, but he was long gone before I even knew I was pregnant."

Ulrich grabbed the washcloth and soap and began to bathe Millie while she talked. She stared at him a moment, her eyes still swimming in tears and a tiny crease between her brows. Then she turned around. He sensed it was easier for her to tell him everything when he wasn't looking into her tearful eyes.

"My uncle was very religious. I think, in his eyes, the mere fact I was female was already a sin. My mother, his only sister, had me out of wedlock. She died when I was about three and the county placed me with my uncle since he was my only living relative. He never forgave me the sin of being illegitimate. He never married and he spent the rest of his life trying to beat whatever irritated him, out of me. The ranch where the sanctuary is was supposed to be my inheritance, but after the babies were born, he said I was going to hell and didn't deserve his land. I loved these mountains, always have. That's why I've stayed on here."

"What happened to your babies?"

"I'm not really sure. The little girl was given to a missionary family and I think the boy went to a farming family somewhere in southern Colorado. The adoptions were handled privately through the church and I was never allowed access to the records. The church is long gone, along with any way I might have to find them." She turned and smiled sadly at Ulrich as he rubbed shampoo into her hair. "Believe me, I've tried. I went through my uncle's records after he died, but there was nothing at all about my babies. It was as if they never existed, as far as he was concerned. I've wanted to know what happened to them, if they were all right. Most of all, I need to tell them I didn't want to give them up. They were taken from me."

She bowed her head. With her wet hair plastered against her skull, her shoulders slumping and the line of her vertebrae showing down the middle of her back, Millie looked like a lost child. Her shoulders rose and fell with her sigh and her voice shook. "I miss them so much. I wasn't conscious when they were born and I never even got to see them. Never held them. I don't even know what they weighed at birth. I think about them every day, especially on their birthday."

Ulrich nodded as he worked the rich lather into Millie's hair. "When were they born?"

"July 10, 1971. A lifetime ago. I never even got to tell them I love them."

"You'll be able to tell them. We will find them."

"What? How?" Millie spun around. Her fingers wrapped around Ulrich's wrist and she stared at him, wide-eyed.

Ulrich smiled at her and pushed the soapy strands of Millie's hair away from her eyes. She was absolutely lovely. His cock swelled in appreciation, rising to midlevel and, in spite of the fact they'd made love most of the night, Ulrich wanted Millie again.

"I told you last night, sweetheart. I own a detective agency, and I'm very good at what I do. We will find your children. Now turn around so I can rinse your hair, and then we will make love again before you have to leave for work."

"Just like that?" She turned and bent her head while he directed the spray over her hair.

"Just like that."

Chapter 8

"I can't believe I got to work on time." Millie waved to the night watchman as he drove off, then turned and unlocked the door to her office.

Ulrich touched her hand. It seemed he couldn't go more than a few seconds without touching her when they were near one another. Millie decided that was something she could get used to really fast.

"I'm going to check out that new pair of wolves that just came in." Ulrich kissed her on the mouth and then walked across the compound toward the temporary cages. Millie watched him go, well aware of his taste on her lips, the tight coil of desire in her middle and the fact she already felt a powerful connection to a man she'd known for less than twenty-four hours.

He was utterly amazing, even beyond the fact he could shift from human to wolf. She giggled, then glanced quickly around to make sure no one heard her. If she didn't behave herself, someone might guess what was going on between her and a man they all knew she'd just met for the first time. She'd never live down the teasing if anyone found out. Her employees loved her dearly, but they loved just as much to wonder and speculate about her private life.

If they only knew . . . she'd never imagined the sensual

potential with her multi-speed shower massage, especially when wielded by a man with unlimited imagination and an impossible sex drive. The sharp beads of steaming water, directed at nipples and clit and all areas in between had been a revelation.

Millie stood in the open doorway and watched as Ulrich hunkered down in front of one of the cages. She thought of his big hands roaming gently over her naked body and the way he'd made love to her. There wasn't a position they hadn't tried, not an orifice that hadn't been breached—on either one of them.

He'd shown her a wantonness about herself Millie had never dreamed existed, and his loving thoughts had caressed her mind with unspoken words of encouragement and love. That thought led to another, and she wondered if he could communicate with the animals the same way, mindtalking just as he'd communicated with her, and if so, how much they might be able to learn from the wolves.

He'd certainly learned any and all of Millie's secrets. She turned and went inside the office, thinking of her babies. They'd be grown now, probably married with children of their own. She wished them happiness, she wished them love . . . she wished she knew them.

If Ulrich said he'd find her children, Millie believed him. She had to. The entire situation was beyond bizarre, but she had to believe. She'd seen him shift. A man one moment, a wolf the next. She'd buried her face in the thick ruff of fur at his neck and cried for all the years she'd felt so incomplete, for all the times she'd been without hope. Suddenly, the dreams she'd had for years, the fascination with wolves, the feeling she was somehow fragmented, missing an important part of herself—all of it made sense.

Did her children feel the same? Did they dream of running through the forest on four legs, eyes bright in the darkness, senses aware and alert?

Millie had blamed so much of her incomplete existence

on her missing children. Maybe that wasn't it at all. Maybe it was, as Ulrich suggested, the fact she'd never known her true nature.

She thought of the pill she'd taken this morning. One just like the big ugly capsule Ulrich had swallowed with his morning coffee. She'd know in a matter of days. Maybe she'd finally understand why her life had always felt so incomplete.

Millie sat down at her computer and logged on. They'd be going over the books and paperwork today. An entire day working closely beside the first man to ever make her body sing. She tried, but couldn't wipe the smile off her face. Ulrich Mason was a revelation in more ways than one. He'd revealed a totally new side of Millie West.

She felt young and free, as if the whole world waited for her. Humming to herself, Millie stared at the blue screen while her computer booted up and she thought about the evening to come.

Time alone, again, with Ulrich. A coil of heat speared her from nipples to sex and the muscles between her legs tightened in delicious anticipation. She glanced at the clock. It was only ten after eight, and the day stretched out ahead.

A day spent within sight, sound, scent, and touch of Ulrich. All of Millie's senses reacted at the thought.

She couldn't wait.

* * *

Manda trotted slowly behind Baylor as they made their way back to the cabin. Though the trail was unfamiliar, she had a powerful sense of direction she'd never noticed before. Baylor might be leading, but Manda knew she could find her way back on her own if she had to.

She'd never had this sense of self before. It was so much more than just a feeling, it was an acceptance of feminine empowerment that went far beyond anything she'd read about for human women.

Bay had told her that, in spite of her life as a disabled human, she was, without any doubt, an alpha bitch. Aggressive, powerful, self-confident.

She'd known that long before Bay had tried to explain the difference between alphas and betas and omegas. Maybe she hadn't known the exact meaning behind the terms, but she'd certainly sensed the confidence, the self-assurance she had in this form.

If only she didn't have to think about the sex. Touching Bay, being touched by him, had been wonderful, but he expected more. Deserved more. She knew he wanted full penetration, both as human and as wolf, but her body froze at the thought. She couldn't do it. Couldn't couple with him no matter how much he wanted it.

Blocking her fear, Manda concentrated on the intriguing scents of the night. She picked out the musty smell of mice and knew she ran past a nest in the thick grass. There was another scent that made her mouth water. When she glanced at Bay, he nodded to their right where a huge jackrabbit stood in the shadows. It held absolutely motionless, obviously hoping against hope the wolves wouldn't see it.

Manda had only taken a few bites of the deer Bay had killed, but she ran past the rabbit without pausing. There was always tomorrow.

She reveled in the sounds and scents of the night, running free for the first time in her life. Pushed to the back of her mind, hiding in the darkness beside the ghost of sexual terror was another thing she refused to think about—the women she was about to meet, the face she'd not seen before. Manda's human face.

With that face came a whole new set of worries. What if Bay wasn't attracted to her? What if he didn't want her?

Where the hell was the alpha bitch personality when she needed her? What an idiot. Worrying about what she'd do if he wanted to have sex, afraid he might not want to have sex . . . she should be worried more about her own reaction. She'd always wondered what she might look like, had God not cursed her.

Well, in a few minutes, Manda was going to find out.

Baylor reached the deck first and shifted without thinking. He reached for the door and looked toward Manda. She stood on the top step, one paw raised, her wolven brow furrowed.

"Manda? Are you okay?"

The wolf nodded. Walked up onto the deck. Paced the length and back again.

"Aren't you going to shift?"

I'm afraid. What if it doesn't work? What if I'm still a freak? Cursed?

Bay shook his head and crouched down in front of the wolf. "You'll be fine. Look how easy it was for you to shift and become the wolf? You are an absolutely perfect wolf. You'll be just as perfect as a woman. Your body is ready. You've taken enough of the nutrients to make things work exactly the way it should. Can you look inside and see what you need to do to shift? Is the knowledge there?"

The wolf nodded. *It's there. I know how. I'm just . . .* She looked at him, her eyes glowing. *As much as I hate the body I've had all these years, it's the one I know. What if I don't like the new one I'll have? It's the one I'll be stuck with forever!*

"The main thing wrong with the old body is that you were in constant pain. Shift, Manda. Find the woman you're meant to be. She won't hurt. She'll be strong and healthy, just as you are now, as a wolf. I'm here for you, sweetheart. Shift."

He tried to project a sense of confidence, but at the same time, Bay ordered Manda to shift. He commanded her with his voice, taking a position of power over her. And something in Manda responded. She glared at him. Then she shifted.

Bay sat back on his heels and looked up. He never would have recognized this woman as Manda if he were to pass her on the street. Almost six feet tall with broad shoulders and long, long legs, she stood straight and healthy, her blond hair falling about her shoulders in thick, soft waves, her breasts high and firm, her nipples dark pink against her fair skin.

She was beautiful. Without any doubt, the most glorious creature Bay had ever seen in his life. He stared at her for what seemed like forever, struck dumb by her shimmering beauty. Then he slowly rose to stand in front of her, took her hand in his, bowed over it and raised it to his lips.

He felt as if he should kneel once more at her feet. There was something ethereal about her, as if she were a fey creature who would disappear with the morning's light. She looked at him, a quizzical expression on her face, head tilted, a tiny wrinkle between her brows.

"What?" She held her hands out to her sides, almost helplessly. "What's wrong with me? Why are you looking at me like that?"

Her voice was soft, melodious, pitched just a bit lower than average. It raised shivers along Bay's spine.

He grinned. He almost laughed, but managed to control himself. Instead he reached for her hand and led her to the front door, opened it and took her inside the cabin. He noticed that she placed her feet with care, as if expecting to stumble, but each footfall was sure and true.

Bay led her straight to Shannon and Jake's bedroom, tugging Manda along behind him when she seemed to hold back. Both of them were well aware this was the one room with a full-length mirror on the closet door.

Manda followed quietly. Bay had the feeling she was

still assessing all her body parts, testing arms and legs to be sure they worked. Her concerns hadn't quite reached appearance yet.

He took her into the large master bedroom and turned on the light. Then he grabbed her by the shoulders and walked her to the full-length mirror. Obviously afraid to look, she kept her eyes closed and her head bowed until he kissed her on the cheek and whispered, "Look. My lovely, lovely Manda. Look at yourself."

Manda raised her head, opened her eyes, and burst into tears.

Sobbing without any semblance of control, Manda shoved Bay's arms away when he tried to draw her into a hug. Her tears blocked her first view of herself and she scrubbed at her eyes, but they kept falling and she got the giggles.

"I can't see myself!"

Bay hugged her from behind and kissed the side of her neck. "Then stop blubbering, silly."

"I'm trying. Oh God, Bay, I really am trying but I can't . . . I can't stop. It's so amazing. I'm so amazing. I'm normal, Bay. I'm a normal woman and I want to see!"

Bay reached into a big oak dresser next to them and found a cotton handkerchief in the top drawer. He handed it to Manda and she wiped at her eyes.

Finally she stopped rubbing and stared at the face in the mirror. She was beautiful. And tall! She'd always been so stooped and short, she never dreamed she'd be so tall. Suddenly she reached around behind herself and touched her tailbone. Smooth and firm, her back sloped down to her rounded buttocks. No tail. Not even a stub.

How she'd hated that thing. The tail, more than anything else, had set her aside from other humans. It was the one thing the lab people always remarked upon, the fact she had a tail like a dog . . . or a wolf.

Her hand brushed against Bay's thigh and she jumped. So intent on herself she'd not even noticed he stood right behind her, watching over her left shoulder as she studied her image in the mirror. Blushing, Manda lowered her head. "I was feeling for my tail. It's gone."

"I know." He kissed her neck, just below her ear, brushing her hair back to bare her skin. She had such smooth skin without any tufts of hair anywhere it shouldn't be. His lips felt wonderfully soft against her, his words a whispered benediction.

"Manda, do you have any idea how perfect you are?" Bay's voice cracked as he rubbed his cheek across her shoulder and Manda felt the warm dampness of his tears.

She realized she was shivering, her legs trembled and Bay was crying. Why the hell was he crying? Manda turned into his embrace and kissed him. "Why, Baylor? Why are you . . . ?" She didn't finish her question. Instead she scrubbed her hand across her own eyes, then handed the damp handkerchief to him. "Here, it's the best I can do."

Bay sniffed and grinned, then took the white cotton and wiped his face with it. "Pretty powerful stuff. This. You. Watching your eyes when you saw yourself for the first time. I just realized how very lucky I am to share this moment with you."

"It's because of you I have this moment, this life." She couldn't take her eyes off the image in the mirror. Tall and beautiful and so healthy looking! Her arms and legs were straight and strong, her shoulders wide, her breasts both the same size, full and round like breasts should be. She had a sleek patch of dark blond hair at the juncture of her thighs, soft downy tufts under each arm and perfect, darker eyebrows over the same, familiar eyes she'd had all her life. In fact, her eyes were the only thing left unchanged.

That and the woman inside. She was still a neurotic, frightened wreck, but after the life she'd led, what else could she expect? Manda felt the brush of Bay's engorged penis against her buttocks and jerked away from him before she could catch herself. "I'm sorry. You startled me." She looked down, away from his intent gaze in the reflection.

Bay put his hands on her shoulders and slowly turned her away from the mirror to face him. "Please. Don't be afraid of me. I told you nothing will happen until you're ready. This . . ." He gestured toward his thick erection and laughed. "After a run, I'm always horny. It's part of what I am, what you are. I can't help getting hard, but I have complete control over what I do with it."

"I know that. Consciously, I know you'd never hurt me, but there's a part of my memories that have a stranglehold on me. I have to work through them."

Bay wrapped his arms around her and pulled Manda close against his chest. She felt the press of his erection against her belly, but forced herself to remain calm and relaxed. His hands rubbing up and down her back were soothing, comforting, and after a moment she realized she could accept the pressure of his huge shaft riding over her belly without fear.

"The sad thing is," Bay said, whispering against her hair, "that if you could get past your fears and we could mate as wolves, we'd bond. A mating bond is an integration of thought unlike anything else. It's a total, complete meshing of our minds and memories. You'd know everything about me and I'd know everything about you, possibly even things you've tried to forget. I would know what it is, exactly, that makes you afraid. Then, just maybe, I could help you deal with it."

"We'll have to find another way." Manda slipped out of his embrace and took a deep breath. "I'm not ready for penetration. Just the thought of it terrifies me, but I liked what we did earlier, and as weird as it sounds, I'm so turned on I can hardly stand it! I liked touching you before, and exploring." She giggled and felt her skin prickle with embarrassment. Now that was a new sensation! She covered her face with one hand, and it was all she could do to choke out the words. "I really liked how you taste, the way it felt to lick and suck you. If that's enough for . . ."

"You're kidding, right? You're asking me if it's okay to touch you? If it's okay to let you go down on me?" He laughed, but there was a strangled sound to it. "Sweetie, I was planning to jerk off in the shower. I think I prefer your suggestion to mine."

She looked up at him and frowned. "What do you mean, jerk off in the shower? What's that?"

Oh shit. Bay almost lost it, hearing that innocent question from the gorgeous blonde in his arms. He hadn't quite come to terms yet, with the fact this was Manda. *His* Manda, yet here she was, beautiful beyond belief, talking about taking him in her mouth, touching and tasting him, and then asking what he meant when he said he jerked off?

He cleared his throat. "Uhm, it means I make myself come in the shower . . . you know, with my hand."

Manda stared at him out of those gorgeous amber eyes and ran her fingertip down his chest, parting the dark hair all the way to his navel. His cock rose up to meet her. "I didn't know you could do that. Make yourself come. I used to try it by myself. It was always less than satisfactory." She glanced down at his cock, swollen and pulsing between them. "I'd like very much to see how you do it. Would you mind if I watched?"

Breathing was suddenly really difficult. She wanted to watch? *Oh shit.* "Uh, no. I guess it's okay. If you want."

Manda nodded. It suddenly came to him that they were both naked, both unimaginably aroused after their run as wolves, both evading their needs. Okay. So she wanted to watch. If he didn't come soon he knew he'd explode. Maybe Manda felt the same way. Maybe, just maybe, watching him masturbate would help her over whatever walls she'd built.

Decision made, Bay grabbed Manda's hand and practically dragged her toward the big shower off the master bedroom. Plenty of room for two, lots of hot water. It wouldn't be the first time he'd jacked off under the spray in this room.

It was, however, the first time he could recall he'd ever done it with an audience.

Manda followed, a small smile on her lips. Her nipples had puckered into tight beads and Bay knew she was more than a little interested in what he had planned. He also suspected she was every bit as turned on as he was. Shifting did that to Chanku, though he'd never understood why. Maybe it was the increase in sensual awareness, the way the shift seemed to energize and sensitize everything about them.

The libido was definitely energized after a shift, in women as much as the men. With that thought in mind, Bay turned on the water, waited for it to heat, then stepped under the steaming spray.

Manda followed him. She found the small molded seat at one end of the shower and sat down on it. The shower sprayed across her torso until Bay stepped in between the shower head and Manda. She didn't seem to mind. Her attention appeared to be focused solely on his cock. He was swollen and dark, his foreskin partially stretched back behind the head, the tip already leaking tiny drops of precum.

She seemed inordinately interested in that tiny bubble of white.

Manda raised her chin and looked at him, only it wasn't the Manda he knew. Hell, it wasn't even the Manda *she* knew. This gorgeous blonde was essentially a stranger to both of them. A beautiful, sensual stranger who wanted to watch Bay make nice with his cock in the shower.

Sure. No problem. Feeling unaccountably angry and embarrassed, yet so turned on his body shook, Bay grabbed his cock in his right hand and cupped his sac with his left. Slowly, with years of experience behind the moves, he rolled his foreskin completely back, exposing the swollen crown, then slipped it forward over the tip. Over again, then back, again and again until the familiar rhythm took control. All sense of anger and embarrassment slowly slipped away and left him practically humming with pleasure. He leaned back against the wall of the shower, his cock wrapped in his fist, his balls nestled in his palm, the hot water pounding against his side and shoulder.

How many times had he stroked himself? How often had he used his fist to find a release for the powerful tension in his aroused body?

The difference this time was the audience. Manda watched, expression rapt, lips parted, hands folded demurely in her lap. She appeared mesmerized by each stroke and thrust, her eyes following the movement of his hand along the length of his cock, the way he carefully cupped his balls in their wrinkled sac and rolled them between his fingers.

He couldn't recall the sensation ever feeling so powerful before, the mere act of beating off taken to an entirely new level. He could have gone faster and been done with it, except for the simple fact of Manda watching him. Knowing she watched increased the eroticism of the act, made him feel more, expect more. His cock seemed to expand beyond all proportions, the sensation of his balls against his palm, the stroke of his fist, took on entirely new roles. He felt as if he acted out a part in a truly erotic film.

The shower stall filled with steam. The strong jets of hot water beat a powerful, stinging tattoo against his left side. Manda's tongue slipped between her parted lips, then disappeared inside her mouth once more. Her eyes held a slightly glazed expression. She leaned closer, as if drawn to the tiny beads of white that appeared at the tip of his cock, then quickly washed away beneath the shower spray. Bay stared, unblinking, mesmerized by her beauty, her look of total involvement in the way his hands moved, the size of his erection.

Manda leaned close and ran her tongue over the tip of his cock. She left a trail of fire across the sensitive skin. Bay groaned and held perfectly still, caught up in the moment, in the rough, callused grasp of his hands, the pounding water, the tender sweep of her tongue, the fiery connection they made. She licked him again, but her hands remained in her lap, fingers tightly folded as if she were a schoolgirl awaiting an assignment.

Bay's eyes drifted shut for a moment as pleasure washed over him. This wasn't a shower in a cabin in Maine. He was deep in the jungle, the damp air filled with the scent of his lady, the rain beating on his bare back and shoulders. That wasn't his own fist wrapped around his cock, his hand supporting the weight of his balls. It was Manda. Only Manda.

He wanted her lips on him. Wanted the suction of that beautiful, warm, wet mouth, the scrape of her fingernails across his sac, any kind of touch she was willing to share.

His eyes flicked open. He focused all his attention on Manda's face. As if reading his mind, she leaned closer once more and licked the very end of his cock, circling around the sensitive crown before dipping the tip of her tongue into the weeping slit at the center. Bay groaned and thrust his hips forward as fantasy became reality. She looked up at him and smiled, then leaned close and wrapped her lips around the entire head. Bay almost whimpered. It took all his self-control not to thrust his cock down her throat.

Instead, his hand tightened around the base and then he let go, turning himself over to Manda and her sensual touch. She wrapped her slim fingers around his shaft and her tongue around the crown and nibbled it with her teeth. Suddenly he was in her mouth and she was sucking him deep, past lips and teeth, her tongue stroking the length of him, her mouth sucking him deeper and deeper.

Her fingers found his sac. He moved his hand aside and she cradled his balls. Her nails scraped the sensitive skin behind his testicles, traced the narrow length of his perineum and circled the tight ring of his ass.

Then, without warning, she thrust one finger deep inside his ass. She pressed forward and closed her lips tightly around his cock, just behind the head, at the same time.

Fire flashed from spine to balls. Bay sucked in a gasp of mist-laden air with the shock of her touch. A coil of heat flamed up as if she'd hit him with a blowtorch. He had barely enough strength to cry out, to grasp the sides of her head in his palms and thrust once, twice, into her willing mouth. She closed her eyes and swallowed, holding his cock in place with her tongue and teeth, taking his bursts of ejaculate and swallowing every bit.

When he finally withdrew, legs trembling, lungs pumping as if he'd run a mile, Manda was laughing. *Laughing!*

"I've read about that," she said, leaning close to lick once more along the length of his cock and then grinning broadly when he jumped at her light touch. "I read that you could make a man climax that way. I just never believed it was true."

"Well, believe it, damn it! What the hell have you been reading, anyway? What are you trying to do to me?" Bay tried to sound angry but he burst out laughing. "Sheesh, woman, you just about killed me."

Manda blinked with the look of the innocent. The water beat down on them both and Bay dropped to his knees in the warm spray. He spread Manda's long legs apart before she realized what he intended. She tried to clamp them shut, but only managed to trap his head between her thighs.

Laughing, she squirmed about on the small molded seat, but Bay held her down with both hands and proceeded to explore all her parts with his tongue. He found her clit immediately. Distended and hard, it protruded from between swollen lips as if searching for attention. He clamped his lips over it and Manda screamed.

Shocked, he backed away, but she grabbed his head and forced him back. "Don't you dare stop." She was laughing and so was he and Bay spread her thighs apart and licked and sucked until Manda squirmed helplessly on the slick seat.

He sensed no fear in her, no discomfort in the way he licked and nibbled between her legs. The water began to cool but Bay was so hot he should have been steaming beneath the spray. Manda tasted sweet and sour, tart and perfect under his tongue. Her flavors were something to be savored, but the water was getting cold and Bay knew his time was limited.

He drove his tongue deep and licked his way out, suckling her labia between his lips and licking her clit on every pass. Kneading her buttocks with his hands, he lifted her closer to his mouth. All the while, the water beat a powerful rhythm against his back, cooling faster now, as the last of the hot water ran out.

Finally, Bay took her clit between his lips and suckled, wrapping the tip of his tongue around the base. She groaned and lifted her hips off the seat, just enough for him to find the cleft between her buttocks and locate the tight ring of muscle at the center.

He caught her right at the edge of her climax, driving a finger deep inside Manda's ass just as she'd done to him. He felt her climax explode through her entire pelvic region. Felt the powerful contractions against his tongue and middle finger, the gush of thick fluids over his lips. Licking and sucking, he caught as much of her taste as he could while she clamped her thighs against his head and cried, then whimpered, and finally sighed her release.

Bay reached behind himself and turned off the shower

just as the hot water ran out completely. He wrapped his arms around Manda and rested his cheek against her belly where he could inhale the rich scent of her release.

It took her a moment, but her hands came down to brush the hair back from his eyes while the other touched his shoulder. "I've never felt anything like that," she said. Bay looked up. Manda had her head back, leaning against the wall of the shower. Her eyes were closed and she had a soft, sweet smile on her lips, and little goose bumps all over her chilly body.

"Did that penetration frighten you?" He'd loved the feel of her muscles clamping tightly around his finger. He wished like hell it had been his cock.

She shook her head. "No. You did it so fast I didn't have time to be scared. Then I was climaxing and I guess I didn't care at that point."

He nuzzled her belly again. "I care, enough for both of us. You know I want to make love to you. I don't want there to be any barriers between us."

Manda ran her fingers through his wet hair, stroking him slowly. "I want to think sex, real sex with you deep inside me, will feel as good, but I can't imagine anything better than what we just did."

He laughed and blew a small gust of breath through her pubic curls. He loved her. Loved her so much he ached with the need to hold her, ached with wanting to fill her the way she was meant to be filled. Now wouldn't be soon enough.

"I can say, without any doubt, that when we finally make love the way we're meant to, you will wonder why you feared it. But in the meantime, this ain't bad. Not perfect, but not bad." He chuckled and looked up at Manda, expecting to see her smile.

Instead, she looked troubled. "I don't know, Bay. I want to, but . . ."

"Shhh." He pressed a finger over her lips. "Don't worry.

It will all happen when you're ready. Not a moment before. Now let's dry off before we freeze to death. We need to get some sleep, okay?"

Manda nodded. "Okay." She stood up and took the towel he offered. They both shivered, as much from the aftermath of sex as the frigid ending to their shower. Bay rubbed her hair with an extra towel as she dried herself. She silently accepted his help, but he thought she seemed terribly subdued for a woman having a night such as she'd just experienced.

From a lifetime as a deformed cripple, to shifting into a wolf, to this, the body of a goddess . . . how could she possibly handle it so calmly? Shouldn't she be reveling in all the changes? It made no sense. Bay tried to access her thoughts but her mental blocks were up and shields drawn tight.

He handed her one of the heavy terry cloth robes hanging on a hook by the door. Manda slipped it on without comment. Bay grabbed one for himself, slightly unnerved by the unusual yet powerful feeling that he needed to cover his nakedness.

Sighing, wondering what he should have done differently, or what, if anything, he could do differently tomorrow to bridge the suddenly widening gap between himself and his woman, Bay hung the damp towels over the shower rod and followed Manda down the hall to his bedroom. At least she had chosen to sleep beside him. It was a small concession, but a concession after all.

A man could always hope for more.

Chapter 9

"Millie, love, you should be so proud of what you've accomplished in just the few weeks since you've taken over. This is amazing." Ulrich closed the last of the files and sat back in his chair. "Anton Cheval told me things were an absolute mess when you stepped in."

Millie felt her face grow warm and knew she'd probably turned beet red. She wasn't used to compliments and Ulrich had been giving them to her all day long. She glanced at him out of the corner of her eye. He had a huge, self-satisfied grin on his face.

Bastard! She laughed. "You do that just to make me blush, don't you? Say nice things to me, call me *love*, just to see how red I'll get!"

"Ah, Millie." He slapped a hand over his heart. "I would never do anything so cruel."

"Yeah. Right." She snorted and Ulrich laughed.

"Well, maybe just a little." He stood up and carried the stack of files to a large cabinet against the back wall of Millie's office. "I mean every word and every compliment is no more than the truth, but I love to see you smile, or blush or . . ." He turned around and looked at her with a heated expression in his amber eyes. "Or, shiver from my touch. Damn, Millie, if I don't get to touch you soon I'm going to explode."

He gripped the chair in front of him so hard his knuckles turned white.

"Ric . . ." The shorter form of his name slipped out. It was what she already called him in her heart, the name she thought of when she thought of him. "Ric, I . . ."

He sat down in the chair, hard. Buried his head in his hands. Millie raced across the room and knelt down in front of him. "Are you okay? What happened? What's wrong?"

He leaned his head back, but his eyes were closed and there was a look of such profound but indecipherable emotion on his face that Millie gasped aloud. "Ric, what happened?"

He shook his head. "Not your fault, Millie. Sometimes I'm just an old fool, wishing for what could never be. You stirred an old memory, one best left in the past where it belongs." He tilted his head and looked at her. His beautiful eyes glistened with unshed tears.

"I don't understand . . ."

"I know." He covered her hand with his and looked down while he traced her fingers with his. Then he raised his head and smiled sadly. "My late wife, Camille, called me Ric. No one else ever had the temerity to shorten my name. I hadn't been called Ric in the twenty years since Camille died, not until Anton brought us together last fall. I told you about that, how he was able to send me into the spirit world to be with her." He paused a moment.

Millie couldn't help but wonder exactly what he was remembering when he thought of that one special night with Camille. An unwelcome knot of jealousy settled under her heart.

"When Camille and I were together, that was the name she used for me and it was as if she'd never died." He sighed, but at least he was smiling. "Then it was time for her to pass beyond the veil and my name went with her. I never expected to hear it again. I guess it just caught me by surprise, hearing it from your lips, especially knowing how important you've already become to me."

She wanted to crawl under a table and die of shame, though at the same time, she was damned angry. Was Camille still so important to Ulrich that a nickname upset him? "I'm sorry," she said, well aware her clipped, formal tone of voice projected every bit of emotion roiling through her heart. "I didn't mean to upset you. I won't call you by that name again. I promise."

He touched her lips with his fingers. "Actually, I hope you do. I love the sound of that name, coming from you. I love your voice and everything about you. That, my dear, is why I am an old fool. The worst kind."

Only slightly mollified, Millie ran her tongue over his fingertips and smiled. "Why would you say that? You're certainly not old, and if you're a fool, then so am I."

"Maybe we both are." He sighed heavily, turned away and shuffled some of the papers on the desk, then stood up and pushed the chair away. "I've worked beside you all day and want to touch you so badly I ache. We're done here. It's past time to close. Everyone's gone home."

"I wondered if you ever intended to leave."

"Only with you, Millie. Only with you."

They locked up, waved good-bye to the security guard arriving for the night shift and headed down the narrow trail to Millie's cabin. She'd grown quiet while they turned off the computers and locked up the files. Ulrich wondered if he'd hurt her feelings, mentioning Camille.

For all his years, both married and single, he still felt awkward around women. Unsure of himself, unless he was between a woman's thighs making love. Making her sing. Millie was absolutely unique. He wondered how she'd managed celibacy all these years alone, though the vast number of vibrators and sex toys in the drawer beside her bed was a pretty good clue.

Even so, toys were never as satisfying as the real thing. The Chanku libido was the one trait that appeared to separate average humans from those with the potential to shift, yet Millie had been without a lover for at least thirty or more years. How the hell had she managed?

He sighed. Following Millie was such exquisite torture, watching the sway of her slim hips, the bunch and pull of lean muscle beneath her clothing. She had a beautiful body for a woman her age . . . hell, she had a beautiful body for a woman of any age.

Suddenly, Millie stopped in the middle of the trail and turned to face him. Ulrich blinked back his shock. Tears covered her cheeks, still spilled from her eyes. Why hadn't he sensed her distress?

"I've been thinking of what you said earlier. What you told me last night about making love with your wife's spirit. I know she's very much alive for you, Ulrich. Very much a part of your life. If we continue with whatever it is that's happening here, will I have to compete with a dead woman, Ulrich?"

He heard the emphasis on his full name and winced, but Millie barely took a breath. "I know you loved Camille, but she's gone. Or is she? Will Mr. Cheval bring her back whenever you need your fix?"

"No, Millie. It's not like that at—"

She cut him off with a slash of her hand between them. "Yes it is. You said yourself you were a fool for wishing for what might have been. Your words exactly, that you're still wishing for Camille. I've been alone for over thirty years. Without a man all that time, and yes, I've been lonely, but I've avoided being hurt, too. I won't set myself up for pain, Ric. Ulrich. Whatever."

He stepped close and wrapped his arms around her

waist. She stiffened in his embrace. She'd been so pliable until now, so willing to mold her slim body to his.

How the hell could he make her understand? "Millie, love . . . do you wish you'd been able to keep your children and raise them yourself?"

She pushed away from him and glared. "Of course I do. Why would you even ask me?"

"Do you wish your uncle had been kind and loving? That your mother had married your father and lived for a long time and you'd grown up with a loving family?"

Millie shook her head, as if to clear her thoughts. "Yes, but it didn't happen, so what's the point of wishing? I don't get what you're . . ."

"I wish Camille had not died. I wish we could have raised our only daughter with brothers and sisters. I wish my late wife had not been so selfish and independent, because it led directly to her death. I wish a lot of things. Millie, I wish Camille had known you, because she'd love you as much as I do. What I'm getting at, love, is that life doesn't always turn out the way we expect, but sometimes the curves we're thrown are even better." He laughed and held his hands out.

"Hell, there were days in our marriage I wanted to kill Camille myself. She could drive me nuts. I was every bit as angry at her when she died as I was filled with grief and loneliness. It wasn't my love holding her to this plane. It was anger, pure and simple. I couldn't let go of the anger I felt toward her. That's what was holding her, and that's what I was thinking about when I said I was a fool for wishing what might have been. I was wishing I had felt the same kind of love toward Camille as I do toward you."

"The same kind?" She frowned, obviously not understanding.

"The lasting kind. The deep down, makes me feel good just to be close to you, kind." He held his hand out, then dropped it to his side. *Damn.* Where were the right words when he needed them? "Camille and me? We loved each other, but sometimes it was almost a desperate sort of love," he said, remembering. "We had a child together, but Camille loved her freedom more than she loved either Tianna or me. She died young because she broke rules and never thought of consequences. She always put herself first."

"Oh." Millie covered her mouth with her hand. "I'm sorry, Ric. I didn't mean to bring up bad memories. I just kept thinking of how you'd risked death for one more night with your wife. That was unfair of me."

"No, it was honest. If we can't have honesty, we can't have a relationship."

"Is that what this is?" She slipped back into his arms and wrapped herself around him. "A relationship?"

"Dear God, I hope so."

"Me, too, Ric. Me, too."

He held her hand all the way back to the cabin. She'd never held hands with a man before, not even her cowboy lover of long ago. Never walked along a narrow trail with full knowledge she'd most likely be making love with the man beside her within a few more minutes. She shivered, but it wasn't from the chill in the air. No, it was pure sexual anticipation.

Something her body still hadn't grown used to. Millie chanced a quick glance to her left and realized Ric was smiling at her, and that had to be love in his eyes. Whatever he felt, it was obviously more than mere lust.

Lust alone wouldn't make him this caring, this unsure of himself. He seemed like the kind of man who always knew exactly what he wanted and how to get it, but she sensed his vulnerability where she was concerned. She liked that. Liked knowing she made him feel as insecure and fragile as she was.

Millie unlocked the front door and stepped inside. It

was chilly, and she started down the hall to turn on the heater, but the phone rang.

She answered it while Ric opened the door on the woodstove and stirred the coals left from the morning. A man, his voice sounding so familiar, asked for Ulrich. Suddenly, Millie recognized who was calling. "Tinker? Is that you?" Tinker was Ulrich's packmate, a wonderful man who'd swept into all their lives just a short time before and taken off with Millie's very able assistant, Lisa Quinn.

His big laugh made her smile. Yes, it was Tinker and yes, Lisa was happy and loving San Francisco. Millie chatted with him a moment, then handed the phone to Ric and headed for her room and the shower. Every muscle in her body ached. The shower would give Ric privacy for his call and her a break from all the testosterone she practically tasted when she was around the man.

Not that she minded. No, not at all.

"Mind if I join you?"

As if she could keep him out. Millie stepped back beneath the stinging spray and made room for Ulrich. He was such a big man he took up more than his share of her small shower, especially with a massive erection thrusting out from his groin.

Laughing, familiar enough already to feel a sense of ownership over his parts, Millie reached down and stroked his full length. She loved the feel of it, so smooth and silky to touch, yet hard as steel. "Does that thing ever stay down where it belongs?"

Ric laughed. "Not when you're around. Besides, who says it belongs down?" He reached around her and directed the shower head to spray both of them more evenly. "That call concerned you, by the way. I have Tinker checking on your babies."

"What? How . . . ?" He hadn't said a word. She had no idea he'd given them another thought after this morning.

"While you were back at the cabin making lunch, I got on the phone to Tinker. Normally this is the kind of job Luc loves to tackle, but since he and Tia are still on their honeymoon, I didn't want to bother him."

He grabbed a washcloth, handed it to Millie and turned his back to her. "How about you find something useful to do while I tell you what Tinker's discovered."

Laughing, Millie soaped the cloth and began scrubbing Ric's back.

"Tinker hasn't gotten any information yet on your daughter, but your little boy was adopted by a farming family in southern Colorado. Oddly enough, their last name is Wolf."

Millie stopped scrubbing and stared at Ric's back. "You're kidding, right? That's bizarre. Almost too much of a coincidence."

"Not necessarily. Odder things have been known to happen. They named him Adam. Adam Leyton Wolf. Leyton was a family name. There were no siblings. Adam attended Colorado State. He excelled in his studies and was quite an athlete, but dropped out in the middle of his second year. His adoptive parents went through a contentious divorce about that time and Adam cut off all contact with them. We haven't found any records more recent than fifteen years ago when he left school, but Tinker's still on it. We'll find him."

"Did Tinker get any pictures? Any personal information about him?"

"Turn around. I'll wash you. And yes, Tink's got pictures. A couple, anyway."

Millie did as he directed, but her mind was spinning a million miles an hour. Adam! Her son was named Adam and he'd gone to college and was out there, somewhere. Ric's voice rumbled in her ear as he gently washed her back, then rubbed shampoo into her wet hair.

"There's one from a high school yearbook, another from a newspaper article when Adam was in college. Tink said he'd e-mail them as soon as he got off the phone. It sounds as if Adam was quite a standout in track and field events. No reason given why he left school, but it might have been money since it was about the time his adoptive parents split up."

He gently washed her hair, rinsed it and added conditioner. Millie felt as if she were in shock. As if all her blood had rushed to her head and her heart had nothing to pump, but it was working overtime anyway because she heard the racing sound, felt the vibration in her chest.

She didn't remember Ulrich rinsing her hair and barely realized he'd walked her out of the shower and dried her off with a big, fluffy towel. All she thought of was her son, the fact that when she looked at her laptop, she'd get to see a picture of him for the first time.

"Here." He handed Millie a bathrobe. "Put this on so you don't get chilled. I need to check and make sure the fire's going. Why don't you go boot up your computer?"

Millie nodded and headed out to the kitchen where she kept her laptop. She opened it up and pushed the button, watching as the screen went through all the necessary steps. She plugged in the phone line, dialed up and accessed her mail, found the message from Tinker with two attachments, and paused with her finger over the touch pad.

"Have you got it yet?" Ric stood behind her with nothing but a bath towel wrapped around his hips. He rubbed her shoulders, bringing warmth back into her chilled body.

"No. I wanted you here with me." Why she needed Ric, Millie wasn't sure, but she did. Needed him beside her, needed his solid presence and his strength.

"I'm here, Millie. Let's look."

She opened the first attachment. It took forever on her slow dialup service, but her son's face unfolded, one line at a time. This picture was in black and white, so it was hard to tell the color of his hair. He looked about eighteen and it was a typical high school yearbook photo of a very earnest young man dressed in a dark suit.

The picture was horribly distorted until Ric handed her a tissue and she wiped her eyes. She laughed when the picture suddenly cleared up. Her son. Her very own child. He looked very much like his father, that handsome cowboy who had ridden into Millie's life and out again, staying only long enough to leave her with twin babies. "Oh, Ric." She touched the screen, tracing the shape of her son's face, the high cheekbones and broad smile. That was all hers, the only part of Adam that looked remotely like his mother. "Thank you. Do you think Tinker will be able to find him?"

"Tink's good. Luc's even better and Tianna is the best of them all. They'll be back at the office in a couple days. With all of them working on the trace, I imagine we'll find him before too long, and your daughter as well. You'll have to be patient. At least you've got this much to go on. Your son's a handsome young man, Millie. He looks like you . . . he's got your smile. Here. Open the next photo. I want to see."

She clicked on the second one and a different version of her son appeared, a color photo from a newspaper. He was at a track meet where he'd obviously gone over the high jump with enough room to win the event. His wide, bony shoulders had cleared the bar, his back was bent in a graceful arch, long legs curved over the edge of the bar—his face was a study of concentration, upside down.

"Oh my!" Millie flipped the photo, and once again saw her son. She felt Ulrich's strong hand on her shoulder and brushed her cheek against his knuckles. "Thank you. Thank you so much. I had no idea you'd be able to find anything about either of them so quickly."

"Private adoptions are often difficult to trace, but we

have our contacts and Tink's been working on this all afternoon. Hopefully, he'll have some news of your daughter before too long."

Millie sighed. "I've thought about my babies every day of their lives, but it was always as if they only existed in my mind. Seeing my son, knowing he's tall and handsome and intelligent . . . Ric, it's too much. I feel so blessed, just knowing what he looks like."

"The best part of him looks like his mother. He really does have your beautiful smile."

"Thank you." She reached up and touched his cheek. Then she turned in her chair and hugged him, hard, her cheek pressed against the hard planes of his belly. "I feel so torn. I want to sit here and look at the pictures forever, but I so want to see you naked. I have a lot of years to make up for." She stood up slowly, sliding against his lean body and kissed him at the base of his throat where his pulse beat powerfully against her lips.

"Sweetheart, you have no idea how pleased I am to hear you say that." Ric didn't even hesitate. He swept Millie up in his arms and carried her back down the hall to the bedroom. She snuggled against his chest and realized she felt more loved, more complete at this moment than at any other time in her life.

She loved her job, she finally knew where at least one of her babies had gone, and the most wonderful man she'd ever met was hauling her off to bed to make mad, crazy love to her. She burst into giggles. It really didn't get much better than this.

* * *

Heart pounding in fear, Manda awakened out of a terrifying nightmare. She lay beside Bay, eyes wide and breath hissing in and out of her parted lips. He slept soundly beside her, but the images in her head wouldn't go away. Men taping her arms to a table, laughing men, and all of them had the heads of wolves with huge teeth and slavering jaws.

The same dream, she'd had year after year, only this time they were naked, their bodies aroused, their intent obvious.

Bay stirred beside her. His hand touched her shoulder and she felt his warm breath against her cheek. His voice was rough with sleep when he whispered, "You okay sweetie?"

"I'm fine. Go back to sleep."

"Mmm . . . okay. Love you."

He snuggled close against her back and one arm flopped heavily over her waist. His hand went unerringly to her breast, cupping the weight in his warm palm. Manda smiled as the fearful dream faded into her subconscious where she knew it lived with a million other horrible things, just waiting to come out and scare the crap out of her in the middle of the night.

She lay there pressed closely against Baylor's warmth and tried to sleep. Her mind hadn't stopped spinning since she'd shifted, but now she was even more awake. They'd crawled into bed shortly after showering, exhausted from the long run, their bodies sated from mutually shared climaxes.

Well, her body was sated. She wasn't sure about Bay, especially since she'd only pleasured him with her mouth and her hands. He said he was fine, that he could wait until she was ready to try more, but he'd still been partially erect when they crawled into bed, his penis almost as large as it had been before she made him come.

He'd fallen asleep almost immediately, sleeping the sleep of the just, she figured. He actually seemed more satisfied with the climaxes he'd wrung out of her than what she'd given him. That thought alone was enough to keep her awake. He was so unlike the men she'd read about, the few she knew. Manda had so much spinning through her head that sleep had been a long time coming. In fact, that was one of the things that had kept her awake . . . thinking about coming.

Bay seemed to know exactly what to do to bring her to orgasm. In fact, he knew her body better than Manda did. It felt so strange, lying here without any pain at all. Pain had been an inescapable part of her life for over two dozen years, something she was never free of. Now, the lack of pain seemed strange, almost unnatural. She cupped her breast in her hand, amazed at the smooth skin, the perfectly rounded shape. She felt warm to the touch, and her fingers were sensitive to her soft skin, her tightly puckered nipple. Everything about her was different, from her well-formed feet to the thick mane of blond hair.

Different and strange. How odd, to think of this perfectly glorious woman's body as strange. She'd hardly had a chance to look at herself, to see what she looked like.

There was no one to bother her, no reason she couldn't go take a closer look. It was her body, after all, and she certainly didn't feel like sleeping. Slowly, carefully, Manda lifted Bay's arm away from her waist and slipped out of bed. He stirred, then settled back into sleep. She walked quietly down the hall, aware how clearly she saw in the dark, as if that part of her wolven nature remained active even after shifting back to human.

A fire still glowed in the big fireplace in the front room. Manda padded quietly across the multi-hued carpet covering the floor and went into the master bedroom. This was Jake and Shannon's room, but Baylor said he generally slept here as well. That would explain the oversized bed. She couldn't help but wonder about the details.

She stared at the bed for a long moment, imagining Bay with another man as well as a woman. She knew he was a highly sexed, sensual man, but that was a bit much to wrap her thoughts around. The visual just wouldn't compute, no matter how hard she tried, though she had to admit, the concept of three people having sex together at the same time absolutely fascinated her.

Manda stared at the bed and her mind was spinning.

She tried to picture what must have happened in this bed any number of times, but the visual of two men and a woman all having sex continued to elude her. She finally gave up, dragged her fingers slowly along the edge of the down comforter and then headed into the bathroom. It was large and well lighted, with mirrors over the sink and a full-length one on the door. Quietly she closed the door behind her, flicked on the light and looked at the mirror.

A stranger stared back, wide-eyed and wondering. A beautiful stranger with an amazing body. Manda reached out and touched her image. Her fingernails were absolutely perfect. Short ovals instead of curved, black claws, set at the ends of long, slim fingers. She turned her hands over and looked more closely, silently celebrating the perfectly normal shape of her hands and fingers. Next, she turned and looked over her shoulder at the soft sweep of her spine where it met the flair of her buttocks.

She was lean and muscular, her body well-balanced and healthy. "And no tail. Thank goodness for that!" She turned back to the mirror and lifted her breasts in both hands, surprised by their weight, the smooth, round flesh that fit so perfectly into her palms. Her areolas were a soft raspberry pink against her fair skin and the nipples just a bit darker. She ran her finger over one soft nipple and watched it pucker and grow until it grew hard and taut. It felt and even looked like a pencil eraser against her fingertip.

Her old body hadn't reacted like this. Not at all. Not this perfectly. She rubbed the other nipple and it quickly matched the first. *Amazing!*

Manda tried standing on her toes and felt the stretch of healthy muscles in her calves and thighs, the smooth movement of her joints. Knees, ankles, hips . . . all functioned as they should, smoothly and without pain. She reached over her head and watched the way the motion lifted her breasts.

She glanced at the door. What if Bay caught her, posing

like this? Would he laugh at her foolishness, or would his eyes glow with the same desire she'd seen earlier?

He wouldn't laugh at her. Not Bay. Never Bay.

Her breasts tightened and a coil of need spiraled from womb to sex. Manda almost moaned aloud at the rush of hot desire, the warm flush of arousal she felt, merely from thinking of Baylor. Imagining his look, the knowledge that he found her body exciting.

Hell, Manda found her body exciting. She was touching a stranger. Living inside a stranger's skin. She hadn't had a chance to really look at herself earlier. Hadn't been able to try out all of her suddenly smoothly working parts.

She ran her fingers over her flat belly, swirled a fingertip inside her perfect little navel. Grinning at the sensations her touch aroused, she slipped her hand lower and tangled her fingers in the soft thatch of hair covering her sex. One fingertip brushed against her clitoris. The spark of sensation made her think of Bay in the shower, his hand wrapped around his cock. That's what he called it. *Cock*. Not penis. It was a cock.

Men. They seemed to have a name for everything.

He'd called this little nub her clit, and the warm folds covered in hair, her pussy. That sounded so much nicer than the clinical terms of *clitoris* and *vagina*. Warmer. Friendlier, even. She was inordinately curious about that part of her new self. Manda's twisted body hadn't allowed her the freedom of motion to actually see what she looked like down there, but it was a simple thing to climb up on the counter and spread her legs wide under the bright bathroom lights.

She grabbed a hand mirror and scrutinized this new body, fascinated by the layers of sensitive tissues protecting her sex. So this was what kept Bay so fascinated! He certainly didn't mind spending a lot of time touching and tasting her down there.

Manda rubbed a fingertip over her clit. It was sticking up a bit more than it had earlier, almost like a very tiny penis. She wondered if Bay's cock was as sensitive as her clit. She couldn't recall if she'd ever seen him not hard, but she knew she wasn't aroused all the time. At least she hadn't been before, not the way she was now.

Were all men like that, or was it just the Chanku? Bay said they had really strong libidos. Even with that bit of knowledge, she knew there was an awful lot he wasn't telling her. Like exactly *what* he did with Jake and Shannon at night. He obviously didn't share their bed merely because he was lonely, and he said they had sex together, but all of them? At the same time?

She tried once again to picture it. No luck. She couldn't quite fathom the three of them all at once, even though he'd said they were together. How? Hell, she couldn't imagine herself having sex with one man, much less two. Not yet. Maybe not ever.

Swinging her legs around to dangle them over the edge of the counter, Manda sat there beneath the warm lights and wondered at all she still needed to learn. Her life had been so wrong, so unnatural, but at least it had been familiar. Would she ever feel normal? Ever be a real woman for Bay?

For herself?

She heard him only moments before he tapped lightly on the door. "Manda? Are you okay in there?"

"I'm fine. The door's not locked. You can come in."

Blinking against the bright lights, Bay entered the room. "What are you doing?"

No point in lying. "I was looking in the mirror. I wanted to see what I looked like. I need to get to know my body. It's so different." She glanced up at him and saw compassion in his eyes.

"I can't imagine what you're going through right now. I wish I could, but your thoughts are blocked. Will you let me in? Let me share what you're thinking?"

Was it really that simple? "How? I still have a hard time

with that. I honestly don't know why or when I'm blocking you."

"Remember what I told you? Think of a window. Just open it and let me in."

It really wasn't all that hard. She opened her thoughts as if pulling up the window. Suddenly Bay was there. He put his arms around her shoulders and held her face against his chest. She heard his heart beating, felt the warmth of his skin, the soft tickle from his chest hair against her cheek. Her thoughts stopped whirling and spinning and Manda felt herself relax.

Bay's searching thoughts reminded her of a small mouse running through a series of rooms, barely visible, but still there. He wasn't intrusive, but he was still very much a presence in her head. Suddenly, he paused. Manda felt a surge of energy, a sense of anger, of outrage and violent passion held tightly under a stout leash. She pulled away, blinking rapidly to separate herself from the powerful wash of Bay's emotion.

"Is that true?" Bay glared at her, his eyes narrowed, his lips a thin, white line. "What I saw in your memories. Did those terrible things really happen?"

He couldn't possibly have seen that, could he? "I don't know? What are you talking about?" The space between them stretched into miles.

"You said you were raped. You never said you were still a child, that it was more than once, nor did you say that one of those times the men used a wolf. You never said the lab workers who were supposed to care for you set this up. Shit, Manda. What kind of monsters held you captive all these years? Who in the hell was Papa B?"

"He was the man who rescued me." She turned her head aside. Away from her reflection, away from the man. She couldn't look at Bay. Couldn't face the anger in his voice, the condemnation in his eyes. Did he hold this filth against her? Would he always look at her and see someone who disgusted him?

His hands clasped her shoulders and she was suddenly pressed against his body. His lips moved against her hair and his voice was rough, as if the words were difficult to say.

"Oh, Manda. My sweet Manda. He rescued you, and then allowed that to happen? Why? You did not deserve treatment so foul. You did nothing wrong, Manda." His voice broke and he held her even closer. "Nothing. Nothing would warrant anything so hideous. What they did was evil. It was wrong. Do you understand me? That was wrong! They took an innocent child in a painfully twisted body and tortured her. What kind of monsters were those men?"

Shivering with relief, body trembling with the myriad emotions and memories suddenly opened to the light, Manda knew she could stay here, with Bay's arms around her, forever. His words carried so much emotion, such an amazing sense of love and empathy. He understood. Bay actually understood.

He sighed and the pressure of his anger seemed to fade away. "No wonder you flinch when I touch you. Shy away when I mention bonding, our mating as wolves. No wonder. Ah, Manda my sweet. I am so sorry if I tried to push you."

He rubbed her back with his palm. Manda rested her cheek against his chest where his heart thudded, strong and steady, beneath her ear. She felt his bare skin all the way to her toes, every inch of him pressing against her nakedness.

It was the first time since she'd known him he remained completely unaroused, his cock soft and flaccid against her belly. He told the truth. He understood. Manda was safe with him. Bay would always keep her safe.

Chapter 10

Ulrich stood in the doorway to Millie's office and watched as she shut down her computer for the day. Her thick blond hair was pulled back in a ponytail and she wore a black turtleneck sweater with a sheepskin vest for warmth against the unseasonably cool weather. Her black jeans fit her like a second skin, tucked into her heavy hiking boots. She looked absolutely lovely, and he would rather do anything in the world besides deliver the message he held in his hand.

"Ready to go?"

She glanced up and smiled. "All ready. The moon's full tonight." She looked around quickly, double-checking, he knew, in case someone else might be nearby. "I can't wait, Ric." Her voice was a husky whisper that sent shivers along his spine. "I've thought of nothing else all day, knowing I'm ready, knowing we'll bond tonight. It's more romantic than any wedding, more exciting than anything I've ever dreamed."

She stood up and went to him and he wrapped his arms around her and wondered if she might change her mind after he told her. Oh, she'd definitely shift. She was more than ready. Had probably been ready for the past few days, but he'd not wanted to rush anything. It wasn't like they were kids, their bodies pliant and adaptable like the young ones in the pack. No, he and Millie were definitely going to be the old-timers at Pack Dynamics.

Damn but he loved her. Hated the thought of bringing her any kind of pain. He nuzzled her hair with his lips and tried to think of the kindest way to break the news.

This past week had been wonderful. Courting Millie, falling more in love with her every day. He'd never expected to find love again. Not after Camille. There'd been so many nuances to their marriage and relationship. She'd been the one to introduce him to his Chanku heritage, and in that respect, she'd changed his life forever.

Still, as much as he'd loved Tianna's mother, she'd frustrated the hell out of him. No matter how much he had wanted things to be different, he knew Camille rarely put anyone but herself first.

Not until that Samhain night, when Anton had parted the veil between the living and the dead. That night Camille had chosen death, alone, when she could so easily have insisted Ric follow her into the shadows.

He would have, too. That night. As much as he hated to admit it, Camille had been a drug for him, a memory of love he'd held on to long beyond its time. But that night, that one very special night, she'd been generous and giving. Camille had accepted her fate and wished him and their daughter well . . . and embraced her death.

Did she know then about Millie?

If Camille were to return right now and ask him to follow, he'd not be tempted at all. Not with Millie waiting for him. Loving him. Damn, he hated having to hurt her, but putting off the truth was even more unfair.

It was unusually cool for the middle of June, but she'd had to work late tonight and the moon was coming up almost full in the evening sky by the time they headed back to her cabin. It appeared larger than ever, with a stiff breeze blowing and the air crystal clear. Ric seemed quiet, but he was often a quiet man, retreating into his thoughts when they walked, coming to life when they made love.

She kept glancing at his profile, the strong line of his jaw, his long, straight nose. Taut lines defined him. Hard, lean muscle, broad shoulders, powerful, muscular thighs. She searched constantly for imperfections, anything to make her question the feelings growing for him, but no matter how hard Millie looked, she hadn't found a damned thing yet for the negative column.

She felt giddy and nervous, anticipating her first shift and all the changes that would come with it. She rubbed her arms, scratching at the itchy, crawly sensation Ric had said was perfectly normal after taking the pills. It had grown worse over the past couple days, but that would pass once she finally made the shift.

It hardly seemed real. Tonight, maybe in less than an hour, she would run on four legs beneath a brilliant moon. She'd change completely, her body morphing from human to animal and back again. As thrilling, as unbelievable as it seemed, the shift itself was more exciting than frightening. What scared her spitless was the fact she'd be partnered tonight for the first time in her life. Finally, after a lifetime alone, she'd have someone connected to her on levels well beyond what even a normal marriage entailed.

Could she handle that kind of intimacy? Millie figured she'd done all right with Ric around for a week, but how did that compare to the rest of your life? How would it feel to have him in her thoughts? He popped in occasionally now and then, generally during sex, but it was more like taking a phone call in her head.

After a mating bond, Ric said there'd be no secrets. Of course, he'd already found out all about the sex toys in the nightstand beside her bed. Now, though, he might even learn things about her she'd forgotten, and vice versa. He'd told her about Camille, the fact their marriage had been open, that both had taken lovers. Would he want other lovers after they bonded? It wasn't like they were really getting married, after all . . .

"Millie, we need to talk."

She stopped, brought up short by his soft request, one foot resting lightly on the bottom step. Instead of going inside, Ric led her to one of the chairs grouped around a small table. As courtly as ever, he held a chair for her. Millie sat down. Ric took the chair across from her. Concern rolled off of him in waves, a sense that all was not well. She felt another tremor of nerves and her heart pounded uneasily in her chest. "What's the matter, Ric? I can tell you're upset. What's wrong?"

"Sweetie, I wish I had better news for you." He sighed, then gave her the direct, honest look she'd learned to love. He wrapped both of her hands in his. "Tinker's still checking on the kids and today Luc and Tia got home and went to work on the trace as well."

"Did you find Adam? Is he okay?"

Ric shook his head. "No further word on Adam. When he dropped out of college, he really dropped out." Ric smiled and shook his head. "Tinker found some leads that might guide us to him, but nothing we're sure of. Tia, though . . . Tia found your daughter." His grip on her hands tightened. "There's no easy way to say this, but it appears she died when she was twelve years old."

Millie's breath caught in her throat. Her baby dead? How? She couldn't even imagine her as a twelve-year-old. It was impossible to think of her gone. Millie's throat felt tight. Her eyes burned, but she would not cry. Not now. It was too late and her tears were all gone. She'd shed them years ago.

She cleared her throat. It took a couple tries to force the words out. "What happened?"

Ric squeezed her hands. *Squeeze. Release. Squeeze.* She found the gentle rhythm oddly comforting.

"Her parents were missionaries in a small Tibetan village. They were attacked by bandits and murdered. All of them. The entire village burned to the ground. It was destroyed so completely and the area was so isolated, no remains of her or her family were recovered. I can't even take you to a cemetery to mourn her loss. I'm so sorry, sweetheart. So very sorry. I only wanted to bring you good news. I never expected something like this."

Millie slipped her hands free of Ric's and stood up. She had to move, somehow had to find her center. Her chest ached with a pain she couldn't describe. Pressure constricted her lungs and it was hard to breathe. This was more than her own pain. She felt Ric's. He ached for her, broadcasting his anguish without realizing he flooded her with his own heartache.

Millie sensed his deep sadness at having delivered such horrible news, but even more powerful was his fear. He was terrified she might reject him over what he'd had to tell her.

Never! She turned quickly and leaned over the table, close to him, and covered his big hands in hers. "Oh, Ric. My babies died for me the day they were born. I've mourned their loss since they were taken away from me, but never once did I hope to find out what happened to them or where they'd gone. We still may find Adam."

She took a deep breath. She was not going to cry. It was too late for tears. She had to keep reminding herself that she'd used them all up over thirty-six years ago. Another breath. Another. Her heart rate slowed. Emotions returned to the dark corner where they could do no harm. "Did you find out what her name was? It would be nice to have a name."

Ric's voice was gravelly. He cleared his throat to speak. "Amanda. Her name was Amanda Jane Smith." He coughed, cleared his throat again. Blinked back the tears flooding his beautiful eyes. "According to the information

Tia found, she was a beautiful tomboy, smart and sassy and full of spunk, a tall, coltish girl with long blond hair."

He stood up and held out his arms. "Ah, Millie." It was the most natural thing in the world to slip into his embrace. "I imagine she looked just like you did when you were that age. I am so sorry to be the one to bring you such sad news."

Millie reached up and cupped his face in both her hands. "Don't be, Ric. I'm thankful you're the one to tell me what happened. I wanted to know. You've given me a painful message with more compassion than I could imagine. I love you, Ric. I've never said that to another man, not even to my children's father. I love you more than I ever dreamed imaginable, and if you still want me, I want to run with you tonight. I want to make love beneath that beautiful moon. Most of all, I want your promise you'll never leave me."

He turned his head and kissed each palm. "I love you, too, Millie West. And you have my promise. I will never leave you."

He stepped back, glanced around, and began stripping off his clothes. "It's easier to shift without clothing."

"Now? But what about dinner?" He'd totally caught her off balance. She hadn't realized he meant to go now. She had a wonderful meal all ready to stick in the oven and her practical side was thinking of cooking times and table settings. It was so much easier than thinking of the daughter she'd never known, now forever lost to her, but Ric was already practically naked.

"Don't worry about dinner. We're wolves, Millie. The forest is alive with game. Tonight we hunt."

"Oh." She hadn't expected that. Frowning, aware of depths to this new reality she'd never considered, Millie slipped off her boots. The rest of her clothing followed until she stood there on her front porch and faced Ulrich, both of them clothed only in moonlight. A man she'd not even known a mere week ago. A man who had already changed her life in ways she'd never imagined.

And tonight, beneath the moon and stars, he would become her mate. Paired with her for the rest of their lives.

"Link with me, Millie. Open your mind. See how I shift. You'll find the knowledge inside, if your body is ready."

Panic sliced through her. "What if I'm not? Ready, I mean? Will it hurt? Will I be able to come back?"

"Relax. Follow my lead." *Are you with me?* He paused and stared at her, gave her time to figure it out, and then the most amazing thing happened.

Yes! Oh, Ric, it suddenly makes sense, in a weird, convoluted way.

Okay. Watch now, but watch with your Chanku senses.

She concentrated on his eyes, following them down from his tall, human height, to the level of the wolf now standing on her porch. She hadn't actually seen the shift, but knew instinctively what she had to do. It was such a simple thing, after all. Shifting from human to wolf. Why hadn't she noticed before how very easy it was?

There was a moment of dizziness when she felt mildly disconnected. Then she was sitting on her haunches on the porch, seeing the world through new eyes. She hadn't imagined how colors would change. Hadn't thought of seeing through wolven eyes, but now colors took on new, muted hues in tones of gray and green, even in darkness.

The forest loomed, dark and inviting, filling her nostrils with the pungent yet distinctly separate scents of pine, cedar and fir, plant and creature. Sounds assailed her ears—individual calls of night birds and insects and, from the direction of the compound, the cry of howling wolves. Their voices blended in a beautiful harmonic sound, one she'd always found poignant and indescribably moving.

Tonight, though, the symphony took on new meaning. She knew every wolven voice, recognized the unique quality to each call. Even the gender behind each voice was clear and distinct. Shaking herself out of the spell the wolves cast, she lifted her foot and stared at the long, curved nails. Short hair covered each toe, the bottoms were protected with thick, black pads. It was hard to tell in the moonlight and with her new visual parameters, but she thought her coat was much lighter than Ric's. Possibly brown, with a reddish cast.

Millie decided she liked it. Liked everything about this new body. She stood up and shook herself, aware of Ric sitting quietly to one side, watching as she introduced herself to her new form. *You gonna sit there all night?* she asked. She yipped once, and then, as if she'd been a wolf her entire life, bounded over the porch railing and landed lightly on the ground below.

Ric raced after her. They took a trail leading away from the compound, away from roads and people and any other cabins. Running with ears back and tails high, two wolves raced the moonlight.

There was no room for grief. Not tonight. Her daughter had lived and died and she'd never had a chance to hold her, to see her, but at least she knew her fate. Besides, wolves didn't cry. They had no mechanism for tears of grief. Strengthened by that knowledge, Millie charged into the darkness that was not nearly so dark as before, following a swath of moonlight along a forest track.

Amanda was dead. She'd never even known her daughter, not even been the one to choose her name, and now she was dead. The words beat like a refrain with each touch of Millie's paws to the hard ground, each gasp of breath from her powerful new lungs.

How does one grieve for a lost child? How does anyone ever forget? How do you forget what you've never known?

But she'd loved her. She'd loved them both. Millie had loved those two little bodies kicking against the walls of her womb. She still recalled the way it had felt, a tiny elbow or foot reminding her of separate little people growing inside her body. She'd loved them more than life itself, but she'd awakened to nurses who wouldn't face her, to a doctor decidedly absent, to the cold, calculating man who was her uncle.

He'd not told her he was taking her babies. Hadn't given her time to prepare, to escape. She'd done the only thing she could. She'd buried all her emotions away, grieved powerfully, yet wondered all these years.

Adam might still live. Amanda was gone.

Ric nuzzled Millie's shoulder. *Follow me,* he urged. *We need to go here.*

She followed him without question. He led and she knew she would always follow, always accept his lead, not because he dominated, but because she trusted. Trusted him as she'd never allowed herself to trust another man before.

Up they ran, until they reached a barren rise bathed in silvery moonlight. Ric led her to the highest point and she wondered if this was the place, if this was where he would mate with her. It didn't matter. Nothing really mattered tonight.

Her baby was dead. Nothing else was important.

Suddenly, Ric stopped his pacing and stared at Millie. His eyes glowed in the pale light, shining in some otherworldly hue and his thoughts were clear and heartfelt and more meaningful than Millie could ever have dreamed.

I love you, Millie West, but our mating has to wait. Tonight we honor your child who is lost. Tonight I honor you.

He turned his muzzle to the sky and howled. The sound started soft and low, spiraling upward, carrying his feelings, his frustrations into the heavens. A song of grief, but even more powerful, a song of enduring love.

Millie had never known love could be this strong, emotions this powerful. She stood beside him, raised her muzzle and howled a counterpoint of sound, a loving benediction to her lost child. She might not cry tears, but this sound she made, this song torn from her very soul, carried away the grief, carried the anger and the years of misery and lifted her spirit aloft.

The moon remained passive in the blue-black sky, unfeeling and cold. Not the warm-blooded male standing beside her. The one who would be her mate. Not tonight, but soon. Tonight they dedicated to sadness and loss, but that burden would be lifted.

Howling with Ric beside her, Millie gave up a lifetime of sorrow and prepared for whatever might follow.

* * *

The phone call woke him. The conversation insured he'd stay awake. Bay rolled over and reached for Manda, but her side of the bed was empty. Startled by her absence, he sat up and looked around the room. It was still dark. He checked the clock by the bed. Barely midnight, but it was only nine in California. No wonder Jake had caught Bay sleeping. Now, where the hell was Manda?

Shaking off the phone call, Bay climbed out of bed and padded down the hall. Checked in the living room and couldn't find her. Went into Jake and Shannon's room, but she wasn't there, either. Growing uneasy, he opened the front door and stepped outside.

Manda sat alone in the big porch swing, wrapped tightly in an afghan, sobbing as if her heart would break.

"Sweetie? What's wrong?" The night chill had him shivering by the time he'd reached Manda, pulled her to her feet and wrapped her in his arms. "Why are you crying?"

"Oh, Bay. I'm still a freak. No matter how I look, I'll never be normal." She curled against his chest and cried even harder.

"You're not a freak. You're a sensitive young woman who's lived a nightmare. It won't go away overnight, but things will get better." He slid his palms up and down her bare back. His cock pressed between them, a constant reminder of the one thing they hadn't been able to do. Not that she hadn't tried. Manda had been willing to do almost anything to achieve penetration, but her fears and panic attacks over the past week had only grown worse.

"You'll get tired of waiting for me. I know you will. I want to make love. Really I do, but I can't."

"I know." He thought about the phone call he'd just taken. "Don't worry. Help's on the way. It's only been a week and I know I promised you more time, but Shannon and Jake just called and they're headed home."

"How will they help? She doesn't know about . . . everything, does she? You didn't tell her . . . that." Her hands clutched frantically at his shoulders.

Bay held Manda tight, swung her into his arms and sat down on the porch swing. He settled her on his lap, snuggling her against his chest. She curled up close like a frightened kitten. "I didn't have to tell her. She sensed our problems because she's my packmate, sweetie. I've told you before—Shannon and I are also lovers. I know that's confusing, but it only means she'll love you as much as I do. Shannon guessed a lot of what's going on. She knows you were caught in midshift all those years. She guessed a lot of the rest, so yes, I did tell her a lot about your past. Be glad she knows, because she also knows how to help you."

Bay's cock pressed against her buttocks. He was so hard right now, he knew if she moved only a little, he'd probably come. If Manda noticed his erection, she didn't say a word, but she glared at him, as if he'd betrayed an enormous trust.

He'd had no choice. None at all, not if they were ever going to break through the tangled web of memories and nightmares that still controlled the only woman he would ever truly love.

Bay brushed her tangled hair back from her face and wanted to cry right along with her. She had circles under her eyes from lack of sleep, and silvery traces of tears down her cheeks. She was beautiful and afraid and she broke his heart. The last thing he wanted to do was hurt her. He kissed her forehead and smiled at the frustrated pout on her lips.

"Shannon knows you're afraid. She knows why and it doesn't change one thing about how she or Jake will feel about you. She's been with Keisha Rialto, Anton Cheval's mate. I've told you about Keisha. How she was assaulted by those men? Keisha gave Shannon some pointers on what it took to get her through the trauma. She sends her love, too, and says she'd be here in a heartbeat if it weren't for the baby."

Manda raised her head. "She's got a baby?

Bay nodded. "Yep. Just about a month old, now. A beautiful little baby girl, a husband and . . ." He started to say lovers, but Manda probably wasn't ready for that. He needed to get her past the first big hurdle. "She's happy, Manda. Truly happy with her mate. In spite of her assault a few years ago, she and her mate, Anton, make love and she has no fear. Not anymore. She was terrified at first, but she got past it with the help of her friend, Alexandria and with Xandi's mate, Stefan. They helped her because they're her packmates."

Bay kissed her. Manda's lips were salty with the taste of her tears. He brushed the line of her cheek with his fingertip. "Shannon knows what to do," he said, whispering into her thick fall of hair. "If you'll let her into your heart, I think we'll all be able to help you past the fears controlling your life."

Mentally crossing his fingers, Bay hoped he hadn't made the biggest mistake of his life. This had to work. He needed all of Manda in his life, not merely as his friend and lover, but as his mate, the one person alive who would know him as well as he knew himself.

Without that final bond, the forging of the most intimate link, they would never find the true relationship all

Chanku yearned for. He rested his cheek against her sleek hair and sighed. Manda would be his mate. She had to be. He would accept nothing else.

Manda idly flipped the pages on the book she'd been trying to read. She stretched her long legs out and soaked up more of the afternoon sun and wondered when Bay would return. He'd gone to town for supplies but Manda preferred the quiet here at the cabin. She'd gone with him once, and as much as she'd loved riding on the back of the big BMW motorcycle, the friendly townspeople made her nervous and shy. After a lifetime as a freak, she still wasn't comfortable in this new body.

She wondered if she'd ever relax and live a normal life.

A snort burst out of her. Normal? Like turning into a wolf was normal? At least when they shifted, when she ran in the forest, she felt complete.

As complete as she could, without making love to the man who would be her mate.

The deep rumble of a motorcycle caught her attention and Manda's heart rate immediately sped up. Bay was back, a lot sooner than she'd expected. She put her book aside and stood at the porch railing, her hands clutching the smooth, sun-warmed wood.

The big bike rounded the last bend before the cabin and she froze—it wasn't Bay. This was a different motorcycle, similar but not the same, and the man driving had a passenger on the back. A woman. Long red braids hung down her back and Manda knew immediately this had to be Shannon and Jake.

They were early. They were here . . . and she was all alone. Petrified, Manda clung to the railing and watched the big motorcycle make a lazy circle into the driveway and stop.

The woman got off the bike first and pulled her helmet off. Her hair was sweaty from the helmet and stuck every which way and she looked ridiculous, but the man didn't seem to care. He took his helmet off and leaned close and kissed her.

"Hi," she said, the moment they broke the kiss. "I'm Shannon. This is Jake and you have to be Manda. Wow! Bay wasn't kidding when he said you were beautiful!"

She walked up the steps, her stride self-confident and smooth, and all Manda could do was hang on to the railing and hope she didn't do something to embarrass herself.

"It feels so good to be home. I've about had it with people and cities and traffic . . . and sitting on a motorcycle for fourteen hours straight!"

"Fourteen hours?" Manda spoke without even thinking. "That's a long time."

Shannon laughed. "Tell me about it! There's a local group of riders called the Iron Butts, and I think Jake's trying to earn his membership. He can have it! They do a thousand miles in a single day, which we've just about done, and believe me, it's not my idea of fun."

"Woman. You are such a wuss! Where's your sense of adventure?" Jake bounded up the steps behind Shannon and swatted her on the butt.

Shannon yelped and swatted him back. Jake twisted out of her reach and made a face, but he directed this one at Manda, making her feel as if she were in on the joke. Manda realized she was laughing. Within just a few minutes it felt so natural, standing here on the porch, listening to Shannon's hysterical stories about their mad dash across the country.

Somehow Jake had slipped inside and brought out cold drinks before Manda even noticed he'd gone. Now he held a bottle of beer in his hand and took a long swallow, obviously enjoying every drop. Manda was drinking wine, which she'd never even tasted before, and it was really good. Shannon had a glass as well, and they were sipping the golden liquid and talking, and she wasn't sure how it had happened, that absolute strangers were making her feel so comfortable.

But were they really strangers? Bay never said much, but Manda knew they were all lovers. By virtue of her love for Bay, did that make them her lovers as well? She took another sip of the chilled wine, wandering along that convoluted trail of thought.

It was almost an hour later before Bay returned. She barely heard his bike come rolling up the driveway, but she sensed his presence, his joy at his packmates' return. Did he feel her joy as well? He came to Manda first, kissed her hard and possessively, and she loved the fact he'd staked his claim in front of the others. It felt right, made her feel loved and just a little bit more self-assured. Then he kissed Shannon full on the mouth. Manda saw Shannon's hand caressing Bay's butt and she felt a small shudder of jealousy that another woman was so familiar with her man.

Except that other woman had a greater claim on Bay than she did. Shannon and Bay had actually had sex. Shannon knew what it felt like to have Bay buried deep inside. Manda was still running that through her mind when she got the biggest surprise of all.

Bay threw his arms around Jake and the two men kissed. Shannon just stood there smiling like it was no big deal, but Manda knew her mouth must be hanging open. She'd never seen a kiss so blatantly sexual, especially one between two men. Her breasts got all tingly and she practically dripped between her legs, watching the two of them together.

When they finally broke apart from each other, both of them were breathing hard. Manda had a feeling they really hated to stop, and there was no way anyone could ignore the fact both Bay and Jake were extremely aroused.

Manda was definitely aroused. Her body's reaction surprised her even more than the kiss she'd just witnessed. She'd never felt so horny in her life!

Jake spoke first, his voice a little breathless, his intense gaze burning into Bay's. "God, I've missed you. I need to run, man. You up for it? My butt is so sore from sitting, I gotta get some exercise."

Bay turned to Manda. "Honey? Will you be okay if we go for a while?"

Still in shock from that amazing kiss, Manda merely nodded.

Shannon spoke up. "Don't be long. I'm going to make something for us to eat."

Jake shook his head. "Don't worry about us. We'll hunt if we get hungry. Right now I just need to stretch my legs."

"Yeah. Right." Shannon kissed him, sliding her body along the front of Jake's. He groaned into her mouth, and when they broke apart, both were breathing hard.

Manda sensed something else going on, but she merely nodded when Bay suddenly stripped out of his clothes and shifted. Jake took longer, unzipping the leather riding suit he wore, carefully removing his clothing and folding each item. Naked, gloriously aroused with his cock thrust hard against his belly, he glanced at Manda and grinned. "Shannon's been on me to be more careful where I throw my clothes. Living in a hotel room for almost a month gave her lots of time to enforce new housekeeping lessons."

Shannon laughed. "You got it." She turned to Manda. "I just told him no sex unless he picked his clothes up off the floor. It's amazing how fast he figured out how to fold things."

Jake leaned close and kissed Shannon, then shifted before Manda got past the shock of not one but two naked men on the front porch. The two wolves raced down the steps and headed for the woods. Shannon stood up. "I imagine they'll be gone a couple hours. I think I'm going to go take a shower."

"Do you really think they'll be gone that long?" Manda felt as if her head spun on her shoulders. So much had happened in a few very brief minutes. She gazed across the meadow toward the nearby woods and felt completely off balance and out of her element.

Shannon gave her a look that was part sympathetic, part pragmatic. "Honey, they've missed each other terribly. Jake and Bay don't just love each other as friends. They *are* lovers. They're packmates. It's all part of who and what we are."

Lovers? They were going into the woods to make love? Manda knew they had sex but she still hadn't quite figured it out. Not completely. The logistics of two men making love went beyond her small store of sexual knowledge. She turned to ask Shannon more, but the other woman had gone inside.

Manda stared at her glass of wine and thought about the men in the woods. Would they have sex as wolves or as men? The image of those two perfect bodies, both in their human skins, both aroused, their bodies pressed close together, was enough to make her sigh with regret while her own body thrummed with need. She pictured rippling muscles and arms and legs entwined, though she really didn't have a visual for the mechanics.

As much as she and Bay had touched and tasted and explored, she still didn't have a good idea of what a real sexual experience was going to be like. Poor Bay. He must be so frustrated by her lack of cooperation as well as her lack of understanding.

Hell, *she* was frustrated. Trapped by her own fears, held prisoner by a past she'd been unable to control, her body seething in an almost constant state of arousal. It seemed to grow each day, made worse by the powerful libido since her full switch to Chanku. Bay hadn't exaggerated when he'd said it could be overwhelming. She thought of sex day and night. She and Bay had tried every position possible, short of penetration, and yet nothing seemed to ease her need for more.

It wasn't like they hadn't tried going the whole way, but every time, when Manda would be so turned on she was practically mindless with need and positive her body's arousal outweighed fear, panic managed to overwhelm desire.

There had to be a solution. Somehow she had to get past the blind, unacceptable terror that ruled her body. Manda needed answers, and she needed them now. If Bay thought Shannon would be able to help, what was the point of waiting? Her fear couldn't be as powerful, as painful, as the needs seething inside. She couldn't go on this way, punishing Bay, punishing herself for a past over which she'd had no control.

Manda heard the shower go off and stood up before she could talk herself out of this. Her head spun just a little, and she glanced at the empty wineglass in her hand. It couldn't hurt. Didn't alcohol help relax a person? Maybe Bay was right. Shannon was a woman, she was Chanku, she'd made love with both Jake and Bay. Maybe Shannon had the answers Manda needed. If not . . . well, damn. She didn't want to think of that. Living as a freak was almost preferable to this miserable sexual limbo, but that option was gone forever.

Thank goodness! Striding forward on her perfect long legs, Manda went in search of Shannon.

Chapter 11

She stopped in the kitchen and refilled her wineglass. Since she'd never had alcohol, Manda had to guess how much she could drink before it was too much. She already felt the effects from just one glass.

Of course, maybe a little liquid courage would help. She was more than willing to try whatever worked.

She knocked lightly on the bedroom door and heard Shannon's invitation to enter. The shades were drawn and the room in semi-darkness, though it was still early afternoon. Shannon sat in the center of the bed, combing out her long, wet hair.

She was entirely naked.

"I'm sorry. I can come back later." Manda ducked her head and turned to leave.

"No. Stay." Shannon smiled and patted the bed beside her. "I left my clothes off on purpose. Please don't be embarrassed."

"I don't understand."

Shannon's smile lit up the room. "Of course you don't. Most people don't understand me, but they love me anyway." She laughed and her amber eyes twinkled. "Hon, I can tell just by looking at you that you're a child in an adult's body, sexually speaking. It's obvious you don't know the first thing about sex, other than what you've found on the Internet, and of course what Bay's managed to show you in his own endearingly male way . . ."

"Bay's . . . he's been very patient." How could she possibly explain what she'd put the poor man through? And how did Shannon know all these things about her? When Bay said he'd told Shannon about Manda's past, he hadn't told her everything . . . had he? Manda ducked her chin and took a sip of her wine, but her thoughts spun out of control.

"Hon, your body must be a frothing stew of hormones since you became Chanku and you're probably going nuts, especially if you're not comfortable with sex."

She couldn't believe he would betray her! "Did Bay tell you all this? Did he tell you *everything* about me? I thought . . . I didn't . . ."

Shannon shook her head. "He didn't have to. All I needed to know is that you've been part wolf since you were twelve and you were mistreated by the people you thought had rescued you. You might be a couple years older than me, but as far as sex, you're a baby. If you didn't have issues I'd be worried. Here." Once again she patted the soft down comforter beside her. "Sit with me. We need to talk. You ask questions. Any questions. I'll do my best to answer."

Feeling horribly exposed, Manda hesitantly sat down on the edge of the bed. She'd never been so close to a naked woman, but she realized Shannon had a damp towel thrown across her lap, so in that respect, she wasn't totally naked. Maybe she really did know how to help. Manda took another sip of the wine. That definitely helped. "You're sure you're not too tired?"

Shannon laughed and shook her head. "I am never too tired to talk about sex. Well? What do you think of Jake?"

"Jake?" Manda was sure her voice squeaked. "Your Jake?"

"There's no other." She leaned close to Manda and winked. "All I can think of is that right now, he and Bay are out there fucking like bunnies and it makes me so hot I can hardly stand it."

"Oh." Manda's clothes, a comfortable pair of sweats that she guessed Bay had snatched for her from Shannon's closet, suddenly felt too tight. "I've never . . ." She wasn't even sure what two men even did together. Their kiss had seemed awfully hot, but she knew there had to be more. A lot more. She swallowed. Shannon must think she was an absolute twit.

Shannon seemed perfectly oblivious. "I love watching when Jake fucks Bay. It's hard to imagine that huge cock of his even fitting inside Bay's cute little ass, but the looks on both their faces . . ."

"You've watched?" Wide-eyed, Manda leaned closer. There was no denying the rush of heat to her sex or the taut pucker of her nipples. She noticed Shannon's nipples had puckered up just as tight.

Almost like an invitation. Manda licked her lips and didn't even try to take her focus off of Shannon's perfect breasts. She took a quick gulp of wine.

"Oh, have I ever." Shannon laughed, but her voice had grown huskier, her eyes brighter. "The first time was before Bay had even made his first shift. We were here and he'd been taking the supplements, so his Chanku sex drive had definitely kicked in. The three of us were having sex." She sipped at her wine while Manda drained her glass.

Shannon reached over the bed behind her and came up with an open bottle of Chardonnay. She filled Manda's glass again without asking. "Anyway . . ." She clinked her glass against Manda's in a conspiratorial toast. "Bay was doing his best to eat me alive. He has the most amazing tongue."

Manda gulped, thinking of how his tongue felt between her legs. It dawned on her that she could accept without jealousy the fact he'd gotten a lot of practice with Shannon.

"Jake knelt behind Bay and took it really slow, getting him ready with a lot of lube. He grabbed him by the hips while Bay was working wonders on my clit. Every time Jake shoved his cock inside Bay, Bay's tongue went deeper inside me, and the look of pure lust on Jake's face . . ." She leaned back against the headboard, as if lost in her own ecstasy. "Bay groaned when Jake pressed deeper. I can still feel those vibrations against my clit. Amazing. Absolutely amazing."

"I guess I never really thought of it before, the way men had sex." Manda scooted up next to Shannon and leaned against the pile of fluffy pillows. Maybe it was the wine, maybe it was just Shannon's open appreciation of her own sexuality, but Manda felt as if she could say or do anything with this woman.

"It's like two women . . . where there's a will, and all that." Shannon turned and smiled at Manda. She was close, mere inches away and her mouth was so perfect and inviting, her breasts full and round.

Manda realized she couldn't stop staring. The towel had slipped away from Shannon's waist and the perfect triangle of deep russet hair between her legs drew Manda like a beacon. She suddenly realized she was reaching for Shannon and snatched her hand back, horribly embarrassed.

"Do you have any idea how much I want you to touch me?" Shannon leaned close and kissed Manda softly on the mouth. There was nothing at all threatening about her kiss. Her lips were soft, her breath sweet with the taste of the wine. Manda kissed her back before she even realized what she'd done.

Shannon seemed to take her acquiescence as an invitation to touch and it was fine, really. In fact, Manda decided it was more than fine, it was wonderful to have the uncomfortable sweats peeled slowly from her body, to have Shannon's lips and tongue laving a trail across her throat and her breasts, licking and sucking her suddenly responsive nipples.

Manda groaned as Shannon took the wineglass from her nerveless fingers and finished tugging her sweatpants over her feet. The air was cool against Manda's heated flesh and she shivered, but her body's reaction was due as much to the woman slowly parting her thighs as the wash of air on naked skin.

There was none of the urgency she felt with Bay, none of the sense of impending assault, though she knew that was never his intent. Shannon's touch was sensual yet non-threatening, her mouth on Manda's breast as warm and comforting as it was sexually arousing.

Fingers spread her thickened labia and stroked the warm, wet petals of her sex. Lips suckled at first one breast, then the other. She kissed a trail along Manda's ribs, suckled at her navel and dipped lower to taste her more intimately.

Manda arched her hips and sighed as Shannon licked and nipped between her legs. It felt similar to Bay's touch, but gentler, more precise. Manda's climax grew closer. She felt small tremors with each touch of Shannon's tongue. Clutching at the blankets, Manda arched her hips even higher, hovering much too close to the edge of orgasm.

Then suddenly Shannon was gone.

The bed dipped and Manda opened her eyes, blinking owlishly and feeling terribly abandoned. Shannon smiled at her, sat up and reached beyond Manda to the small bedside table. "I've got an idea. Don't mean to leave you hanging, but I am so horny, and I really love penetration. Lots of penetration." Shannon held up two plastic vibrators. At least that's what Manda figured they must be. She'd read about them but had never seen anything quite like these. They were both flesh colored and shaped to look just like large penises.

Manda blinked. "Oh. My." She reached out and touched one. It was soft around the tip, every bit as large as Bay when he was really erect. She tried to imagine putting it inside herself and couldn't.

"They're brand new. I got them just before we left for San Francisco. Ever used one?"

Manda shook her head. Fascinated, she took the one Shannon placed in her hand and turned the base. It vibrated to life with a low hum. "This is amazing."

"Put it in me." Shannon spread her legs and leaned back against the headboard.

Manda looked at the vibrator clasped in her hand, then at Shannon's pouting sex. A thrill spiraled from breast to womb, the sense of something illicit yet unbelievably exciting. Manda crawled between Shannon's legs and brushed the woman's dripping sex with the tip of the vibrating penis.

Shannon threw her head back and grabbed her knees with both hands, spreading her legs wider. Giggling, Manda touched her nipples instead and Shannon jerked, laughing. "Damn. You learn fast. Do it again!"

This time, Manda found a trail from Shannon's sternum to her clit, dipped the vibrator between her pouting red lips, then back over her clit. Shannon's hips lifted toward the vibrator.

"Oh . . . God. More. Inside me. Push it in really deep. You have no idea . . ."

Manda looked at the buzzing thing in her hand and shrugged. It looked huge, but she held it at the entrance to the dark, damp opening between Shannon's legs and slowly pushed it in. It was absolutely fascinating, watching the way Shannon's body stretched and shifted to accommodate the vibrating cock, almost as if she slipped it into a warm and pliant glove. Manda kept pushing, slowly and carefully, until it was almost completely buried. There was a tiny appendage at the base, and it seemed logical to turn that so that it pressed against Shannon's clit.

Obviously, she'd made the right decision.

Shannon screamed, grabbed her own breasts, tugged at her nipples and thrust her hips forward, forcing the vibrator even deeper. As if she'd done this before, Manda worked the vibrator in time with Shannon's thrusting hips, fascinated by the power of her orgasm, the knowledge she'd been the one to cause it.

By the time Shannon slumped forward and grabbed Manda's wrist, Manda was ready to come just from watching.

"Oh shit. I forgot how good that feels." Shannon took a couple of deep breaths. "You've got to try it."

She took a minute to catch her breath and then knelt between Manda's thighs with the second vibrator in her hand. It all felt so strange, sitting on the bed with a woman she hardly knew, heart pounding, gut clenching, body tingling with suppressed need. She felt a little woozy and knew the wine affected her, but the most powerful sensation was not the fact she'd had too much to drink. It was the arousal coursing through her body, the sensitivity to her skin and breasts, her nipples and clit.

She couldn't help herself. Manda rubbed her palm across her nipples and watched, fascinated, as both of them puckered into tight beads. Then she reached down, grabbed her legs and held them, just as Shannon had done. Even before the animated piece of plastic touched her clit, Manda felt the first ripples of an approaching climax. Fascinated by her body's reaction, she didn't even flinch when Shannon slowly, carefully, pushed the thick head of the toy inside her sex and tilted the vibrator so that it vibrated against her pubic bone.

The powerful vibrations seemed to pull something from deep within Manda. She felt her climax growing, spreading, gaining strength, felt the deep throbbing vibrations against her womb expanding to every corner of her body.

Something seemed to open up deep inside, something

that ripped at her emotions with as much power as it tore through her body. Contractions slammed into her center, spread to her fingers and toes with a tingling shock of awareness, an out-of-body explosion that practically lifted her off the bed.

She cried out, an incoherent groan that might have been Bay's name, might merely have been a prayer. Sobbing, shuddering with the powerful rhythm of her orgasm, Manda doubled over and grabbed Shannon's wrist, not so much to pull her away as to hold her still while her body rippled and clenched around the plastic cock buried deep inside her body.

A second climax rippled through, not as powerful as the first, but every bit as satisfying. Manda's body clasped the vibrator, inner muscles clenching, trying desperately to hold it close as Shannon slowly withdrew the vibrating toy.

Manda didn't mean to. She hadn't planned this, but she suddenly found herself wrapped in Shannon's arms, crying against her bare breasts. Her body still clenched and pulsed and her fingers and toes felt numb, but she'd had something penetrating deep inside her body and she'd climaxed. She hadn't freaked out, hadn't panicked, hadn't wanted to stop.

She hiccupped, then giggled. Shannon held her at arm's length. Manda burst into laughter and asked, "Do you do that to everyone the first time you meet them, or is it only me?"

Shannon snorted, grabbed a tissue out of a box by the bed and wiped Manda's eyes. "Only you, sweetie. That was a first. Wow! You don't do anything halfway, do you?"

"I have *never* done that before." She glanced at the pair of vibrators lying on the bed and shook her head. "That was pretty amazing. Really, really amazing." She looked back at Shannon and they both giggled.

"Want to do it again?" Shannon reached for the vibrator.

They both heard the sound of steps on the front porch at the same time. "Sounds like the men are back." Manda glanced toward the door. Instead of fearing what might come next, she felt a powerful rush of anticipation.

"Damn." Shannon stuck the vibrators back in the bedside drawer. She shot a glance at Manda. "Want to give it a try with the real thing?"

Manda sat very still for a moment, thinking of what she'd just done. Logically, if she could so easily accept a vibrator deep inside, there shouldn't be any problem with Bay's cock penetrating her. Another glass of wine to help the nerves, maybe a whole lot of foreplay . . . She glanced up at Shannon. Maybe her new best friend beside her. The visual of Bay and Jake having sex sent a sharp spike of need through her body.

Maybe, just maybe, with all of them together . . . the options suddenly seemed mind-boggling, especially considering how she'd freaked out just last night with Bay when he'd barely pressed his cock between her legs.

"I do," she said. "But I want you and Jake there, too. I want to see the men together, and I want to see them with you. I think that will help, just being there with everyone at once. I won't feel as if I've been singled out."

"You're a very wise woman. That's how Keisha got through her trauma. She joined her packmates mentally without actually experiencing physical sex until she was ready. Maybe you can do the same."

"Do you think the men will mind?"

Shannon rolled her eyes. "You're kidding, right?" Grinning like a fool, she stood up and then leaned over and gave Manda a quick hug. "I think it will make the men absolutely ecstatic. Come on. They're out there in the front room wondering what we're up to. I think it's time we let them know."

* * *

It was too damned quiet. Neither Bay nor Jake had taken the time to dress after their run, and while they'd shifted immediately after returning, they paced in the front room like a couple of angry wolves. Bay kept staring at the closed door to the master bedroom. Damn, it was making him crazy, wondering what the women were up to. If Shannon did anything to make Manda's fears worse . . .

The door opened and the men stopped in midstride. Shannon stepped out first, gloriously naked. Her hair spilled in a tousled, fiery mess around her face and her eyes were shining. Manda walked out behind her.

She was naked as well. Bay flashed a quick look at Jake, then crossed the room to his woman. "Are you okay? You look . . ."

Her smile told him a lot, but not nearly enough. "I'm better than I was. Shannon's got a plan."

"Oh, crap." Jake laughed and grabbed Shannon up in his arms. "When Shannon's got a plan, it's time for everyone to run screaming from the room."

"Thank you, Mr. Trent, for your vote of confidence." Shannon pushed herself out of Jake's embrace, but she had a big grin on her face. "We are all going to shower and get squeaky clean. Nothing personal, but you two reek of wolf and sex. Then we're going into the big bedroom where Jake, Bay, and I are going to make crazy love and Manda's going to join in with a mindlink. She'll be in my head and experience penetration from both of you jerks, at which point she's going to realize it's no big deal and then she'll really join in."

"No big deal?" Jake grabbed his erect cock and held it in his right hand, pointed toward Shannon. "This, my love, is a big deal. It's a huge deal."

Bay ignored Jake and his teasing. He watched Manda. She looked at Jake's erection, then at Bay's. Both of them must look huge to her, but she didn't appear frightened, not the way she'd been when they'd tried to make love last night.

Are you okay?

Her head tilted up and she looked into his eyes. She was smiling. *I'm okay. I can do this, Bay. Shannon makes everything seem so easy and natural. I can see why you love her. I love you.*

I love you, too.

"You coming?"

Bay turned toward Jake. "Yeah. We're coming. Be right there."

Manda headed toward the kitchen.

"Where ya going?"

She laughed. "For another glass of wine. I think it helps me shed my inhibitions."

"Well, in that case, bring the bottle." Bay followed close behind her. He loved watching the gentle sway of her hips, the little dimples at the base of her spine. The fact she'd come out here, unclothed in front of Jake and Shannon without showing any fear or embarrassment, stunned him.

It also made him very curious about what she and Shannon had been up to. Curious and aroused. He wanted Manda so badly he ached. The image of the two women, touching, tasting, doing whatever women did. Damn. What *had* they been doing?

He didn't realize he was broadcasting. Manda stopped, turned around, stood on her toes and kissed him hard on the mouth. "You'll never know," she said, giggling. Then she grabbed the bottle of wine out of the refrigerator and led Bay back to the shower.

Manda decided she really liked both Jake and Shannon. They laughed and teased and treated her just like an old friend. As far as they were concerned, she'd always been normal. There was no mention of her freakish appearance before her first shift, no mention of the fact she and Bay still hadn't mated.

Hell, they hadn't even had sex yet, but the only one who seemed concerned was Manda. For the first time in her life, she actually felt just like everyone else. Normal. Feminine and attractive. She sat on the big bed in the flickering light of candles set about the room, still sipping on her wine while Bay toweled her dry. She'd had more than enough to drink, but the lazy, relaxed buzz kept her nerves away. It wasn't something to make a habit of, but tonight . . . tonight Manda figured she needed all the help she could get.

Arousal simmered like a banked fire and kept all her senses on edge in spite of the wine. Shannon lay next to her on the bed, sprawled out on her belly while Jake rubbed her back and butt, payback, according to Shannon, for going almost a thousand miles on the back of a motorcycle in one day.

Manda leaned forward while Bay took an inordinate amount of time to dry her, but she couldn't keep her eyes off Jake. Kneeling behind Shannon, the sexy blonde worked on his mate's stiff muscles. His own muscles bunched and flexed in the flickering light. Manda had never experienced such an intense physical reaction from merely watching another man, not since Bay had come into her life, but Jake was absolutely gorgeous. She thought of the two men making love, their sweat-slicked bodies locked together, straining and groaning as one dominated the other.

"What are you thinking about, sweetie?" Bay ran his fingers through Manda's hair and gently worked out the tangles. "You've got your thoughts locked down tight."

She almost snorted her wine. Thank goodness she'd been blocking! "I didn't mean to." Manda took a last sip of her wine and handed the empty glass to Bay.

"Would you like more?"

She shook her head. "I don't want to fall asleep." She

hiccupped and slapped her palm over her mouth. "Oops."

Bay chuckled as he lifted the glass out of her loose fingers.

Manda's gaze strayed back to Jake. He rubbed Shannon's shoulders now, but his cock slipped up and down the crease of her buttocks. Manda clenched her own butt, imagining how that would feel. She glanced at Bay. He watched her watch Jake.

She blushed.

Don't be embarrassed. We all like to look. And touch.

I was thinking of you and Jake together. She glanced away, not so much out of embarrassment. She just knew the heated desire spiraling through her body had to show on her face. Hot and cold and so intense it was almost painful. *Shannon said you probably had sex during your run.*

Oh she did, did she?

Manda swung her head around. Bay had a huge grin on his face. *Yeah. She did.*

Got a problem with that?

Yes, she said, almost defiantly. *I didn't get to watch.*

He blinked. Good. She'd managed to shake him with her answer.

Then he grinned. *We can do something about that.* Bay leaned over and kissed her, hard. Then he crawled over her legs and knelt behind Jake. He patted Jake's left hip. Jake looked back, cocked an eyebrow and wiggled his butt.

Manda knew she must look bug-eyed as Bay found a condom in the bedside table and casually slipped it over his erection. Then he grabbed a tube of what looked like some sort of cream.

Do you want to help?

Manda nodded, mesmerized by the sense of the forbidden, the feeling that all the rules she thought she'd known had just blown out the door. She moved close to Bay's side and took the tube from him. Squirted some in her palm and stared a moment at the clear, cool gel that was obviously a lubricant. She lifted the solid weight of Bay's erection in her free hand. Spread the slippery stuff over the latex covered crown of his cock. *Is that okay?*

What about Jake?

Manda's breath caught in her throat. *You want me to put some on Jake, too?*

Inside. So I don't hurt him.

Manda's skin went hot, then cold all over. She realized Jake had quit moving. She sensed his anticipation, his body's desire for her touch. She scooted close with the small tube in her hand and touched the taut muscle of Jake's right cheek. The skin jumped and he arched his back. Manda hissed in a quick breath.

It's okay. Go ahead.

She shot a quick glance at Bay, took a deep breath and squeezed the cool gel into her palm. Jake kept his face turned away and it all felt somewhat anonymous, moving closer, running her finger along the crease from his tailbone to the tight ring of muscle guarding entry.

So intimate, touching him there, watching the pink flesh pucker and then soften. She pressed with her fingertip, ran her fingers past and down until she found the sensitive area of his perineum, then back up along the narrow crease of his ass.

This time she pressed harder, gained entrance and withdrew. He felt hot inside, and the ring of muscle clasped her finger. She thought of the play she and Bay had engaged in for the last week, the touching and teasing that, so far, had not led to more than occasional shallow penetration.

There was no risk for Manda here. Jake obviously wanted her to relax the tight muscle and ready him for Bay. She pressed again, with more lube this time. One finger, in and out, then two. She felt the tension ease and her fingers slipped inside all the way. Jake moaned and pressed back against her hand. Manda added a third finger, twisting this time. She felt a shudder go through Jake's body.

Guide me inside.

Once more Manda shot a quick look at Bay. He wasn't smiling anymore. A trickle of sweat ran down the side of his face. The intense look on his face made her gut clench with a hollow spike of need. As if she moved in a dream, Manda lifted his heavy cock in her hand and pressed the head against Jake's ass. Bay held perfectly still. Shannon lay quietly beneath Jake.

Jake had begun to tremble. Manda opened her thoughts. Once again, she'd been blocking without realizing. Now her mind shuddered beneath the sensual onslaught. Images and sensations, the seething mass of their combined arousal. Shannon, her sex gaping in wait with Jake's cock poised at the mouth, Bay's struggle for control as he pressed against the slick entrance to Jake.

The most powerful sensations of all, the greatest needs, were Jake's. Aroused to a shivering frenzy, body tense and ready for both penetration by Bay and the need to fill Shannon, he shared his arousal, filled each of them with his needs, his visceral craving for completion.

Caught up in Jake's powerful shared images, Manda wrapped her fingers around Bay's cock and pushed him hard against Jake. Both men groaned as Bay slipped past the tight ring and drove deep inside his packmate. Then Manda guided Jake's cock between Shannon's legs. Shannon arched into his thrust and the three of them pressed together with Jake in the middle. Manda sat back on her haunches, feeling a part of, yet separate from the writhing bodies on the bed.

Once again she realized she'd closed out their thoughts. Once more she found that window and opened it wide.

Manda doubled over beneath the wave of impressions. Sensation! So many feelings from three separate minds. Flooded with awareness and images, with the powerful love and respect each of them felt for one another, finding herself, for the first time ever, included in the whole.

She experienced everything—every touch, every thrust and probing penetration—as if it happened to her. The fullness of Bay's cock inside Jake, the heat and tightness Bay felt with each deep thrust along Jake's tight channel. She was Shannon, penetrated all the way to the hard mouth of her womb when Jake plunged deep inside. Manda slipped back into Jake's mind. He was the most highly aroused, the one experiencing both Bay's powerful thrusts and Shannon's warm, clenching pussy.

Shannon was the first to climax. She reached for Manda's hand and held her tightly, arched her body against Jake's and cried out. The added physical touch strengthened the mental link, tugged Manda into the maelstrom of feelings, of clenching muscles and rippling flesh.

She felt her own orgasm spiral out of control. Cried out with the shared feeling of Jake's cock filling her, pressing hard against the mouth of her womb, filling her with hot bursts of his seed as her vaginal muscles clamped down on his thrusting shaft.

Penetration without fear. A climax from both Shannon's point of view as well as Jake's. Long moments later, Manda blinked herself back to the present, realized she still knelt beside her three packmates, but now the fingers of her left hand were buried deep inside her sex and her right still clasped Shannon's hand.

Manda shook her head to clear her thoughts. Bay's hips slammed against Jake and both men groaned. Manda still trembled in the aftermath of orgasm. She'd not had sex, but her body didn't seem to care. She'd still participated, still wanted more.

Whether it was the wine or the sex toys or merely the fact Manda felt more loved than she ever had in her life, whatever combination of events and happenstance it might be, she had just experienced sex without panic. Wanted more. Wanted to feel the length, the heat, the solid weight of Bay deep inside.

Now she watched. Her body and mind experienced. She shared feelings and sensations. As if immersed in virtual reality, Manda became Jake. She felt the dark slide deep inside her bowel, the growing pressure of a second climax building.

Shannon had separated herself from Jake, turned around and now took his heavy erection in her mouth. Held his sac in her palm and his cock between her lips.

Manda felt Shannon's tongue, the pressure of her lips and teeth, the heat from her mouth. She cried out when Bay thrust hard and deep, and arched her back as Jake's need spiraled from spine to balls to explosive ejaculation.

Jake groaned. Manda's reality shifted. She was Bay. Surging forward, buttocks clenched, cock plowing deep inside Jake. She experienced the heat, the pressure, the convulsive tremors milking her cock. When Bay shouted his release, Manda sobbed her own. When Jake collapsed and rolled to one side so as not to crush Shannon, Manda toppled to the bed.

And when Bay slowly fell forward, his arms wrapped tightly around Jake's waist, Manda crawled close and laid her head upon his thigh. The four of them, replete, exhausted, satisfied, a single unit, no longer separate one from the other.

Manda's body trembled, but so did Bay's. She felt a hand sweep through her tangled hair and recognized Jake's gentle touch. Felt lips on her shoulder and knew Shannon kissed her.

Felt strong arms pulling her close, warm lips on her own, a heart full of laughter spilling into her mind.

Bay. Loving her. Ready to take the next step. Together.

Chapter 12

Millie trotted along behind Ric, marveling at how natural this felt, this amazing wolven existence. What had seemed impossible a few short nights ago was now almost more comfortable than life on two legs. She'd always loved wolves. Living as one far exceeded her wildest dreams.

She'd actually learned to enjoy the hunt, the rush of the chase, the burst of adrenalin when Ric deferred to her smaller, faster leap and she took a deer by the throat or outraced a speeding rabbit. The taste of hot blood on her tongue might have totally grossed her out before. Now it was all part of her life as a wolf. Her almost perfect life.

Only one final act remained to bring her full circle. She'd not yet mated with Ric. Not as wolves mate, in the deep forest. She'd yet to commit herself to him forever, their bodies tied, minds linked until they were no longer Millie West and Ulrich Mason, but a single entity, two strong-minded, stubborn people bound forever, together as one.

She'd been so sure a few nights earlier, but doubts had crept in after that first night on four legs. She knew she'd been emotionally overwrought, but it was all so new, so intense.

She'd mourned her daughter's death. Reveled over possibly finding her son. She hadn't quite accepted the new reality of her own life. It was all so new. She was still new.

And so terribly unsure of herself, where Ric was concerned.

So, what's your excuse now, Millie, m'love?

She turned to Ric, tongue lolling, head tilted just so, as the truth filled her heart. *Fear, Ric. Pure and simple. What if we're bound forever and you change your mind?*

Playfully, he nipped her shoulder. *I don't think it's my changing mind you're worried about. You're afraid you'll miss your freedom, aren't you?*

She bowed her head, forced to face her fears. It took her a moment to phrase what had truly bothered her, what kept her awake nights, worrying. *No.* She sighed loudly. *It's not that. I'm afraid of what you'll see in my past. What you'll know about me when you learn my deepest secrets.*

He nuzzled her shoulder, and she felt his warm breath against her thick coat of fur. *Very little I don't already know, my dear, sweet Millicent. You're worried what I'll learn about your girlhood fantasies and fears, aren't you? You lived with a perverted man after your mother died. You did what you had to do to survive. The way your uncle treated you was not your fault. He was wrong. You were a child.*

Her blood rushed cold in her veins. Millie stared long and hard at Ric. How had he known? They'd not bonded. Not yet. She'd buried those memories, the way her uncle had delighted in punishing her, the often prurient response he'd managed to wring from her maturing young body.

She'd locked the memories away. The memories, but not the guilt.

Ric licked her muzzle and leaned his head against her shoulder in a rare sign of submission. *We didn't need to bond for me to know your thoughts. You're an open book to me, Millie. I should be more concerned about what you'll find in my convoluted history.*

Millie hung her head. So much regret, so many terrible memories . . . *We both have secrets, Ric. So many things best left buried. Maybe we should just . . .*

Ric straightened up, held his head high and stared at her, his amber eyes glowing green in the light of the moon. *Come with me now, Millie. I love you. You love me. It's time.*

She stared at him, at the beautiful dark wolf with the sharp ears and flag of a tail and saw instead the man, the powerful alpha male who claimed her as his own. Human or animal, he would always love her. She didn't doubt his feelings.

How could she continue to doubt herself?

When Ric turned and trotted down the trail, back toward a silent woodland glade where they'd rested earlier tonight, Millie followed. Usually attuned to the sounds of the forest, the scents and sights so powerfully unique in this wolven form, tonight she saw only Ric. Scented Ric.

Needed Ric.

He picked up the pace and they were running now, flying down the narrow trail, brush whipping at their shoulders, eyes alight and tails flying. Feet barely touched the thick mat of leaves and pine needles beneath, yet their run was almost soundless, so adept were the two of them at passing through these woods unnoticed.

Millie felt as if she raced the wind. Raced with Ric, the man she loved. Nothing could stop her, now. Nothing could halt what they'd both set into motion.

Ulrich slipped through a narrow breach in thick brambles near a still pond. He burst through to the other side and stepped into a meadow bathed in moonlight with Millie close behind. When he turned to confront her, she almost ran into him.

Millie skidded to a halt. Ears perked forward, tail high, she held perfectly still, then lowered her tail just enough to show that in this, at least, she deferred to him.

Panting from their run, Ulrich eyed Millie just as warily as she watched him. His thoughts whirled and shifted, more wolf than human right now, so caught up in the rich scent of the bitch who faced him across the small patch of grass, he thought he might explode with wanting her.

He'd been patient. It hadn't been easy, but he'd waited. He'd given her time to grieve, time to adjust to this perfect wolven body. They'd made love in every human position, found every possible way of reaching pleasure. She'd introduced him to sex toys, he'd plied her with bondage. They'd taken turns with the blindfold, with restraints and without.

He'd suffered through nipple clamps and vibrators, plugs and all other indignities and loved every moment, but nothing came anywhere close to standing here in a meadow bathed in silver, with moonlight glistening off the tips of their fur and the light in Millie's eyes challenging the glow in the midnight sky.

She lowered her head and watched him, a slight curl to her lip. She was an alpha bitch preparing to submit, and he knew submission would not come easy. Ulrich moved closer and growled, then leapt to one side when she snapped at him. He opened his thoughts and found Millie, her mind a jumble of lust and fear, excitement and trepidation.

He raked her back with one broad paw, twisted when she tried to block his body with her own, then mounted her. Quickly, efficiently, his powerful front legs grasping her shoulders, his jaws clamped on the side of her neck, back legs planted firmly in the damp earth.

Thrusting hard and fast, he found her tight sex and rammed the narrow length of his wolven cock deep within her folds. She yelped and tried to pull away, but the large knot at the base of his penis slipped inside, swelling as he thrust deeper, harder.

Holding them together. Tying their bodies.

It had been so long. Not since Camille had he known this sense of unity, the knowledge and assurance he was no longer alone. Millie's thoughts poured into his mind, incoherent at first, a mass of confusion and disconnected memories. They slowly drew together into a comprehensible pattern. What he saw angered him and made him love her even more. He'd only scratched her surface before now, but this . . . this was pure, unadulterated history, the world as Millie remembered from her earliest recollections, her childhood unabridged.

Ulrich experienced Millie's loss and pain when her mother died, something the toddler saw as abandonment. He felt her unfathomable grief over the loss of her own babies, her shame each time her uncle found some obscure reason to punish her.

She'd known from an early age he took sexual satisfaction from spanking her, knew he loved the feel of her firm bottom beneath his palm, but she was a young woman with powerful needs, and to her shame, she'd often responded. Knowing what the man did was wrong, she'd still felt a certain excitement when he beat her. Then she'd wallowed in overwhelming guilt, putting the blame entirely on herself. She realized now that her powerful libido was merely a manifestation of her Chanku spirit, but then she'd suffered.

And she'd needed. Now, Ulrich celebrated her joy as understanding spilled into her, and with it, forgiveness. Her uncle had not been a good caregiver. What he'd done was molestation, pure and simple. But the uncle, like Millie, was Chanku. He had died without ever knowing. Ulrich felt the forgiveness as it blossomed inside Millie. Forgiveness for a twisted man who lived a life of desperation, forgiveness for the girl she'd been, so unaware of her true self.

Celebrating silently as his mate found her center and learned to understand her deepest fears, Ulrich continued thrusting, driving against Millie's womb. There would be no offspring. Too many years had passed for them to conceive, but this joining would stay with them, would keep them tied emotionally, mentally, and physically, for all their days.

Something deep inside Millie made her fight him at first. This was wrong, her body wasn't ready, she wasn't ready. Then he slipped inside her sex and she felt the huge swelling that held her fast, locked her to Ric while his hot semen flooded her passage, while his memories flooded her mind.

Something deep inside her burst free.

She bowed her head and accepted, opened her mind and invited him in. He came, with reverence, with empathy, with complete understanding. And somehow, in that perfect sharing, Millie understood her life and Ric's, her uncle's, and even the woman who had been Ric's first love.

Camille was indeed a contradiction in terms and personalities. Strong willed, somewhat selfish, and a little bit spoiled, she'd loved with all her heart, but it hadn't been enough. Millie finally understood Ric's mixed emotions when it came to his late wife.

Understood and accepted. She felt his pride in his daughter Tianna, his love for Tia's husband, Lucien, a man who had become the son he'd never had. Most of all, Millie saw and accepted the true depth of Ric's love for her.

Any doubts there might have been fled with the final thrust of his hips, the tight clenching of her powerful vaginal muscles holding him tight inside her body.

The orgasm she felt in this form was every bit as powerful, though totally different from that experienced in her human body. It came to her then, as her muscles rippled and tightened around Ric's cock, as her heart pounded in her chest and her ears lay flat against her head, just how amazing this was. How unbelievably amazing, to be Millie

West, middle-aged woman, sanctuary supervisor, lover of Ulrich Mason, one moment, and the next, a she-wolf, powerful denizen of the forest, lover and bonded mate to the perfect alpha wolf now locked so tightly inside her body.

Unbelievable. Impossible. Perfect.

Locked together, both panting with exertion and emotion, they dropped to the ground, bodies twisted around so they might face one another while waiting for the huge knot tying them together to subside.

I love you. Ric's voice rang loud and true in her heart.

And I love you. That's amazing. Impossible. Wonderful. So different from sex as humans.

That wasn't just sex, Millie m'love. That was lovemaking. That was a mating bond to beat all other bonds. In fact, it was utterly fantastic. You are utterly fantastic.

She tilted her head and her ears perked forward. Then she shifted. A woman now, still tied to Ric in his wolven form, long human legs tangled with the wolf. She was almost preternaturally aware of the stuffed feeling of his wolven cock inside her, of the amazing differences in their bodies. She touched the thick ruff of fur at his neck and clenched her vaginal muscles around the unfamiliar knot of flesh filling her sex.

Then she threw back her head and laughed aloud. "You're damned right I'm fantastic, Ric Mason. And don't you forget it!"

Still laughing, she leaned close to hug the wolf and wrapped her arms around the man. Both of them naked and altogether human, lying together in the damp grass, bodies sated from lovemaking, hearts full.

It just couldn't get much better than this.

Ric disentangled himself from Millie's embrace, stood up and grabbed her hand. The night was warm and summer finally seemed to have arrived in northern Colorado, but the water felt icy when they stepped into the shallow end of the pond. They bathed quickly, both of them shivering and giggling, but Ric's arousal, his need for Millie, hadn't abated a bit. It seemed perfectly natural to make love once more. Millie held Ric's broad shoulders and wrapped her legs around his waist while frigid water lapped against her hips. He pressed into her, his fingers digging into the soft curves of her buttocks, his cock lifting her with each powerful thrust.

With him, she was a girl again, but this girlhood was right and pure. She knew sexual freedom for the first time in her life, the freedom to love and be loved on her own terms by a man of her own kind.

When she had come and he was finished, when they were both trembling and panting once again, Ric carried Millie out of the cold pool. They shifted at the water's edge, reclaiming dry, warm wolven coats of harsh fur.

Together they raced the narrow trail back to the cabin. There would be no hunting tonight. No howling at the moon. Millie wanted a warm shower, a big, soft bed, and Ric beside her. She felt empowered, as if she'd done more than step fully into the world of Chanku.

Tonight, for the first time in her life, Millie felt as if she'd finally, irrevocably, embraced the woman who was Millie West, past, present, fears, anxieties, and all. There were no secrets left. No guilt. No fear. She'd met her past and, with Ric beside her, conquered every demon.

* * *

Night had finally fallen and Shannon was the first to shift, but Jake went right behind her. Manda snuggled close to Bay and watched them go, two wolves scrabbling over the hardwood floors, their mental burst of laughter filling her mind. It appeared to be a race to see who would get outside first.

She sensed more laughter when they reached the front door and argued about who was going to shift and open the damned thing, but Shannon appeared to win that argument. Both of their voices faded into the quiet buzz of distant thought.

"That was really amazing."

"What? Those two shifting?"

Manda punched him on the shoulder. "No, you doofus. Sex. You and Jake. Then you and Jake and Shannon. Oh my." She shook her head and laughed when a spiraling shock of need spread from her breasts to her sex. "I had no idea how intense that could be."

Bay rolled to his back and brought Manda with him. "It was intense because you were here. I love you, Manda. I love you so much it hurts, knowing you're still afraid of me."

She lay on top of him. His cock was huge and hard, pressed tightly between their bellies. It would be so simple, just to ease up on her knees, to see if she could actually fit him inside without freaking out.

"Maybe it's not just you. Maybe I'm getting past some of the things that scare me." She couldn't credit the wine. Not now. The slight buzz she'd felt earlier was long gone, but her need for Bay hadn't faded at all. If anything, she wanted him more than ever. Watching Shannon and Jake together had given her a powerful visual of exactly how much she was missing.

The memories of her horrific attacks had faded. They weren't completely gone, but she had to believe that was a good thing. All that had happened in her life made her the woman she was today. She had to learn to accept and move forward.

It was definitely time.

She wasn't going to miss out on life anymore. Not if she could help it. Trembling just a bit, as much from desire as fear, Manda raised up on her knees and straddled Bay's thighs. His cock popped up and she sensed his growing arousal, but she felt his hesitation, as well, his concern that she might not be ready. She hesitated a moment too, took a deep breath and then reached out and wrapped her fingers around the base of his cock.

He was warm and solid in her grasp, and she'd done this much before. Held him. Tasted him. Manda stared at Bay's erection, noticing the difference in color in the broad, smooth head where the blood ran hot and the huge veins traversing his length. His foreskin had peeled back behind the crown and that, for some reason, gave his cock an almost vulnerable look. As if the protective sheath had parted just for Manda.

It was not something to frighten or hurt her. It was merely a part of the man she loved, something designed to bring both of them pleasure, not pain.

This she could do. She wasn't being restrained. Bay wasn't forcing her to do anything. He was merely lying there, watching her, his eyes shimmering with love. Before she could wallow any deeper in her stupid fears, Manda raised up on her knees, pressed the smooth crown between her thighs and slowly eased down over his full length.

She was so wet and sensitive that her muscles clenched in reaction, then relaxed and welcomed Bay inside. She experienced a brief flash of remembered fear, then a melting, a sense of pleasure so profound it brought Manda to tears. Her fingers curled into the dark mat of hair on Bay's chest as his hands slowly, gently, cupped her buttocks. He didn't hold her so much as allow her to rest on his palms, but it was enough.

Lifting herself up, she felt the smooth slide of his cock inside her sex and pressed her knees against his tense thighs. He grasped her tighter, using his strength to raise and lower her body. His knees came up behind her hips, supporting her, encircling her.

Pleasure grew and blossomed deep inside and something powerful and dark broke free from her mind. Manda could have sworn she watched the black cloud form overhead then slowly, silently dissipate, taking with it her fear and frustration from so many years' existence in her own personal purgatory.

As the darkness left, sensation increased. Her breasts tingled and her nipples tightened. Bay's soft chest hair beneath her fingers tickled and the muscles in his thighs bunched with each downward stroke she made.

She realized her eyes were closed. Manda opened them and glanced at Bay, surprised to find him grinning at her.

"You're doing it again," he said, thrusting his hips up to meet her downward stroke. "You're blocking me. Open your windows, sweetie!"

Laughing with the pure joy of the moment, Manda threw her mental shutters wide and gasped at the myriad sensations flooding her mind. Not only her own sensitive reaction to this most amazing penetration, but Bay's. She knew, now, what it felt like to have a cock, to have it deeply embedded in the rippling, clenching warmth of feminine muscle. She felt each twitch and turn, not only from Bay's point of view, but her own.

Sensation doubled on sensation, an overload of awareness, as Bay not only shared his feelings but the way in which he perceived her feelings.

An overwhelming, unbelievably exciting overload of sensation suddenly spiraled from somewhere deep in her center to coalesce in a pinprick of heat, a melding of fire and ice, of arousal and excitement centered right between her legs.

Unexpected. Powerful. Not frightening. Not at all frightening! Still, Manda screamed when her climax hit. Screamed and arched her back, knees slamming against Bay's hips, fingers digging into his chest, her muscles caught in a spasm that felt as if it would never release.

He thrust into her again, then again as she slowly folded over against his chest. She felt Bay's muscles tense, heard a long, low groan starting deep in his gut and felt the hot rush of his ejaculate for the very first time, deep inside her body.

His hips continued rocking slowly against her. Manda sobbed, her tears spilling across his chest, her body shaking with the aftereffects of her climax and a lifetime of anguish.

This was the way it should be. This was right and perfect and she never wanted to return to that place in her mind, that place where the darkness had always lain in wait.

It's gone. Forever gone.

Giggling, crying, she raised up and stared at Bay. "Ya think? Good lord, Bay. That was amazing. Absolutely amazing."

He reached for her and brushed the tangles of hair away from her face. "You're amazing, Manda. You and your wonderful ability to heal. You're a lot stronger than you give yourself credit for."

She leaned down and kissed him. His tongue tested the seam of her lips and she opened for him. As they kissed, he grew hard and solid inside her once again.

This time, Bay rolled Manda over and knelt between her legs. She looked up at him, at the beautiful smile for her alone, at the powerful muscles and broad shoulders. Not holding her captive. No, protecting her. Loving her.

Without a second thought, Manda arched her hips, driving him deeper inside. Taking Bay all the way, without panic, and definitely without fear.

Later, when Shannon and Jake returned, there was no question of sleeping arrangements. With the scent of the forest clinging to their night-chilled bodies, the two crawled into bed beside Bay and Manda.

Manda lay there for a long time, smiling into the darkness. Just a couple of weeks ago, she'd been entirely alone in the world. Now, surrounded by warm bodies and tangled limbs, she finally understood the concept of the healing power of love.

Bay broke a few more eggs into the pan when Manda wandered out into the kitchen. The sun had barely topped the tree line, but it cast a beam of light sparkling with dust motes across the kitchen.

Still looking half asleep, Manda stretched up on her toes and kissed him, filled a cup with coffee and sat down next to Jake at the table. Shannon was in the shower, bacon fried with a frantic snap and pop in the big cast-iron pan, and Bay couldn't recall ever feeling so content.

This was his family. These people meant more to him than he'd ever imagined. He didn't want anything to change.

Well, one thing. He definitely wanted one thing to change.

Later, tonight maybe, they'd run as wolves. He and Manda might finally mate, somewhere in the forest he would take her as a wolf, make love to her, bond with her. Never before had he come close to anything as powerful as the bond between mates, but if what Jake said was true, it would be a life altering experience.

Bay grinned, slowly stirring the eggs in the pan, thinking of the night ahead with the woman he loved. The woman who, even now, leaned over Jake's shoulder. Jake had his laptop in front of him and was busily taking notes on a pad beside it.

"Whatcha doin'?

Jake turned his head, grinned at Manda, kissed her on the nose and laughed at her look of total shock. Bay bit back another grin. Manda would get used to Jake's kisses eventually. She'd already adjusted to so much more than he'd expected.

One day, she might even make love with Jake . . . and

Shannon, as well as with Bay. The thought of all those bodies tangled together slammed into his gut. His cock immediately reacted.

Of course, it reacted whenever he thought of Manda, but adding his packmates to the equation took him even higher.

Jake sat back from his laptop and turned his attention to Manda. "Tia and Luc are doing a search for a couple of missing kids, well adults, now. They asked me to help," he said. "Ulrich Mason, Tia's dad, has met a woman who had her out-of-wedlock twins taken away from her as soon as they were born. This was like thirty-six or more years ago. She's always wanted to know what happened to them. Ulrich asked for help, so we're all taking different paths online to see what we can find."

"How horrible!" Manda set her coffee cup down and looked at Jake's notes. "That poor woman. Have you had any luck?"

Jake shook his head. "Well, yes and no. We ran into a dead end on both the boy and the girl. Tia got fairly good stuff on the girl. We know she died about twenty five years ago, so we're basically trying to follow up on the son. See if we can come up with any new leads."

Manda took a sip of her coffee and looked at Jake's notes again. Bay noticed a frown creasing her brow. "Wow. That's a coincidence. Their birthday was July 10, 1971. That's my birthday, too."

Jake turned and stared at her. "Were you adopted?"

Manda shook her head. "No. 'Fraid not. I was an only child. My parents were missionaries in Tibet, but they were killed when I was twelve."

Bay hoped Manda didn't notice the sharp look Jake shot in his direction. He immediately narrowed his band of contact. *What's going on?*

We know that Millie West's daughter was adopted by

missionaries. They were killed in Tibet during a raid by insurgents. The daughter was supposedly killed as well.

That's an awful lot of coincidence.

My feelings exactly. Don't say anything yet. Let me talk to Ulrich.

"You two ready for some breakfast?" Bay turned away and grabbed three plates out of the cupboard.

Manda smiled at him, obviously unaware of the brief conversation he'd had with Jake. "Definitely. I'll get the toast." She shoved her chair back. Bay watched her moving around the kitchen with grace and ease and marveled at how comfortable she seemed in a house filled with strangers.

What would happen when she learned the details of Jake's search?

Shannon wandered out into the kitchen, wrapped in a cotton robe with a bright green towel around her damp hair. She kissed Bay on the cheek and leaned over Jake's bare back with her arms draped lightly over his shoulders. She looked back over her shoulder at Bay. "There'd better be a plate for me in that stack, buster. I'm starving."

"Coming up." Bay ladled eggs and placed strips of bacon on four separate plates. Manda buttered and stacked the toast on another plate and grabbed silverware out of the drawer. It all felt amazingly domestic, comfortable in the way of long-time friends with a lot of history together, but it wasn't that way. Not at all.

Their history as a small pack had, essentially, started just last night. Off to such a tremendous start, and now Jake had information that would most likely rock Manda's fragile world. Bay watched the graceful sway of her hips as she walked, the smile that lit her eyes, the shiny fall of her hair sweeping across her shoulders, and felt his heart tumble in his chest.

When she'd remembered her parents' death, he'd felt

her grief. Could he put her through something like this? Finding out those weren't her birth parents after all? Learning that the mother who gave birth to her still lived? How would it feel to discover the past she thought she knew as truth had been based on lies?

Another thought hit him as he carried plates to the table. Until Manda knew the truth, they couldn't bond. Mating was out of the question while he carried secrets about her past. Whatever he knew would become part of Manda's knowledge.

He caught Jake's eye and knew his packmate had come to the same conclusion. They needed to reach Ulrich. Needed to find out everything they could about the search for Millie West's babies. Then, somehow, Bay had to find the best way to tell Manda the truth—that everything she knew, every part of her history, had all been a terrible lie.

Bay picked up his fork and stared at the plate in front of him. Finally he managed to choke down a few bites. Everyone raved about his breakfast. Bay thought it tasted like sawdust.

"I'm headed for the shower. Maybe that will wake me up." Manda carried her plate to the table, leaned over and kissed Jake, then Shannon, and finally reached Bay where he sat sipping a last cup of coffee. "I'm learning. See?"

Then she planted one on him that promised a lot more than a mere after-breakfast kiss. Tongue and teeth and the soft slide of moist lips over his. Bay reached up and snagged her around the neck with his left arm, tumbled Manda into his lap and took control.

Long minutes later, they finally broke apart, both of them panting for air. Shannon and Jake applauded. Manda fanned herself, but she grinned ear to ear. Her hair was mussed, her eyes sparkled and her lips looked swollen.

Bay lifted her off his lap and steadied her on her feet. "Go. Now. Or you won't get that shower you want."

"Well, I could be persuaded . . ."

Bay laughed. "No. You can't. I have to clean up the kitchen."

Manda swatted his shoulder and sashayed away. "You are acting like such a grownup. Well, it's your loss." She slipped through the doorway and headed down the hall.

Bay turned to Jake and Shannon. "She's right, you know. It is my loss. Damn it all, I need to find out the truth before tonight."

Shannon frowned. Obviously Jake had filled her in on Manda's possible relation to Ulrich's friend. "Why the rush?"

Jake answered for Bay. "She's ready to bond. They can't."

Shannon nodded. "I hadn't thought of that. She'll know what you suspect, but you need proof before you say anything at all." She stared toward the hallway, then back at Bay. "She's fragile, Baylor, but she's not made of glass. I think you need to give her more credit."

Bay nodded. "Manda's definitely stronger than she looks, but what we're talking about means an entirely new history, a new reality for her. She's been traumatized enough. I don't want to tell her anything until I know for sure. It was bad enough convincing her that Papa B didn't have her best interests at heart."

"Papa B?" Jake frowned. "Who the hell is he?"

"The guy who supposedly rescued her after her parents were killed. She thinks of him as her savior, but the guy turned her over to scientists who treated her worse than a lab animal. What they did to Manda makes Josef Mengele look like Mother Teresa."

"Any idea who Papa B was?" Jake grabbed his laptop off the floor and opened it up.

"She said he was with the government, but she wasn't sure exactly what he did. Remember, this was a totally traumatized, twelve-year-old girl in a strange land, whose parents were brutally murdered in front of her. Hell, she saw her mother gang-raped before they killed the poor woman. Manda was in a small closet with a wicker door, just inches away from everything. After all this, she wakes up half wolf, half human, looking like a freak, no clue what's happened. People ran from her in fear, all except for a young American man who helped get her out of the country before the surviving townspeople could kill her. They thought she was cursed. Hell, Manda thought she'd been cursed by an angry god until I shifted for her. I've tried to see who Papa B was, but his form is always indistinct in her mind."

"What a nightmare." Shannon rubbed her arms as if warding off a chill. "You need to call Ulrich, find out anything you can. What's Millie look like? If we can get a photo, that might at least point to a family resemblance."

"Good idea." Bay turned to Jake. "I'll give him a call now, before Manda gets out of the shower. You see if you can find out anything at all about Papa B. He might be the link, though Manda said he's dead."

The photo arrived as an e-mail attachment just moments before Manda walked into the kitchen. When Bay raised his head and looked into Shannon's eyes, he knew there was no way they could keep the truth from Manda. It wasn't just Millie West staring at them from Jake's computer.

It was Manda. A little older, a whole lot wiser. Hair the same color, smile just as wide, the very same cocky tilt to her hip.

He sensed Manda's presence before she actually entered the kitchen. Prepared himself for questions for which he had no sure answers. She stopped behind him. Touched his shoulder.

"Who's that? She looks familiar."

Bay swallowed. "I'm not sure, sweetie, but we think she could be your mother."

"Oh, no." Manda laughed. "That's not her. My mother had dark hair and she was short and round. Plus, she never, ever smiled. Not like that. Not like she loved life." She paused, and Bay wondered what thoughts had stopped her. As usual, Manda had closed the window to her mind. "She hated everything," she said, speaking very softly. "Me. My father. Our life in Tibet. No, that's definitely not my mother."

"You've never told me your full name." Bay took Manda's hand in his. "What's your last name?"

Wide-eyed now, Manda stared at him. "Smith. Amanda Jane Smith. Everyone called me Manda. I never even think of my full name anymore. What's that lady's name?"

"Millie West. But she had twin babies who were given up for adoption, a boy and a girl. The little girl was adopted by a missionary couple by the name of Smith. They named their little girl Amanda Jane."

Chapter 13

"Why did you take my picture?" Millie followed Ulrich out onto the front porch. He wished he had more information, but there was no point in keeping anything from his mate. She'd get it out of him sooner or later.

At least this was good news. Very good news. He'd merely hoped for more details. "Remember the young woman I told you about, the one Baylor Quinn went to check on in New York?"

Millie nodded. "Yes. Have you heard from him? How is she? Is she Chanku?"

Ulrich turned around and leaned against the porch. "Yes. She is. She has an interesting history. We're still checking on details, but it appears she was born on July 10, 1971. Her parents were missionaries, both of them murdered during an uprising in a small village in Tibet. Only Manda . . ."

"Manda? As in Amanda?" Millie grabbed his hand in both of hers. "My daughter? My daughter's alive? You think this young woman could be . . . ?"

Ulrich nodded. "Her name is Amanda Jane Smith. I haven't gotten a photo from them yet, but after sending your picture to the kids in Maine, Baylor said she looks just like you. I do have Bay's cell phone number. It's up to you, Millie. Do you want to call her?"

She stared at him, her eyes filled with tears, her lips parted. Then Millie blinked and wiped her eyes. "In a little while, Ric. When my heart stops pounding. Tell me everything you know about her. Please?"

Ulrich walked her to the closest chair. He sat down, then pulled Millie into his lap. It felt so perfect, the way she curled against his chest. "Baylor said she's had a pretty rough time of it since her parents were killed. Up until then, she was a fairly typical little girl who lived in a small village in Tibet. Her parents' violent deaths changed all that, when it appears the trauma of the event forced a partial shift on her."

"How could that happen?"

"She lived in the area where we believe our race originated, obviously ate just enough of the local vegetation to allow for a partial shift, but she wasn't ready or mature enough for a complete shift."

"But where has she been all this time?"

"That's the sad part of her story. She was supposedly rescued by a man she knew only as Papa B, but Baylor said she was badly treated, more as a scientific oddity or lab animal for all the years since. Since she was caught halfway into a shift without knowing what caused it, she had no way to undo the damage. We know shifting can be a subconscious act for incipient Chanku when they're frightened or otherwise traumatized, sort of a fight or flight reaction. It wasn't until Baylor found her and gave her the nutrients that she was able to complete the shift to wolf and back to human. She's still learning how to be human as well as how to be a wolf."

"Oh, Ric. That poor child! She's going to hate me." Millie's fingers tightened around his.

"Why would she hate you? You've done nothing to hurt her."

"She's going to think I didn't want her. She'll blame me for what happened."

"I doubt that, my love. I doubt that very much, but we can wait. There's no reason to rush. Maybe after you see a photo this will all feel more real to you."

Millie nodded, but he felt her body trembling and held her close. Being a parent was never easy. Parenting shape-shifters was doubly hard. He nuzzled her hair. "Let's run. It's a beautiful day, it's your day off and things always make more sense to the wolf."

"It's true. Why is that? I feel it whenever I shift."

"Life is simpler to the wolf. Food, water, warmth, and sex. It's all in the basics."

Millie slipped off of Ulrich's lap and stepped inside the cabin to undress. He always got such a kick out of her modesty.

"Well, I'm all for the basics," she said, tugging her shirt over her head. "Especially that last one on your list."

With that she raced past him, a reddish blur in the sun-light streaking over the porch railing to the thick carpet of grass below. Ulrich stripped his clothing off where he stood and followed Millie's trail through the thick brush.

She led him on a merry chase, one that had him practi-cally gasping for air by the time he realized she headed in the direction of the meadow where they'd first mated as wolves.

Ulrich cut through a small grove of trees and climbed a narrow ridge covered with aspen, raced down a shrub-tangled valley and approached the meadow from the op-posite end where Millie knew to enter. Slowing his headlong dash, Ulrich found the narrow cleft between two steep, rocky walls where the pond drained and worked his way up to the meadow.

She stood on the opposite side of the pond, facing the trail where she'd come in. Waiting for him. Sunlight glis-tened off her thick red coat, turning it to gold with glints of brass. Her tail waved lazily behind her and she was ob-viously unaware of Ulrich watching.

He could stand there all day, his gaze resting on the she-wolf who was his mate. After so many years alone, to find someone as perfect as Millie seemed unbelievable. The sun beat down warmly on his back and the sound of bees and the chirping of birds created a soft background hum to the low rippling song of the creek. It fell lazily into the pond at one end, leaving with just as little haste at the other.

It was a day, a place and a time created for lovemaking. Ulrich shifted, standing tall and proud at the water's edge. "Millie?"

She whipped around at the sound of his voice, shifted almost immediately and burst into laughter. "Damn you, Ulrich Mason! I was going to surprise you!"

"It's not easy to sneak up on an old wolf, Millie." He stepped into the pond, a good thirty degrees warmer than it was the last time they'd made love in its shallow depths. "C'mon in. The water's fine."

She shook her head, laughing softly, loving him so much she wondered what kept her heart inside her chest. After a lifetime alone, how amazing to have found a man who not only understood her better than she knew herself, but one who loved her as she needed to be loved.

Completely. Without reservation.

Millie stepped into the pond, surprised by how warm the water felt against her legs. It was shallower as well, losing depth as each day moved them closer to summer. When she met Ric at the center, the water barely touched her hips.

It was the most natural thing in the world to wrap her arms around Ric's neck and press her body close to his. He lifted her with his broad palms and her legs wrapped perfectly around his slim waist. There was no need to use her hands to guide him as his wonderful cock slipped neatly, naturally into her waiting sex. Hot, powerful, yet for this mating, so very gentle.

They rocked together. She felt his thoughts slip easily into hers, felt his love, his compassion, even a sense of curiosity about the grown woman who was her daughter. Would she be like Millie? Would she accept the two of them as family?

Had she bonded yet with Baylor? So many questions, but no rush to answer any of them. It would all come in time and they would learn what they needed to know when that time was right.

Millie felt the familiar rush of heat, the clenching in her gut that seemed to encompass her breasts and her womb, her clit and everything in between in a wonderful tide of sensation. She shivered as her arousal grew, peaked, spilled over into rolling coils of heat and light, clenching muscles and rippling sex.

It was never so easy for Ric. She smiled against his chest as he thrust his hips harder, faster, until he was pounding into her and his fingers pressed tightly against her buttocks.

His muscles tensed as he lifted Millie with each powerful thrust. Driving into her, withdrawing and back again, harder, faster, filling her with his heat and length, amazing her with his strength. Strength not a bit diminished by either the years or the miles.

He came in a rush of breath that escaped on a groan, a tensing of muscles, a powerful thrust of his cock so deep he bottomed out against the mouth of her womb.

Millie linked her legs tightly behind his back and rode the second climax as it rippled through her body. More powerful this time, deeper, filling her once again with that wonderful shared sense of lovemaking with the man who truly was her soul mate.

Gasping, arms trembling with exertion, Ric lowered both of them into the quiet pond. Their skin was so hot the water felt cool as they dipped down to chin length. He pressed his forehead to hers, sighed deeply in one, long shuddering breath and kissed her.

Millie closed her eyes against a huge rush of emotion and the tears that threatened to spill. She tightened her legs around his waist. Her breasts pressed against Ric's chest and her vaginal muscles still pulsed rhythmically around the solid length of his cock.

"You're so right, my love. It's all much easier to understand when you race through the woods on four legs." She kissed him back. "But I'm not sure whether to feel anxious or afraid or excited about meeting Amanda for the first time."

Ric brushed her hair back from her eyes. "Put yourself in your daughter's place. How would you feel, meeting your mother for the first time?"

"I don't remember her. I'll never have the chance to know. She died and I was left with my uncle when I was very small."

"Then make it right for Amanda. Be the mother for her you wish yours had been for you."

It all sounded so simple when he phrased it like that. "What gave you so much common sense, Ric?" She nuzzled the smooth skin where his neck and shoulder met, licked him there, then nipped him, leaving a mark. Her mark, just as Ric often marked her.

"I raised a daughter, Millie. I didn't do a very good job, but even so, she turned out to be a lovely young woman I am very proud of. If my daughter can still love me in spite of my mistakes, think how much Amanda will love you? You haven't had the chance to screw up!"

She felt his chest shaking and bit him again. "You're laughing at me?"

"Never, Millie. Not at you. With you."

"I certainly hope so." She slipped out of his embrace and rinsed off in the warm water. When she waded to shore, Millie shifted at the water's edge. She looked back over her shoulder in her most provocative wolven stare. *Again, Ric. I want you again.*

He shifted and lunged up out of the water, a huge male wolf in his prime. *You're insatiable. I love that in my bitch.*

I certainly hope so. I've got a lot of years to make up for.

This time when he took her, hard and fast in the soft meadow grass, Millie howled her release, howled for love and the pure joy of her existence.

"Before I talk to her or meet her, I want to do it, Bay. Not after."

Baylor looked up from the computer. "Meet who? Do what?"

Manda stood in the doorway, arms folded over her breasts, looking terribly determined about something. When Bay answered, she flashed him a look of pure exasperation.

Shannon laughed out loud. "He is so male, Manda." In a singsong voice she asked, "Need an interpreter, Baylor?"

Bay glared at his packmate across the table. "Jake. They're picking on me again." He'd been so involved in the search for Manda's twin, the meaning of Manda's conversation flew over his head.

Jake glanced up from his computer. "Before Manda meets or even talks to her mother, she wants to do the bonding thing with you. Or she did a few minutes ago. She may have changed her mind by now."

"She does?" Bay swiveled around. "You do?" She'd been so distant all day, so closed up since seeing the photo of Millie West, he'd decided to back off and give her space. Had he guessed that wrong, too?

Manda nodded. "I feel as if that's more important. It's something I have to do."

Bay shook his head. "No, sweetie. It's something you want to do, or you shouldn't do it at all. Are you really sure you're ready?"

She shook her head. "No. I'm not, actually, but I didn't think I was ready to have sex as a human, either. When we did that, it was great." She shrugged her shoulders. "I know I love you. I know you love me and you'd never do anything to hurt me."

Suddenly Bay was standing in front of Manda, but he honestly couldn't recall moving out of his chair. "I do love you and you're right. I would never hurt you." He leaned close and kissed her. Manda trembled when she kissed him back. He brushed her thick hair back from her eyes and looked into their amber depths.

Her thoughts were closed to him, shuttered behind those damned blocks she always kept in place. Bay pressed his forehead against hers. "Open your windows."

She giggled when he whispered, but her thoughts were suddenly there for him, her fear, her need, her simmering arousal that never seemed to fade. All for him.

Bay glanced over his shoulder. Both Jake and Shannon watched with unabashed curiosity. "We'll be back later. Don't wait up."

Ignoring their raised eyebrows, Bay took Manda's hand and walked out onto the front porch. The night was dark, but tiny pinpricks of light from fireflies sparkled in the surrounding forest.

Bay pulled Manda against him, fitting her perfect butt against his groin, and nuzzled his chin in her hair. He sniffed, catching a scent he'd not noticed earlier, the rich, ripe musky odor of a bitch in heat. Need slammed into him. He inhaled again, filling his nostrils with the most potent aphrodisiac he could imagine. He wondered if Manda knew she was reaching the most fertile time of her cycle?

The choice to reproduce was hers alone, but any male around couldn't help but be affected by her heady aroma.

He'd first experienced the effects when Shannon's cycle peaked shortly after Bay's first shift. He'd never experienced anything as intense as the sex the three of them shared during those times.

Had Jake noticed Manda's scent? Hell, Bay hadn't even noticed until just now. She must be coming into her cycle right now, while they stood together on the porch.

He took another deep breath and shuddered with a fresh spike of arousal. Would this make Manda more receptive to mating? He wasn't really sure how it affected a woman, but he couldn't help noticing how it affected him. Forcing his surging libido under control, Bay held Manda tightly against him and stared out toward the forest and the twinkling lights blinking in ethereal splendor against the dark.

Manda watched them as well, her back pressed tightly against his front, but she felt so fragile in his arms. He had to ask her, no matter how painful it would be should she change her mind. "Are you certain you're ready to mate, sweetie? You know I'm willing to wait."

He felt the warmth of a single tear on his wrist. Then another. Her thoughts filtered into his, confused, uncertain. *I don't want you to wait. I don't me to wait either, but I don't want it to be my decision. I just want it to happen. Too much has changed too quickly. It's like everything I believed in all my life has absolutely no basis in fact.*

She turned around and wiped the tears from her eyes with an angry sweep of her hand. Her voice cracked and broke on a sob. "I believe in you, Bay. You're solid and strong and you cared about me when no one else even saw me as human. You understood me then and you still loved me. I know you love me now. Sometimes knowing that is all that keeps me sane, but I want more. I want all of you. I want you in my head and my heart, I want to know that you're in every waking thought I have. Shannon told me what it's like with Jake. She told me how she never felt complete before they bonded."

She stopped, took a deep breath that sounded suspiciously like the woman who had been part wolf. Bay rubbed her arms, fully aware Manda needed to say this. She had to speak without any input from him. This was her time, her voice, and he loved her all the more with each word she said.

"Bay, I want that feeling and I want it with you, so whether I'm afraid or not doesn't matter. What matters is that we find the bond we're meant to have. If I fight you, ignore me. If you think I've changed my mind, I haven't. I can't willingly take you into my body as a wolf, but by God if that's the only way to bond with you, I'll do it. I'll do anything for you, Bay. I want you that much."

He pulled her into his arms and hugged her against him. She cried harder, the tears dampening his shirt, her trembling body and racing heart telling Bay exactly how hard it had been for her to give voice to her feelings. As he held her, her scent enveloped him and desire raged, potent and vital in his blood.

Could he mate with her, knowing how terribly she feared the act? How could he take her if she fought him and still make it an act of love, not aggression? Somehow, he would have to manage. Somehow, control the raging beast in his blood and find gentleness and patience. He took a deep breath and let it out, finding his center. Calming himself and his raging need.

Slowly now, with infinite care, he unbuttoned the flannel shirt she wore. Manda stood still, like a small child, and allowed him to undress her.

Her feet were bare so he unfastened the snap at her waist, lowered the zipper and slipped her pants down her long legs. She stepped out of them, placing one hand on his shoulder for balance. The only sound was the occasional sniff of her receding tears and the soft conversation in the background where Shannon and Jake talked about the ongoing search for Manda's twin.

When she was totally naked, Manda shifted, but she stood patiently, waiting for Bay. He undressed quickly, shifted and nudged her with his muzzle, then slowly walked down the stairs. Manda followed, and the two of them headed into the forest.

Her scent was stronger now, and the wolf responded. Bay quickly forced his bestial side under control and concentrated on Manda. He didn't sense fear so much as numbness. She had moved beyond fear into acquiescence, but he honored the mere fact she wanted to try, the fact she was willing to do anything to mate, to bond with him.

He wondered if he could ever show such bravery, knowing Manda's past, understanding the fears she'd hardly been able to acknowledge on her own. He kept walking, taking her farther into the forest than they'd gone before, deeper into woods that were totally unfamiliar to her.

Jake had brought Bay here in the past, running with him when they hunted or merely explored the acreage surrounding the cabin. There was a meadow they'd found. Surrounded by high granite cliffs with a long fall of water splashing into a dark, deep pool, it had struck both men with its simple beauty and left them with a sense of wonder, that such a place could remain hidden here in these ancient woods.

Bay picked up the pace and Manda followed. She ran beside him, her mind once again shuttered, her thoughts completely hidden. He tried to control the powerful tide of arousal racing through him, but Manda's scent was ripe and filled his nostrils with the musk of a bitch in heat, the powerful scent of estrus so rich and enticing he barely controlled his need to stop now, to mount her without warning.

By the time they reached the meadow, Bay's blood coursed through his veins like a river of fire. His cock surged hot and heavy, dripping already with the first milky drops of ejaculate. His breath rushed in and out of his lungs and he trembled with the effort it took to fight his raging need.

Manda stopped at the edge of the pool and shifted. Bay shifted as well, but he was still erect, still breathing hard with nostrils flared and eyes narrowed. She turned and studied him for a moment. "I can do this. I want to do this. All I ask is that you don't stop, no matter what. I'm afraid, but I'm not afraid of you, Bay. Just the act. The thought of a wolf penetrating my body, hurting me."

"I won't hurt you. I could never hurt you." He clenched his hands into fists and struggled for more control. His skin felt prickly, hot and cold by turns and he couldn't recall his cock ever being this hard or this ready. He hoped like hell he wasn't lying to her.

Manda smiled and sighed. "I know that, but the little girl who got raped doesn't quite believe you. You're going to have to show her how different it is when you love someone."

She shifted then, hitting the ground on four feet, her tail raised and ears laid back against her perfect wolven skull. Bay kept his human form. He knelt beside Manda and wrapped his arms around her neck, nuzzling the thick fur and rubbing behind her ears. Her scent tantalized him and made his heart pound harder, his erection grow longer.

Manda licked his cheek and watched him out of amber eyes.

He ran his hands over her perfect wolven body, sliding his fingers through the thick, coarse hair. So perfect, this body. As perfect as the human body she'd just shifted out of, but her heart was the same as it had always been. Her courage was the same. He thought of how courageous she'd been to keep on when all the world saw her as a freak. He tried to tell her this, his mind coming up against her barriers once again, so he spoke the words aloud.

"There is no other woman like you, Manda. No woman as brave, as powerful, as perfect. No matter what you've had to face in your life, you've survived. You've done more then just survive. You've come through everything stronger than before. There aren't many women, or men, strong enough, courageous enough, to keep on when faced with the kind of terrible things you've been through. I love you. I want you to be my mate, my bonded mate, for all time. You honor me, that you want this as well. I can only hope and pray that once we link, your barriers will disappear forever." He pressed his head against her shoulder. "Ya know, I'm getting so tired of asking you to open your windows. Maybe they'll stay open for me after we bond."

She whined, a small, nervous cry. He wrapped his arms around her and buried his face in the thick ruff at the back of her neck. His cock rested between her hind legs and he hugged Manda close to him, but for just this moment, Bay locked Manda out of his mind. He shifted, thrust his hips hard and fast and entered her, his wolven cock sliding swiftly into her narrow channel, the engorged gland at the base locking them together before Manda had time to realize what he'd done, much less panic.

She turned her head, snarled and bared her teeth. Her ears lay flat against her skull and she tried to twist away, but it was too late. His forelegs held her tightly at the throat. His cock with its swollen knot locked their bodies. With a final growl, Manda could only lower her head and accept.

Bay opened his thoughts and flooded her with love. With his praise for her courage, her perfect body, her loving heart and bravery when she had so much to fear.

Thrusting hard and fast, he felt her body responding,

felt her barriers softening, falling away to leave her mind open and accepting. He kept up the steady barrage of positive, loving thoughts. Manda planted her feet in the soft turf and gave up all pretense of aggression.

This was unlike any sexual experience Bay had ever had. His body rippled with the power of each thrust and he felt her response in the tightening of muscles around his cock, in the rich, musky she-wolf scent that enveloped him in a rising tide of lust.

Manda's thoughts skittered at the edges of his mind and he felt her subconscious need to keep the barriers locked in place, but her arousal grew with each powerful thrust and the walls slipped. Bay sensed the first cracks in barriers even Manda didn't know she had.

He stepped through into a nightmare of images, a labyrinth of twists and turns, of darkness and light, her memories flashing through his brain, downloading as if from one program to another and bringing with them all the agony, all the fear she'd lived with for most of her life.

He experienced her parents' death, her mother's brutal rape, and felt her absolute terror when the villagers found her in the morning. He saw the fear on their faces when they first saw her, knew her confusion when those she'd known as friends turned away in horror.

So fast, the images, so many things but he glimpsed one that made him pause, a face among a lifetime of faces that sent shivers along his spine. He made note, remembered and moved on, past the horrible treatment in the clinics, the rapes and molestations she endured, the few friendly souls who honestly wanted to help but had no idea where to start. He remembered the names and faces of each one who had ever hurt her or brought her pain, and promised himself he would someday hunt them down.

Every one of them.

It might have been hours. Was, in reality, only minutes but it left both of them exhausted, falling to the ground, bodies still linked. Manda blinked and stared at Bay out of eyes filled with self-knowledge, with new information of his past as well as a different understanding of her own.

There was a new confidence in the way she tilted her head, the way her ears pricked forward. Then suddenly, without warning, she shifted and the wolf lay tied to the woman, his cock still pulsing deep inside her sex.

"Don't," she said, and she sounded breathless as if her heart pounded every bit as hard as his when she touched his shoulder with her fingertips. "Don't shift. I need to do this. I want to feel you inside me, just this way. The other time with the wolf, it hurt terribly. I was terrified and I thought I was going to die. I love you Bay, whether you're human or wolf. I don't ever want to be afraid again. Never." She tilted her head and smiled at him. "Besides, this doesn't hurt at all." She laughed and shook her head, glancing at the point where his furry body pressed against her sleek one. She giggled. "Nope. It actually feels really good."

She brushed her hand over his shoulder, tangled her fingers in his thick coat and pressed her hips closer to his body. He felt his cock twitch against her womb and knew the bulbous knot subsided. Even though he was small enough now to pull out of her, Bay waited.

Manda wrapped her arms around him and lay beside him in the cool grass. Her top leg looped over his side, the other was trapped beneath his body. They stayed that way for a long time. Bay had never known such contentment. There was a sense of another in his thoughts and he recognized Manda's presence. He wondered if she felt him in her mind, and without asking, he knew it was exactly the same way for her.

As he lay there beside her, Bay gave himself permission to think about what he'd learned during their link. Slowly, carefully, he retraced the images in Manda's memory, searching for a closer look at her savior, the man she said had rescued her. She'd called him Papa B.

Bay knew and hated him by another name. Papa B was no savior. Another of Manda's childhood beliefs was about to disappear, and Bay wondered if she'd found his memories of the man during their link. Did she know how much grief he'd brought to the Chanku?

Secretary of Defense Milton Bosworth might be dead, but his twisted legacy of hate lingered on. Bay raised his wolven head and stared into Manda's eyes. He watched as recognition dawned and her shutters slammed down in her mind.

No matter. They were linked, now. Without any effort at all, Baylor shifted. It was the man, not the wolf who opened the barriers Manda had just dropped into place. Opened them wide and shared what he knew of the creature who had hoped to control the Chanku, the one who had kidnapped Ulrich Mason and planned to develop a breeding farm for shapeshifters.

Angry, to think Manda had been this animal's captive and pawn for so many years, he let her see everything he knew. Showed her the horrible deeds her so-called savior had been guilty of, and when she collapsed in near hysterics, sobbing as if her heart would break, he held her close and called himself every kind of bastard under the sun. *It wasn't your fault,* sick to think he'd taken his anger out on Manda. *It was his, sweetie. All his fault.*

Bay wasn't sure if she heard him, but her pain cut him to the core. When Manda's tears finally subsided and she let him into her darkest memories, Bay cried with her, rocking her in his arms, his tears falling in the thick sweep of her hair.

Chapter 14

Bay sat alone on the swing on the front porch, staring out into the dark forest. He should have been celebrating tonight, not sitting here calling himself every kind of fool. He'd finally bonded with Manda, found his true soul mate in that most perfect young woman, but all he could think of was the anguish their bond had brought to her.

She slept now, with the aid of a couple of sleeping pills Shannon had found for her. Bay had barely gotten her home on his own. She'd been afraid to shift, afraid to face Jake and Shannon, afraid to link with Bay.

Jake sat down on one side, Shannon on the other, but Bay took scant comfort in either their sympathy or their love.

"What the fuck happened tonight?" Jake's arm resting solidly across Bay's shoulders took some of the sting out of his question.

"I screwed up. I lost control and totally screwed up."

"You mean with sex? I sensed she was coming into heat and wondered about your control. You didn't force sex on . . ."

"No. Not that." He sighed. They were his packmates. He had to tell the truth. Let them know what a bastard he'd been to the woman he loved. "I'll admit, her scent was really intoxicating, but she was ready. More than ready. The sex was great, the link amazing, but the mating bond . . . well, it's total. Some of the things I learned about Manda were so awful, so utterly horrific . . ." He shuddered. "I didn't handle it well. Not at all."

Shannon rested her head on his shoulder. "Okay. What happened? We need to know if we're going to be able to help you fix whatever went wrong."

"You've heard Manda talk about Papa B? The guy who saved her? The man she revered as a saint? It was Milton Bosworth."

"Holy shit!" Jake sat back and stared at Bay. "Our Milton Bosworth? The guy you worked for? The bastard who tried to have Shannon kidnapped for breeding?"

Bay nodded at Jake. "One and the same. My old boss. It makes sense. He must have learned about the Chanku through Manda. I always wondered how he found out about them. When he rescued her, he must have figured there had to be more just like her. When he couldn't find them at first, he decided to breed his own population. He wanted an army."

"Manda?" Shannon's harsh whisper spoke volumes.

"Yeah. The rapes that Manda blamed on lab technicians and other employees? All orchestrated by Bosworth. Even the wolf, though I don't know what the fuck he was trying to prove with that. She managed to block out so much—even surgeries. Bosworth used hormone therapy to force egg production and Manda went through numerous procedures over the years when they tried to harvest her ova for fertilization."

"Were they successful? Are there children out there we don't know about?"

"No, Jake. Thank goodness. Manda subconsciously managed to inhibit any eggs from maturing. She was wolf enough for that process to work, but until the bond, she didn't remember any of this. She's survived a lifetime of horror by blocking memories she couldn't deal with. She had to trust somebody, and unfortunately, she chose Bosworth, which meant she had to blame everyone else for the bad things that happened. I screwed up her entire defense mechanism when our bond forced open all those shutters she'd managed to keep closed. It explains why she constantly blocked all of us from mindtalking. She was terrified of letting her secrets out, not only because she wanted to hide them from us, but because, subconsciously, she knew she couldn't handle them."

"We shouldn't leave her alone." Shannon stood up. "Knowing Manda, she's blaming herself for everything awful that ever happened and probably thinks you hate her."

"What?" Bay stood up. "Why would she think that?"

Jake stood as well. "C'mon, bro. Never argue with Shannon. She's always right."

Bay slanted a quick look at Shannon, waiting for her usual quick comeback.

She merely shrugged her shoulders. "He's not cracking wise, Bay. I am always right. Come with me, boys. All is not lost."

Manda lay alone in the big bed and thought about all that had happened tonight. She'd never known such joy, such a sense of belonging, of being loved, as she had when Bay's mind linked to hers. She'd seen his past, his memories, and truly understood the good and loving parts of the man that made up the whole.

His childhood hadn't been any better than hers. His own father had murdered his mother. His sisters had disappeared for years and he still celebrated the fact he'd found them again.

He was a man of great conviction, of honor and integrity. Knowing that, she'd taken his wolven body inside hers without fear, had found such amazing sexual satisfaction she already wanted to do it again. That wasn't going to happen. Not now.

Seeing Papa B in Bay's mind still made her tremble. Bay's memories of his old employer, so riddled with hate, had been such a shock she'd swept them aside in the beginning, just the way she'd learned to do with all bad things. They'd immediately gone into that part of her mind even Bay couldn't access. A dark, hidden corner Manda always stayed clear of.

Now, though, Bay had blown the cover wide open, turned all those horrible memories out into the light where there was no hiding them. Seeing them all together like that . . . well, it was too much. Too awful. She'd not realized how many truly awful things had been hiding in there.

She'd had no idea what a terrible person she was, either, to have been protecting a monster like Milton Bosworth all these years. He hadn't helped her. No, he'd used her to get closer to others of her kind. Because of Manda, Ulrich Mason had been kidnapped, Shannon put at risk, and who knew how many of Bosworth's people killed over the years. If he'd never saved Manda, he wouldn't have known anything at all about the Chanku. All of her friends would have been safe.

Even more important, Bay would have been safe. He wouldn't be living with the guilt of hiding bodies or covering up those killings. The men he'd killed would still be alive.

They'd only been following Papa B's orders, after all. They would all have been a lot better off if the insurgents had just killed Manda, along with her parents.

Only they weren't her parents. Only God knew who her real father was, and some woman in Colorado was her mother, only she obviously hadn't wanted Manda and that had been the start of everything, hadn't it?

She sighed. That wasn't true. Her real mother hadn't

wanted to give her babies up. Not really. At least that's what she told everyone. How could Manda know that was true?

Nothing made sense anymore. She wished she hadn't taken those pills from Shannon. Her thoughts were so confused right now and she'd be thinking more clearly without a brain dulled by sleeping pills that weren't helping her sleep. Somehow, she needed to get out of here. She had to free Baylor from any commitments he'd made to her. It wasn't fair to tie him to a woman who, no matter how she looked, would always be a freak.

Manda stared into the darkness and, without thinking, shifted into the wolf. She felt better this way. More complete, and she knew she was faster on four legs . . . if she only knew where to go. Wondering how to plan an escape when she hadn't a clue what to do, Manda curled into a tight little ball in the darkness and wondered how she could possibly face the man she loved ever again. Even worse, how could she ever go on without him in her life?

Manda awakened slowly. Her mind felt foggy and she was so wonderfully warm, blanketed by warm, furry bodies on all sides. Blinking slowly awake, she realized she was surrounded by wolves.

Shannon and Jake penned her in on either side, and Bay snuggled into the spot where her nose met her tail. His chin rested on her hip. She couldn't escape if she wanted, not with the three of them so close.

But why? Didn't they hate her? She'd brought them nothing but grief.

Bay raised his head first. *I love you. How could you possibly think I hate you?*

But . . .

No buts. Forget everything. It was all part of a past you couldn't control. You've got a whole future ahead of you now.

Shannon stretched and snuggled close to Manda's side. *He's right, you know. We've all got things in our pasts we're less than proud of.*

Jake popped up on Manda's other side. *Well, you might. I, on the other hand, am now and always have been, perfect.*

Yeah. Right. Shannon huffed loudly. *Manda, ignore him. He's also always been a pain in the ass. Just ask Bay.*

Jake popped up again. *Did I hurt your ass, Baylor? I was really careful, and it's such a cute, tight little ass.*

Nope. Ass feels great. In fact, if you're not busy later . . .

He's busy all right. Shannon glared at Jake. *However, I've got some new toys, Bay, and I'm more than willing to try them out on your ass . . .*

Jake popped back into the conversation. *Wait a minute. What about me?*

What about you?

Manda felt like her head might fly off her shoulders, whipping back and forth to catch the banter going on around her. Why were they joking? Weren't they mad at her? Wasn't she the cause of all their problems?

No!

She flattened herself to the bed and her ears slapped down against her skull. She'd never had all three of them yell at once. The mental shout was a bit overwhelming.

Bay was the first to shift. Shannon and Jake followed suit, and they stared at her until Manda shifted as well.

She sat there in the middle of the bed to see what would come next. If they weren't angry with her, then what were they?

"Worried. Sweetie, Bay, Jake, and I are just worried about you." Shannon rubbed Manda's arm, concern obvious in her expression and touch. "We love you. You are, for better or for worse, a part of our pack. What hurts you, hurts all of us. Somehow, we need to help you make the hurt go away."

"Oh."

Bay took her hand as he scooted back against the headboard. He dragged Manda onto his lap. "I love you. I am so sorry I forced you to see things you weren't ready for. I wish there were a way to make you understand how badly I felt when I realized . . ."

Manda pressed her fingers over his lips and looked at each one of them, then back at Bay. She felt his thoughts even as he spoke the words. He really did love her. They all did. They didn't blame her for anything. She felt something blossom deep inside, an awareness that hadn't existed before. A sense of worth, of her own value as a survivor, as a person worthy of Bay's love. Of Shannon's and Jake's as well.

Each of them accepted her. The only one with the problem accepting Manda appeared to be Manda herself. She smiled and shook her head. Bay was right. It was over.

Well, not everything. There was something poking her in the butt and it wasn't her tail. She slipped around on Bay's lap and slid down his long legs until she was eye level with his cock. "I'm not the only one who had a rough night." She glanced at Shannon and caught the twinkle in her eye. "I think Bay needs some attention to make him feel better."

Shannon nodded. "Oh, I agree. Whole-heartedly."

"What about me?"

Manda smiled at Jake. "You can help us take care of Bay, too."

"That's not quite what I meant." Jake sat back on his heels, but he was obviously enjoying himself. His cock slapped up against his belly and he idly stroked himself.

Manda's head filled with their feelings. Her bond with Bay obviously opened her to the naturally comfortable link among the packmates. She'd never imagined this sense of unity, the feeling of belonging, of family.

Nor had she realized the intense arousal with three

other interactive libidos jockeying for attention. Most powerful of all was Bay's. She looked down and saw she'd wrapped her fingers around his erection without even realizing it. It seemed perfectly natural to lean down and take him in her mouth, but the minute her rump tilted up, Jake moved into position behind her.

She'd not done this before, not ever taken a man this way, but she felt Bay's encouragement, sensed his approval when Jake found some lubricant and began slowly massaging between her legs, using his long fingers to spread the cool gel from her clit to her ass.

She wasn't certain exactly what Jake's intentions were, but his touch was mesmerizing. She had trouble concentrating on Bay's cock and she couldn't keep track of Jake's fingers, of where they would penetrate next. His soft strokes and gentle dips over her clit, between her vaginal lips and even slipping through the tight ring of muscle at her butt had a hypnotic effect. Slow and easy, building her arousal at a snail's pace with the lightest, least invasive of touches.

Shannon knelt over Bay and parted her thighs on either side of his head. He found her with lips and tongue and shared Shannon's flavors with Manda. She felt his tongue between her own legs as he traced Shannon's clit and then dipped inside to taste.

Manda shared the tastes, the textures of her packmate even as she explored Bay's cock with her tongue, her lips and her teeth. So caught up in both Bay and Shannon's sensations, she hardly felt Jake's initial breach of her tight sphincter muscle.

He entered her first with one finger, then two, stretching her slowly and carefully. She waited for the expected pain, but there was nothing beyond pure, unadulterated sensation. She had no idea she had so many nerves there!

Once his fingers had softened her for penetration, Jake replaced his fingers with the head of his cock. Slowly, so carefully, he pressed deeply into Manda. She shared the way it felt with all of them, the sharp sting as his cock breached the restrictive ring of muscle, the initial pressure followed by the soothing slide of smooth male muscle finding entry deep inside her body.

Shannon cried out as Bay brought her to climax with his mouth. Manda knew her shared images had tipped Shannon over the edge and she smiled around her mouthful of Bay's cock when Shannon rolled away to one side. Manda felt the rippling shivers of Shannon's orgasm as if from a great distance and it pushed her own level of arousal up another notch. Now, she concentrated on Bay's flavors and Jake's slow but steady penetration. His balls pressed tightly against her perineum and she knew he'd filled her completely.

Expecting pain, she was amazed by the sensuality of the act, the trust and love that went into this deliciously sinful penetration. Jake wrapped his arms around her waist and lifted Manda, pulling her close to him as he sprawled backwards on a pile of pillows.

Bay turned and knelt between both their legs and Manda suddenly realized his intentions. He planned to enter her at the same time as Jake! Before she had a chance to even acknowledge her fear, Shannon was in Manda's mind, sharing the amazing sensation of two men loving her at once, easing Manda's fears and raising her level of arousal even higher.

Instead of fear, she looked on Bay now with longing. She wanted him inside her, wanted the delicious fullness of her two beloved men. Jake held perfectly still, but his hands cupped Manda's breasts and his breath was warm against her neck. She felt enveloped by him, protected and loved.

Bay leaned close and touched her clit with his tongue, then licked gently between her swollen folds. She arched into his mouth, slipping just a bit free of Jake. He lifted his hips and filled her again and his fingers caught her sensitive nipples, pinching and twisting, holding her still when Bay licked her once more.

Then Bay took his cock in one hand and slowly aimed it between her legs. Manda felt the smooth crown sweep over her wet and almost painfully sensitive clit, then the pressure from the broad head poised at her entrance. Teasing, rubbing slowly back and forth, Bay made her wait for him.

She bit her lips hard and tasted blood, but it kept her from screaming through this equally wonderful and horrible anticipation. Bay's soft laughter when he realized just how anxious Manda felt had her ready to curse him. She wanted someone to move. Jake or Bay, it didn't matter so long as someone took her off this precipice.

Bay lifted her thighs over his and pressed forward. She felt the slow, steady slide of his cock and wondered if there'd be room for both men, wondered if Jake and Bay felt each other deep inside her body.

And then she knew. Images and sensations spilled into her mind. She was Jake, gritting his teeth against the amazing sensation of Bay's cock gliding slowly along his full length, separated from his solid erection by nothing more than a thin membrane. Just as quickly, Manda was Bay, pushing slowly past Jake's cock, feeling Jake's length and breadth and Manda's rippling muscles and lush heat. When he finally touched the hard mouth of her womb, he stopped and held perfectly still, as if spending a moment to absorb the myriad sensations.

Then he began to move. Slowly. Surely. Out. Then back in, as deep as he could go. Manda felt stuffed full, her body shivering in reaction to Jake's anal penetration and Bay's slow but steady thrusts inside her sex. Bay rocked back on his heels and, as if they'd choreographed their action, Jake pressed forward until Manda rested between the two, her legs wrapped around Bay's waist, her body filled front and back. Shannon lay beside them and watched, a lazy smile on her face, her fingers stroking between her own thighs.

There was a dreamlike quality to their lovemaking. Manda had never imagined enjoying sex with one man, much less two, but she couldn't recall ever feeling so loved, so content, so satisfied with her body and her feelings.

She arched her back, driving Jake deeper inside, forcing Bay's cock once more against the mouth of her womb. Taking control in her own way, taking her pleasure on her own terms. When her climax raced throughout her body, spearing both Jake and Bay with its power, Manda cried out. She felt herself floating, lifted up by the power of Jake and Bay's simultaneous orgasm, joined by Shannon as she tumbled with them, freefalling into pleasure, bodies shivering in reaction, trembling and shaking, all of them laughing at the miracle that made them one.

Jake was the one who left first, slipping easily out of Manda's body. He returned moments later with a soft, damp cloth and bathed Manda, washing her intimately in an act so personal she should have felt embarrassed.

She felt only love. Shannon lay beside her, stroking her hair and whispering soft, soothing words as meaningless as they were comforting. Bay lay along Manda's other side, his fingers twisting gently in the triangle of blond hair between her thighs, but his mind was filled with love and he shared every thought, every feeling with the pack.

Manda's body rippled with the aftereffects of her climax. She'd never felt anything quite so powerful, so emotionally shattering as the shared orgasm with those who loved her in spite of her background—or maybe because of it?

Did it matter? Bay, Shannon, and Jake accepted her, loved her, wanted her. The sense of acceptance was so alien, she might have doubted its truth if not for the shared thoughts, freely given among them.

Bay wanted to make love again. Jake needed a nap. Shannon was idly thinking about what to fix for dinner. It was like listening to a series of conversations on various levels, understanding each one without really feeling a need to respond.

Though her body was definitely responding to Bay. He shifted. The big wolf jumped off the bed and wandered into the kitchen. She heard him lapping water out of the bowl they kept filled beside the refrigerator. The *tickety tack* of his claws on the wood floor told her he was returning.

Bay jumped back up on the bed, licked Shannon's shoulder, nudged Jake out of the way and curled up at the foot of the bed. Manda dozed, surrounded by warmth and love.

She awakened to the warm, wet sweep of a long tongue between her legs. Jake and Shannon were nowhere to be seen. Bay, furry ears pricked forward, eyes half closed in somnolent pleasure, lay on his side between her thighs. His cold, wet nose pressed against her clit, his tongue swept slowly in and out, deep inside her amazingly sensitive pussy. He might have been half asleep, sprawled between her legs, looking so relaxed as he licked her.

It felt decidedly decadent, lying here with her legs spread and Baylor's long wolven tongue slowly turning her into a molten puddle of need, but once again Manda felt she'd taken another step forward.

She'd hated her body for so long. She'd hidden her past along with her anger and frustration, and lived a mere shadow of what life should be. Now, lying here with another climax slowly building deep inside, accepting Baylor in whatever guise he chose to love her, Manda felt another barrier fall by the wayside.

Bay licked harder, faster. The more he licked, the more sensitive she grew to the rough surface of his tongue, the sharp tip curling against the inner walls of her sex. He rolled over on his belly and his tongue dove deeper, licking deep inside her vaginal walls, finding her clit on the way out, laving her from ass to pubic mound and then driving deep inside her once again. He found her clit and circled it roughly, nipping at her with his sharp teeth, holding her legs down with his broad paws.

Trapped and loving it, she felt the curl of heat spike. A fiery blast of sensation streaked from breasts to womb to clit, and she cried out, doubled over and grabbed Bay by the thick ruff around his neck, her hips pumping in sync with her body's contractions.

He shifted. She held her mate, his broad shoulders clasped in her hands, his lips and chin glistening with her fluids. He leaned forward and kissed her. Manda wrapped her arms around his neck and held on for all she was worth.

* * *

"We should have called." Millie twisted her hands in her lap and stared out the window at the forest rushing by. "I should have talked to her first."

Ulrich flashed her an indulgent grin. "They know we're coming. Manda's ready and it seemed pointless to hang around when I know damned well both of you need to see each other."

"Well, there is that." Millie looked down at the photo in her lap. The beautiful young blonde could have been Millie, some twenty-five years earlier. Had she ever been that young?

She looked at the handsome man beside her and thought, does it matter? She'd never known this kind of happiness when she was a young woman. She wouldn't trade the life she had now for anything, unless it would have been to make it easier for Amanda.

The poor girl had lived through hell, but according to Baylor, Shannon, and Jake, her daughter had come out of it all with a most amazing strength and a powerful sense of exactly who and what she was.

The road narrowed. Ulrich glanced at the hand-drawn map and grinned at Millie. "Less than a mile to go. Jake says they're waiting on the porch."

"You can pick him up already?"

Ulrich nodded. "We've been packmates for a long time. I can't read Baylor or Shannon, but Jake's clear as a bell. He said Manda's alternating between tears and giggles, so I guess she's as nervous as you are."

Millie merely glared at him, but she opened her thoughts and wondered if she could hear Jake, too.

Mother? Mom? I feel you. Can you hear me?

Amanda? Millie's eyes filled with tears. Amanda had called her Mother. She'd never dreamed . . .

Yes! Ohmygod! Mom! I can't believe it! I can't wait to see you. I'm on the porch. I hear your car!

They rounded a narrow bend in the road and the cabin came into view. Sunlight glittered off the windows and four tall, beautiful strangers waited on the front porch, all of them smiling. Waving.

Millie didn't know any of them, but she recognized Amanda immediately. The car was still rolling to a stop when she threw open the door and jumped out. Manda was running down the stairs, arms spread wide, blond hair flying. Both of them were crying and laughing, the center of attention with Ulrich, Baylor, Shannon, and Jake surrounding them.

She couldn't hold her tight enough, couldn't stand not seeing her, but when Millie finally released Amanda, her eyes were so filled with tears all she saw was a blur. Wiping at her eyes and laughing, Millie touched her daughter's hair, her cheek, her shoulder.

She was beautiful. She was sobbing and laughing as

hard as Millie and there was just too much emotion, too much feeling to express. They stared at one another, a lifetime of loss and loneliness forgiven in an instant. Then, as if by common assent, though not a word had been exchanged, the six of them stripped off their clothing and shifted.

It was so much easier this way. More elemental.

Long shadows spread across the meadow as the pack of wolves raced toward the forest. The deer and rabbits were safe. There would be no hunt tonight, no need to kill.

Tonight they ran together, the bond of the pack strong and true. When they finally reached the highest point, a rocky promontory with a view that stretched for miles, six muzzles pointed skyward, six voices blended, a cacophony of howls and barks that said so much more than mere human language could ever convey.

Millie glanced at the beautiful she-wolf who was her daughter and felt an almost painful sense of joy. Somewhere out there, her son remained to be found. Ulrich would find him. She trusted him. He would do exactly as he'd promised. Millie turned to her mate and found the perfect pitch to blend her voice with his.

Epilogue

"There's a nice mattress in the camper. Sure you don't want to . . . ?"

Adam Wolf shook his head and reached for the door handle. The pickup with its dented camper shell rumbled and smoked. He could have told her the tailpipe was about ready to fall off, but that wasn't his concern.

The buxom blonde in the driver's seat raised an eyebrow. "Well, then . . ." She sighed. "Hope you don't mind if I drop you off here. That's my turnoff." She nodded toward a narrow side road angling away from the two-lane highway, then reached out and pressed her warm palm against his thigh. "We coulda had a real good time."

"I'm sure we could have." He smiled and thought of the woman of his dreams . . . if he could call her a woman. Where was she tonight? He glanced at the dark blue sky. Night was falling and it was damned cold for June. He felt like some kind of fool, turning down what was so freely offered, but . . . not tonight. "Well, thanks. I appreciate the lift . . . and the view." He winked, smiled and nodded in the direction of her well-exposed cleavage.

The blonde tittered and held her fingers over her ample bosom, emphasizing the dark cleft between her full breasts rather than hiding anything. Adam grabbed his duffle out of the bed of the truck and stepped back from the road. The blonde waved and her truck skidded when she punched the gas, fishtailed into the turn and disappeared down the narrow country lane spewing black exhaust out of the damaged pipe.

"Well, fuck." Adam looked both directions along the highway and started walking in the same direction he'd been traveling. He could have gone either way. It wasn't like he actually had a destination in mind. If he hadn't figured out the woman was going home to a husband and kids, he might be sleeping in a warm bed between warm thighs, his head pillowed on those exceptionally warm breasts. Just his luck to get a ride from a gal with commitments, whether she recognized them or not.

He heard a car coming up behind him and automatically stuck out his thumb without turning around. Looking anxious never helped, but he was beginning to shiver beneath his lightweight jacket.

The classic Ford pickup that passed him looked absolutely cherry, but it sounded like shit. Adam recognized the make and model immediately despite the new black paint with the immaculate chrome bumper and darkened windows. It was a 1951 Ford F-1, a beautiful old machine that appeared lovingly restored, but something under the hood knocked and sputtered and then just quietly died. When the vehicle coasted to a stop some fifty yards ahead of him and well off the side of the road, Adam wasn't sure if the driver had stopped on purpose or not. Just in case someone was offering a ride, he trotted the short distance and reached for the passenger door.

It opened before he grabbed the handle. Adam bit back a grin. The driver certainly wasn't what he'd expected. His skin was dark, his hair slicked down and perfectly combed. He wore an immaculate navy blue suit, a far cry from the typical rancher in this part of the state.

"Hello," he said, in perfectly clipped English. "I would

offer you a ride but my vehicle appears to have chosen this spot to quit working. You're welcome to wait inside where it's warm and dry, however, Mr. . . ."

"Wolf. Adam Wolf. Thank you, but it's dry out here."

The little man nodded and smiled. "Not for long."

Before Adam could frame an answer, the first drops of rain caught him. He glanced at the sky that had been cloudless just minutes ago. Black clouds roiled overhead. The little man scooted back to the driver's seat. Adam tossed his bag on the floor and climbed inside the beautiful old truck. Stranger things had happened in his thirty-six years. He leaned back against the rich leather upholstery. At least he'd be warm and dry while he waited out the storm.

When the rain ended, he could always take a look at the engine and see what was wrong. Pulling his baseball cap down over his eyes, Adam settled back in his seat to wait out the storm.

The driver's voice intruded. "Did you say your name was Adam Wolf?"

Adam raised his cap and glanced to his left. "Yep. That's me."

"Fascinating."

He paused so long, Adam sat up and stared at the man.

"Mr. Wolf, do you know a woman named Amanda Smith?"

The question hung in the air between them. Amanda Smith. *Manda?* The same Manda who had haunted his dreams for over twenty years, the woman he'd never met, who had directed him with nightly visions so bleak, dreams so compelling, he'd dropped out of school and hit the road in a fruitless search to find her a good fifteen years ago?

Couldn't be. The coincidence was too bizarre. The odds this man knew something about the woman who had haunted him for so long were astronomical.

What if . . . ? The dreams were gone. They'd disappeared from his life mere days ago, vanishing as quickly as they had first appeared, leaving him with a lifetime of questions.

Adam had nowhere to go for answers . . . Once again he contemplated the coincidence. He'd never been one to believe in fate, but he wasn't an idiot, either.

"I might," he said, staring fiercely at the little man. "What's it to you?"

Turn the page for a sizzling preview of
MAKE ME SCREAM!

Coming soon from Aphrodisia!

Chapter 1

Hip deep in drug dealers, rogue cops, prostitutes and assorted bad guys, aspiring mystery writer Devon McCloud frowned and tried to recapture his train of thought.

The PI hero of Devon's book had just discovered the lead witness for the crime family hiding naked in his bed.

The woman stroked my impressive erection.

"Are you going to kick me out?" the buxom blonde asked with a sultry pout.

"Something just came up," I replied.

"I can help you with that," she whispered, stroking my length.

"Put you mouth where your money is," I hissed in a breath when she took my advice. Her mouth closed over me, practically swallowing me whole.

Okay . . . now what? The flashing cursor on the screen of his laptop mocked him.

Out in the courtyard of the little beachfront apartment community he managed as his day job, voices rumbled. His fellow tenants were starting their nightly celebration early.

Above the laughter and conversations, a deep bark

sounded, followed by the shrill voice of his neighbor, Francyne Anderson. Devon's mouth quirked. Petunia, Francyne's one-hundred-and-fifty-pound rottweiler, must be joining the party tonight.

Deliberately shutting out the noise in the courtyard, Devon narrowed his gaze at the flashing cursor.

"C'mon, Mac, be brilliant. What would Trent say?" Trent was the hero of his work-in-progress, *Darkness Becomes Her*. A PI with the prerequisite heart of gold, Trent not only got all the bad guys, he got all the girls.

Devon sighed and rocked back in his desk chair. Maybe that was the problem with finishing the book. Trent had scored approximately every five to seven pages. He, Devon, hadn't been laid in months. Heading way too close to being a year. He didn't have the time, which made him an even more pathetic loser. Who doesn't have time for sex?

Voices rose in the courtyard.

Him, that's who didn't have time for sex. Devon Edward McCloud. With working on his novels by night, writing catalog copy for sex toys by day—which oddly did not help his lack-of-sex problem—while attempting to maintain some sense of normalcy with the rowdy tenants of the Surfside Villas apartment complex, who had the time or energy for sex?

Male laughter vibrated his walls. Opportunity wouldn't hurt either. Of the eight apartments in the old complex, five were occupied by men (six, counting himself), the seventh by a female at least eighty if she was a day. And one vacant unit. Not a lot of opportunity.

He'd just returned to the seedier side of his imagination when a knock sounded on his door. Judging by the lightness of it, his deductive reasoning told him, it was a female knock. Since Francyne never knocked, it could mean only one thing: someone inquiring about the vacancy.

He growled and saved his work before closing his computer. Obviously the intruder could not tell time. The sign on his door clearly stated office hours. Said hours ended—he glanced at the old school clock on his wall—almost two hours ago.

He threw open his door.

The short, blonde woman in a denim miniskirt and yellow tank top hopped back with a squeak.

"Yes?" No point in being polite. Once Blondie got a look at the group sitting around the fire pit in the courtyard, she'd realize this was not the place for her.

She swallowed and licked soft-looking pink lips. "Is-is . . . I mean, are you the manager, the person I need to see about renting an apartment?"

He turned to look meaningfully at the manager sign on his door. "Looks like it, doesn't it?" He tapped the posted hours. "But I'm closed. Office hours don't start again until nine tomorrow morning. Come back then, if you're still interested."

"But I need a place tonight!"

He paused midslam. "Try a motel."

"They're all full. At least, all the close ones." She looked down at her painted toenails peeking out from a pair of ridiculously high-heeled sandals.

He tried not to speculate how short she would be without the heels. He tried not to notice her Barbie-doll build. He also tried not to appreciate the way the firelight from the courtyard played in the silky strands of her blond hair. He failed miserably on all counts.

She looked back up at him, and he forced himself not to break eye contact with her baby blues. She blinked, her long eyelashes creating spidery shadows on her smooth cheeks.

"Please?" Her shiny lower lip gave the faintest of quivers.

"Fine." He spouted off the price of rent, and she nodded. "Don't you want to see it first?"

"No, I'm sure it's fine. The sign said it's furnished?"

He nodded, sure this was a very bad idea but at a loss as to how he could turn her down. Her resulting smile sent a flash of awareness streaking through him. Or . . . did men have hot flashes?

He cleared his throat and stepped back, opening the door wide. "Okay, may as well come on in and get the paperwork out of the way so we can all get some sleep tonight."

"Jamie Cartwright," Blonde Barbie said as she stepped in, extending her hand.

A low growl emanated from behind the recliner. "Killer!" he warned, glaring at the pair of glowing eyes visible from below the edge of the chair.

The woman gasped and jumped back, eyes wide, hand at her throat.

Reality dawned. "No! Not me," he explained, pointing to the eyes. "My dog. That's his name. Killer. I'm Devon. Not killer." He forced a smile. No one would guess he worked with words for a living. He shoved his hand toward her. "Hi."

She took a tentative step forward and allowed him to shake her small hand. "Hi." She looked in his dog's general direction. "What kind of dog is Killer? Is he dangerous?"

"I'll let you be the judge of that." Grinning, he slapped his thigh.

After Devon-not-killer released her hand, Jamie edged toward the door. Did she really want to rent a place with a killer dog in residence?

At that moment, a ball of white fluff pulled itself out from under the dark leather chair to prance toward them. It looked like it had originally been a Pomeranian before something awful had happened to its face.

Its right eye hung lower than the left, and the poor thing appeared to be missing its bottom jaw. Its pink tongue hung out of its face. Seeing her, it stopped and made a low gurgling growl and then said, "Lark! Lark!"

"He's getting better with his barking," Devon said. "At least now it sounds like he's trying to bark." He squatted and rubbed the dog's shaggy white head. "You're getting better, aren't you, pal?"

In response, Killer raised his nose, tongue lolling down the front of his throat, obviously in doggie-hero worship.

"What happened to his jaw?" she asked Devon-not-Killer.

"He got in a fight. He's lucky all he lost was part of his lower jaw." He grinned and patted the dog's back before straightening. "Also lucky for him, I happened to be passing by the pound the day before they were going to destroy him."

She looked from dog to master. "And you just happened to be strolling past the pound and wondered if they had any dogs they were about to execute?"

He looked sheepish. "Not quite. I'm the one who found him and took him there after the other dog left him for dead. When I found out they were going to put him down, fate intervened and . . ." He shrugged. "Well, I decided I must need a dog." His vivid green gaze met hers. "Do you believe in fate, Jamie?" His voice was low, intimate, sending shivers to her extremities.

She blinked, breaking the spell, and looked around his apartment. "Ah, no, not really."

"Neither did I, but Francyne—that's my neighbor—swears by it. She's made a believer out of me. Well, at least where Killer is concerned, anyway." He shuffled through a pile of papers on an old desk and then waved a fistful of blue ones. "Here's the lease, if you want to read it over."

"Is that necessary?" Being in the same room with Killer was beginning to affect her allergies. A sinus headache wove its fingers across her forehead and around her eyes. Eyes that were definitely beginning to itch.

"No, it's pretty much standard. First and last month. No real lease time. It's month to month." He gave a bark of laughter. "Francyne suspects it's because the owners plan to sell it to developers and don't want anything standing in their way in case they get an offer."

"Is that what you think, too?" She stepped closer.

He shrugged, trying to ignore her warm, powdery scent. "I dunno. She's lived here for a couple of decades. I've worked here for three years, and it hasn't happened yet."

Jamie took the pen he offered, sneezed and bent over the table to begin filling out and signing the lease.

"Bless you," he muttered, then added a prayer of thanks while he eyed the cleavage revealed when she bent over the table. The firm globes pushing the neckline of her pink sweater to the edge of decency were roughly the size of small cantaloupes and defied gravity. He salivated and resisted the urge to rearrange his enlarging package.

Jamie sensed the manager eyeing her cleavage and resisted the urge to cover up.

"Drop that vibrator!" a heavily Southern-accented female voice shouted. "Stop that damn dog! Petunia! Drop it right now!"

Jamie paused and looked up.

A huge black dog galloped into the apartment, knocking over a small wooden chair and an end table in its wake.

Hot on the dog's heels was a deeply tanned, small woman with snowy white hair. Dressed in a brightly colored Mumu that fluttered around her slight frame, her small feet shod in white socks and sturdy walking shoes, she was a hair's breadth from catching the animal.

"Petunia!" The old lady rounded the couch to head off the dog who, Jamie now realized, had what appeared to be a purple vibrator in its massive jaws.

The dog faked a left and then darted around the woman.

Before Jamie could form her next coherent thought, the

warm feel of fur against her skin registered, followed immediately by a jarring thump as her rear end met the tiled floor beside the dining table.

"Petunia!" Devon grabbed for the dog's collar, missed and ended up tackling and wrestling her to the ground. Panting, he looked over his shoulder at Jamie.

Sitting with her hands braced behind her back, her legs slightly apart, she belatedly realized he could see clear up to her crotch.

"Are you hurt?" he asked.

Numb, she shook her head and tugged on her denim miniskirt then slowly got to her feet.

"Petunia," the older woman said, grasping the big dog's collar and hauling her to her feet. "What am I going to do with you? Give me that! Release!"

She pulled the dripping purple dildo out of the dog's mouth and grimaced. "Oh, yuck. Now you've gone and chewed up another one." She tossed it into a wastebasket overflowing with paper. Magnified blue eyes peered at Jamie through trifocal lenses. "Hello. How you doing? Isn't she just the sweetest thing, Devon?"

Devon mumbled something threatening-sounding. The woman grinned.

"Bless your heart," she said to no one in particular as far as Jamie could tell. "I bet you're here for the job."

"Job?" Devon and Jamie said as one.

"Sexual-aids product tester." With scarcely a breath in between sentences, she continued. "How do you do? I'm Francyne Anderson. I'm the one who put the ad in the paper, but Devon is the one you'll be working with."